*Sisterhood is
Deadly*

Sisterhood is Deadly

A Sorority Sisters Mystery

LINDSAY EMORY

WITNESS
IMPULSE

An Imprint of HarperCollins Publishers

This is a work of fiction. Names, characters, places, and incidents are products of the author's imagination or are used fictitiously and are not to be construed as real. Any resemblance to actual events, locales, organizations, or persons, living or dead, is entirely coincidental.

EPub Edition JULY 2015 ISBN: 9780062418340

Print Edition ISBN: 9780062418333

10 9 8 7 6 5 4 3 2 1

*To women everywhere
who share their light with others
and shine brighter for it.*

Disclaimer:
This book is not about your sorority.
It's about the sorority you hate.

Chapter One

SISTERHOOD IS POWERFUL.

I have a pillow with that saying embroidered on it. My big sister Amanda gave it to me for my twenty-first birthday, along with a bottle of tequila and a shot glass with the Delta Beta sorority crest enameled on it.

We weren't blood sisters. Amanda was my sorority big sis, a pledge year ahead of me, and she and the rest of the Delta Betas (or Debs, as we're known) taught me the pillars of true sisterhood: loyalty, pride, and willingness to hold your sister's hair back when she's puking tequila on her twenty-first birthday.

The words on Amanda's pillow came back to me as I stood in the chapter room of the Delta Beta house at Sutton College. As a visitor to this chapter, I didn't know anyone's name, but I marveled at the strength of our sisterhood as I held hands with the active sisters and recited the words to our sorority creed—similar to the Apostle's Creed, only more inspiring. There were no strangers here tonight. We were all sisters, bound by our oaths to one another.

For every chapter I visited, the rituals of Delta Beta were the same. The same lit XXXXX, the same book of XXXXXX, the same song lyrics espousing XXXXXX and XXXXXXX. (Details redacted to protect the sanctity of Delta Beta rites.) Here at Sutton College, it was no different. I was proud to call this small chapter of fifty young women my sisters. The rituals were even more meaningful here because Sutton College was my alma mater. This was the house where I was initiated and became a Delta Beta woman. I lived and laughed in these walls, calling them home for four years.

That is the beauty of the Delta Beta sorority. Everywhere I go, anywhere in the world, I have a sister, which is nice for an only child like myself. Maybe that's why I took to sorority life so well as an undergrad and why, after graduation, I applied to be a Sisterhood Mentor.

Nearly all of the national sororities have some program like Sisterhood Mentors. Young alumnae travel to different chapters to advise and assist the collegiate members on all sorts of very important sorority issues. (Don't laugh. There are lots of important sorority issues.) Generally, the programs last for two years, then the consultants and the advisors and the mentors move on to real careers. Me? I'm on my sixth year.

I'm not an idiot. The Delta Beta Executive Council has hinted a few times that maybe I should step down. They even offered me a permanent position at headquarters, something to do with accounting or rush consulting or something. But I always talk them out of firing me; softened by a few wise quotes from our founders, Leticia Baumgardner and Mary Gerald Callahan, the executive council is putty in my hands. They love Delta Beta as much as I do.

I'm Margot Blythe, professional sorority girl.

I was a philosophy major. What do you expect me to do for a living?

The opening ritual completed, the chapter president began conducting business. From my corner, I listened carefully, taking detailed notes. In six years, I had learned that the key to successfully mentoring sisters was often found in the minutiae of these chapter meetings. How they talked to each other, what problems the chapter was facing, and which fraternities they mixed with all provided clues about the state of the chapter. Sometimes it took an alumna to see behind the Tory Burch flats and Lilly Pulitzer prints.

After a full hour of debates on T-shirt designs, scholarship awards, and the next date-party theme, the closing ritual began. We joined hands again, a beautiful gesture of trust and strength. With one voice, we chanted the words to our motto (in Greek, of course, like all serious sororities) and lifted our hands in our secret sign.

It was precisely because we were all doing the exact same thing that I noticed something was wrong. One of us did not form a circle with her forefinger and thumb. One of us did not place the circle over her heart.

One of us fell to the floor, lifeless, before the meeting was officially closed.

Chapter Two

TEN YEARS AS a Delta Beta had prepared me for dealing with hysterical young women. Of course, I'd never dealt with the aftermath of a chapter advisor dropping dead in a chapter meeting. My closest experience with this level of tragedy was when the WU chapter failed to place in Epsilon Chi's Sing-a-thon. Total and complete heartbreak.

Once we'd realized what had happened, I quickly ran to the fallen sister's side, trying to remember my Red Cross training and ordering someone to call 911. Her last gasp for breath sounded like a rattlesnake, her chest strained, her face frozen yet drooping on one side. A sister cried out that she was a lifeguard, and I let her take over the CPR attempt, but it was soon apparent that it was pointless. My duties lay with the living, scattered into small clumps around the room, some sobbing, some silent and shocked. It all happened so fast.

I'd just met Liza McCarthy, the now-shrouded young woman currently being wheeled out by the Sutton medical examiner. I crossed myself like a Real Housewife of New Jersey as I saw the ambulance doors close behind her. She was a sociology graduate student at Sutton and by all accounts a smart, beautiful woman who truly personified the Delta Beta ideal. Our sisterhood had lost a star. And one so young! Liza McCarthy must have been around my age, too young to be felled by a heart attack or stroke or whatever silent killer had interrupted our sorority's most sacred rites.

With the chapter advisor rolling away to the morgue, I was left as the responsible adult on the scene. I herded the pledges into the dining room, the actives into the TV room, and called for volunteers to distribute lemonade and whatever snacks could be rounded up in the kitchen, hoping to distract the young women until the police had finished.

The Delta Beta sorority house was not large. Essentially a dormitory, it felt more like a gracious home, with bedrooms for about thirty initiated members. The first of three floors had a dining room, TV room, and chapter room off an impressive two-story foyer with a curved stairwell. I felt the warmth and comfort of the house envelop all the hyperventilating, confused young women grieving the sudden death that had occurred in their midst.

Even though I knew that Sutton, North Carolina, was a small town, I was unimpressed with the spare police force that showed up at the house, which lacked the gravitas of TV police work. After the paramedics and medical examiner left, only two police officers strolled around, taking notes and photographing "the scene." It seemed they had nothing better to do on a Monday night except make a big production out of a senseless tragedy.

I was busy consoling several girls when I overheard one of the policemen say, "Tell me what happened next," to one of the chapter officers.

Heck, no. That was not happening on Margot Blythe's watch.

I marched over to the policeman to shut him down—but my irritation didn't stop me from noticing that this was one extremely good-looking man. Several inches over six feet tall, with wavy, dark blond hair: Of course I noticed. At a different time, I probably would have approached him differently. Maybe smile charmingly, bat my eyelashes, and even place a hand on that very firm-looking bicep of his . . . but people were grieving, and I couldn't let him take advantage of our pain.

"Don't say another word," I said to the young woman being questioned. Her nose was red and puffy, her cheeks tear-stained, her chapter-worthy shift dress wrinkled and tired-looking.

"We were in the middle of something," said the police officer. I turned to him, my hands on my hips. He wasn't in uniform, but he wore a navy polo embroidered with the police insignia. A name tag identified him as "HATFIELD."

"Mr. Hatfield," I addressed him.

"Lieutenant Hatfield," he corrected me.

"This is a minor. You can't question a minor without a guardian or parent." I'd read that somewhere in a manual. It seemed legit.

"She's not under suspicion, Miss . . ."

"Blythe." I provided my name with all the authority I could muster. I was the chapter's Sisterhood Mentor, after all. "Margot Blythe."

Hatfield's head jerked back, a satisfying reaction. Funny how well people will respond to an authoritarian tone. "Ms. Blythe," he started to say again. "I'm just talking to witnesses. This is a friendly conversation. Nobody's under any suspicion."

"Fine," I said. "But I'm staying right here." I wrapped an arm around the girl's shoulder so she knew I was there for support and protection.

Hatfield didn't welcome me, but he couldn't do much about it. He looked back at his notes and started again.

"You said you were wrapping up the chapter meeting and the girls started to recite something . . .'"

"Objection," I said.

Hatfield raised his eyebrows at me. "What did you say?"

"Objection," I repeated. Did he think I'd never seen *Law & Order*? I'd always liked the 'order' part better—more drama. I looked at the girl. "Don't answer that."

Looking from me to the girl, Hatfield ignored me and repeated the question. "What were y'all reciting?"

"Objection!" I glared at him.

Hatfield looked stunned. "What in the world are you objecting to?"

"You're asking about privileged information!"

"Was a lawyer there? A doctor? A priest?"

Now he was talking crazy. "Of course not," I said. "You are asking about secret sorority rituals. We can't share those with anyone who has not been initiated, and that includes the police."

Hatfield lowered his pad and pen and stared at me, like I was some kind of exotic tropical bird. "Who are you again?"

"Margot Blythe," I repeated hotly.

"Got that," he said. "I meant, why are you here?"

"I'm the designated Sisterhood Mentor to the Sutton chapter for the next six weeks. And in the unfortunate absence of the chapter advisor, it's my duty, as the representative of the Delta Beta Executive Council, to advise these young ladies accordingly."

His posture and expression remained hostile. "You can't object to these questions," he ground out.

"Do you see this badge?" I asked him, hooking a thumb into

my suit lapel, where a small gold pin in the shape of a delta and a beta was prominently displayed. "This badge says I can object."

Hatfield seemed to relax, which I took as a sign that he understood my position and was going to be reasonable. Then he took something out of his pants pocket: a gold shield. "Do you see this badge?"

And that was when I was arrested in front of an entire sorority chapter. It was heartless, in my opinion, to add to the ladies' grief by taking away two of their sisters in the same night.

Chapter Three

It turned out that I wasn't officially "arrested." Hatfield escorted me to his police car with a firm grip on my elbow while I said some not very nice things under my breath that neither Mary Gerald Callahan nor Leticia Baumgardner would have thought befitting a Delta Beta lady. Hatfield told me to sit in the backseat and slammed the door, which was really uncalled for.

Did you know that the rear doors of police cars have kiddie locks on them? Who locks children in the back of a police car? I tried for nearly thirty minutes to get out of the car until the second police officer at the scene, who was both less attractive than Hatfield (unfortunately) and even less personable, got in the front seat and drove off, completely ignoring my protests and the not-so-nice things I was yelling in the backseat.

This officer's name tag which I saw as he escorted me to a cell, identified him as Malouf. The Sutton police station had one large holding cell, which was grim: a square, blank room with benches. All alone, I passed the time redecorating the cell in my mind until Hatfield reappeared.

As much as I wanted to be cool and ignore the man, I also wanted to bust out and return to the chapter. I would have to put my best Deb face on and charm my way out.

Hatfield stood at the door silently while I pretended not to notice him. "This is really unnecessary," I finally said, once my cool patience frayed. "You probably traumatized those poor girls back there when you hauled me off without probable cause, you know."

He chewed the inside of his jaw. I couldn't tell if he was sorry or just embarrassed for what he'd done.

"Aren't you going to say anything? Don't I get a phone call or something?"

When he still didn't answer, that ticked me off. "I know people! You do not want to mess with me!"

Hatfield held up his hands in surrender. "Oooh, I'm scared of the official sorority representative."

I stood up, putting my hands on my hips. "Yes, yes, you've made your point. Your badge is more important than mine. I still think you have your priorities out of whack."

Hatfield's eyes widened before he quickly (and dramatically, I might add) squeezed them shut. "*I* have my priorities out of whack? You put your stupid poems before a police investigation!"

"A poem? This is way more than a poem! You are just putting your ego before the proper oversight of young college women who need someone responsible and caring in their lives tonight!"

Blowing out a rough sigh, he reached for the cell door and un-locked it.

"A rug would be a nice touch," I said as I walked by him.

"In there?" he asked. "Do you know what people do on that floor?"

I looked at the drain in the middle of the holding cell. Hatfield finally had a decent point.

Safely out of the cell, I turned and looked around the town's police offices, disappointed by the lack of activity on a Monday night. No detectives were hustling perps out of interview rooms; no skankily dressed undercover cops drank bad coffee out of paper cups. Nope, it was just me and Hatfield, a few desks, some computers, and a half-filled watercooler.

It was clear that life as a Sutton police officer was boring as heck. No wonder Hatfield didn't know what to do with me. I was so outside his comfort zone.

"Can I make my phone call now?"

Hatfield rolled his eyes. "You don't get a phone call."

"I know my rights."

"You're not under arrest." He paused, seeming a little uncomfortable. "You were accidentally transported here."

For as long as I can remember, I have never been really, truly speechless. Accidentally transported to a holding cell? Of all the inept, low-rent, unprofessional, amateur-hour moves . . . I took a breath to rip this guy a new one. And remind him again that yes, I knew people, and, yes, those people knew people who could maybe, potentially get him fired.

But there had been a tragedy tonight, and I needed information from Deputy Do-Right.

"What comes next?" I asked, "For Liza?"

"Who?" The exasperation on my face made him self-correct. "Oh, Liza. Liza McCarthy. Yes, she'll be checked out and released to her family."

"Checked out?"

"For cause of death."

"I'd like to be there."

"For an *autopsy*?" Hatfield asked, like no one had ever asked that before.

"No. To talk to her family."

Hatfield frowned, deeply. "Who are you? Are you family?"

In a sense, yes. "She's my sister," I said simply. "Delta Betas are there for each other."

Hatfield rubbed a hand over his face like he was exhausted and mumbled something like, "Mother of God."

I decided to spell it out for him. "Look, I know you don't get it. But like I said, there are a bunch of traumatized young women back at the chapter house. With Liza gone, I'm going to have to take responsibility for the chapter, and I'd appreciate your respecting that."

"Right," he bit out. "And I'd appreciate your respecting the legal authority of this police department as we investigate this matter."

Okay, fine. He had another decent point. I saw where he was going with that. A Delta Beta woman always respected the law. But as Hatfield drove me back to the Deb house, I wondered why he seemed to think there would be an ongoing investigation of what a doctor would surely diagnose as a sudden stroke or heart attack.

Chapter Four

FOLLOWING A DEATH in the chapter room and a quasi-accidental arrest, my immediate response should have been to call my supervisor at Delta Beta headquarters in Atlanta. And I did that . . . sort of. I called someone: Casey Kenner, the Delta Beta director for public relations and my best friend at HQ.

The hoarse voice that answered told me I might not have called at the best time.

"Do you know what time it is?" The growling on the other end of the line was disconcerting.

I looked at my rose-gold Michael Kors watch. It had been a present from the UCLA chapter after a particularly difficult semester, grade-wise. I had helped them institute a new study-buddy system and regular study hours. After just a semester, the chapter had reached a C average. They had been thrilled. "It's not that late in my time zone."

"Girl, we're in the same time zone. North Carolina and Georgia are practically neighbors."

Love that Casey. Smart as a whip.

I briefly went over the events of the evening, and as I expected, Casey was all over it. Deaths and arrests were bad for public relations. "You've been there half a day," Casey moaned.

"And isn't it a good thing I was here!" I exclaimed hotly, thanking Jesus that I was sent to the right place at the right time. "The chapter needs me, now more than ever."

Casey yawned audibly over the phone. I forgave the incredibly bad manners at two in the morning.

"I have to call Mabel. She'll want an update, too, but I wanted to give you a heads-up before things get crazy in the morning."

"Thanks." The word was little flat, but like besties always did, Casey came around. "Do you need me? Are you okay?"

Once again, for the fifth or five hundredth time that day, my heart nearly burst with love for a true Delta Beta friend. "I think I'll be all right," I assured myself as much as my friend. "Thank you for asking."

After I got off the phone with Casey, I called Mabel Jones, the Vice President of Collegiate Chapters. She also reminded me of the time, but as soon as I explained what was going on, she forgave me. And because Mabel is a true Deb, smart and sharp even in the middle of the night, she asked me—ME!—to temporarily take over the chapter-advisor position at Sutton College, while the whole mess got sorted out.

It was a huge honor. I was not going to let my sisters down.

AFTER THE CONVERSATION with Mabel, I couldn't get to sleep, wide-awake with ideas and dreams of where I could take my chapter. I was staying in the guest room on the second floor of the sorority house, essentially a supply closet with a spare bed, but I didn't mind; I was used to staying wherever chapters could find room for me. At least I had a door and a place for my suitcase here. I rolled out of the twin bed and pulled on a Sutton College sweatshirt over my nightgown. I headed downstairs to the kitchen to get a drink of water, using the back stairs, where every square inch of wall was covered with Delta Beta history. It seemed as if nothing had changed in fifty years, much less ten. I traced the walls of the hall with my fingertips, in the dim light of emergency bulbs set every few feet into the ceiling. Every step brought back a memory: of college, of friends, of my final days of childhood.

Ten years ago, I had pledged this very chapter of Delta Beta. I was eighteen and fresh from my small hometown in the Florida panhandle. Growing up, I dreamed of going north for college, where campuses were covered in ivy and girls wore flannel and LL Bean boots for necessity's sake. I got as far as North Carolina, which was just fine with me. Here at Sutton College, I had all the ivy and woods and LL Bean that a Florida girl could dream of, plus a winter that was frosty but not arctic-y.

Childhood really lasts through college, doesn't it? Sure, it's in its waning days, but the world still seems as bright as a new penny, hopeful and huge. My four years in this sorority were the last incubation period, my final cozy womb until I burst out, ready to take on the world. And if I had partially stayed in that Delta Beta cocoon by becoming a semipermanent Sisterhood Mentor, well, who would blame me? It was fun. And happy.

Except when people died at a chapter meeting. That was a total bummer.

I pushed open the door to the kitchen and registered movement in the dark. With a jump and a scream, I slapped at the wall and turned on the lights. A young man in khaki shorts and an untucked polo shirt was as startled as I was by my scream. He held his hands up. "I'm sorry! I'm just finishing up!"

I put a hand to my chest, where I found my racing heart drumming a tattoo. "Who are you, and what do you think you're doing?"

Men were only allowed in the public areas of the first floor of the sorority house between the hours of 8:00 A.M. and 8:00 P.M. And they were strictly forbidden in the chapter room. It was inviolable Delta Beta law.

"I'm the house brother," he said nervously. "Hunter Curtis."

Well, that explained it. A house brother was a young man, generally a fraternity member, who was hired to do light housework and/or heavy lifting around a sorority house. It was usually someone who many of the sorority members considered a friend or even a little brother, and there were strict rules about his conduct in the house. Hunter looked trustworthy enough, with friendly brown eyes, sun-streaked brown hair, and worn-in Sperrys.

"What are you doing here? It's after midnight," I asked again, this time with the crazy turned down.

"With the police here, I couldn't finish sweeping up after dinner. So I came back to make sure it was all ready for the morning."

I relaxed a little bit. "I appreciate your hard work, but you really shouldn't be here this late."

"I'm sorry," he said. He seemed like a nice young man, just doing his job.

"We'll let it go this time."

"Okay, Miss . . . ?"

Where were my manners? "Margot Blythe," I said, reaching out to shake his head. "I'm the temporary chapter advisor."

Hunter's expression altered when he heard that. Like I said, people respected strong authority figures.

I locked up after Hunter left via the kitchen door and padded through the halls with my cup of water until I found what I was looking for: four framed displays, hung chronologically. The annual chapter composite pictures featured portraits of each sister, memorializing their youth and beauty for all time. The pictures were alphabetical, and thanks to my last name, I was near the top for my sophomore, junior, and senior years. I went back to my freshman year. Here I was closer to the middle, as pledges were placed after the active members.

Written in calligraphy, my name was under a portrait of a girl I barely recognized. Fresh from having my braces removed the summer before college, I sure liked to show off all those straight, pearly teeth. My natural brown hair was thick and virgin, free of dyes. One of only two brunette pledges that year—I knew what it was like to be a minority. As the composites went on, my hair lightened as more and more highlights were magically added (by the sun, of course).

Now, my hair is almost all brown again. Traveling as much as I do, I don't have time for all the upkeep that a good head of highlights requires. And though the freshman in the picture had hated her full cheeks, now, at the ripe old age of twenty-seven, I appreciated what a little baby fat could do to a face.

I might have given up on a full head of unnatural blond streaks but I hadn't outgrown poor cosmetic decisions, like the thick bangs I'm constantly trying to flatten. Six months ago, I was talked into bangs by a picture of Zooey Deschanel. Turns out, Zooey Deschanel is a better woman than I. I gave it three weeks before I decided to grow them out, but now they just look like an awkward brown flap, just long enough to flip behind my ears, where they stay for about three seconds before slipping out again.

I placed my hand on the faces of my sisters, wishing them well wherever they were. I reached my big sister's portrait, beautiful and self-assured as always, reminding me that a perk of my new role in Sutton would be to spend time with Amanda.

Still not sleepy, I had another pilgrimage to make. I tiptoed up to the third floor. There were fewer bedrooms up here, and most girls didn't like to carry all their shoes all the way to the third floor. It was popular with the older sisters and the really studious ones who liked the quiet. Needless to say, I had lived on the second floor. I tried the door handle at the end of the hall. Luckily, it was open.

The room was nearly pitch-black. There were no emergency lights in here, as it was basically a floored-in attic space where the chapter stored rush props and the random detritus of college women: enough supplies to survive on a desert island. I walked slowly, keeping my hands out in front of me, feeling for furniture or boxes. I stubbed my toe almost immediately, but then I saw the silvery light coming in through a window.

Sorority row sat on the south side of campus, on a rise that wasn't apparent from the street until you were up here, on the third floor, looking over the edge of campus, the town beyond, and the Blue Ridge Mountains in the far distance. I don't remember when I discovered the view from here, but I would escape to this little nook on the days when things got too loud, too dramatic, too much to deal with on the floors below.

The town of Sutton looked like a Norman Rockwell dream, all red brick and straight- edged, with elm-lined streets. Everything made sense up here. The world looked perfect. And it reminded me that perfection was possible. All you had to do was look at the world in the right way. Stay positive, and you'd see the most amazing things. I was pretty sure that Mary Gerald Callahan or Leticia Baumgardner would agree.

Chapter Five

THE NEXT MORNING was bright and clear as I made my way across the Sutton College campus. It was easily the prettiest college campus I'd ever been to, and I'm a bit of an expert. In the last six years as Sisterhood Mentor, I've been lucky enough to visit nearly forty institutions of higher learning across North America.

Wide, tree-shaded pathways snaked through campus, curving among brick buildings built in the colonial style. Students joke that the campus planners were drunk when the sidewalks were built, but I prefer to think that they just liked taking their time when getting to their destination. Kind of like I do.

Though I had a meeting scheduled for nine, I took a bit of extra time strolling through campus. Each building held a special place in my heart; each bend in the path was another precious memory to relive. There, at the Harrison-Peterson Cafeteria, I saw Kirby Jones cheating on me over a spaghetti lunch with an Epsilon Chi. And there, at the War Memorial fountain, my cute exchange-student boyfriend Felipe told me he was married and had three kids back in Chile. And at the ivy arbor next to the psychology building, I found my ex-boyfriend macking down on a Beta Gamma Zeta.

College days were the best.

My destination this morning was the Commons, or the student center, specifically the basement offices of the Panhellenic Council. Panhellenic is a nationwide quasi-governing organization of the national sororities—kind of like the United Nations. Similar to the United Nations, joining Panhellenic is political and voluntary, and their rule-making is toothless. The bite of the Panhellenic is more often carried out at the campus level, and Sutton College was no exception.

In fact, almost fifteen years ago, there was a kerfuffle when the Epsilon Eta Chi chapter invited all the rushes to a kegger at a private house, a no-no. When the Panhellenic advisor took Epsilon Eta Chi's side, it mystified all the other sororities on campus . . . until it came out that she herself had been an Epsilon Eta Chi, causing drama and fallout sufficient for a Bravo reality show. From that scandal on, the Panhellenic advisor at Sutton College has had to keep her sorority membership a secret in order to remain impartial: a good rule I wish other campuses would adopt. It would do a world of good to avoid the underhanded dealings of Epsilon Eta Chis and their ilk.

In her office at the Commons, I sat across from the current Panhellenic advisor, a skinny, perky woman with long, enviably straight, blond hair, and a knack for eye makeup. Now this office showed some imagination in decor, from the rug to the posters; Deputy Hatfield could take some lessons. Every inch of the space showed true Panhellenic spirit, with pictures depicting the most fun times of sorority life. It was like I'd died and gone to Delta Beta heaven.

I made a circle with my thumb and forefinger and nonchalantly put the circle over my heart. The Panhellenic advisor did the same over her heart. We smiled at each other with big, goofy grins, the kind you get when happiness is too hard to keep bottled up.

"BIG!" I yelled, getting up from my chair.

"Little!" Amanda yelled back. That's right: The Sutton College Panhellenic advisor was not only a beautiful, smart Delta Beta, but she was my one and only big sister.

"I can't believe you're here!" she said after we'd hugged each other's breath out.

"When they told me I was coming back to Sutton, I could hardly stand not calling you," I admitted. "But I wanted it to be a surprise."

"Total surprise! Last I heard from you, you were in Atlanta."

"For just a few days," I said. "Before that it was Jacksonville, then Austin, then Portland . . ."

"So glamorous."

I nodded. Living out of a rolling suitcase, doing laundry only every few weeks, and sleeping on spare beds. My life was great but definitely not glamorous. "How's your family?" I asked.

Amanda tossed back her perfectly straight hair. "Fine, I'm sure."

Her reticence wasn't surprising. Amanda had never really talked about her large, West Virginian family.

"Your sisters? How are they?" She had three sisters, which I'd always envied.

"My sisters are all pregnant. For the third time. Each." Amanda added.

"So exciting! Is everyone thrilled about all the babies?"

"Oh, yes," Amanda said flatly. "Especially the welfare office."

There was an awkward pause. Her family was large, and the one time I'd met them, very kind, but I'd known Amanda long enough to suspect that they were very strapped for cash. It was something Amanda never brought up in college, but the tension showed, and I never told anyone about the Delta Beta scholarships she received. Some people are strange about money. Especially proper Southern women.

"Have you heard anything new about the old gang?" Amanda asked, clearly trying to change the topic, which I was happy to do. I updated her on various pledge sisters and friends I'd run into around the country. It was one of the perks of my job. I was still the social butterfly of our Deb chapter, always keeping up with friends in every city even after we'd scattered postgraduation.

"How does Kelly Jo look?" Amanda asked, about a friend of ours who I'd just seen in Austin. "I heard she wasn't keeping well."

"She's twenty-eight," I said. "She looks twenty-eight."

Amanda smoothed a hand over her hair, and I self-consciously did the same with my growing-out bangs. "That's a shame," Amanda said.

"You look great," I said, totally sincere. "Not a day over twenty-two." Amanda was a year older than me, at twenty-eight, but I thought she'd like to hear that.

She smiled, pleased with the compliment. "Can't beat good genes and sunscreen," she said.

"True," I said cheerily, knowing that if Amanda's poreless, glowing complexion was solely due to sunscreen, I was Angelina Jolie.

"How long will you be in town?"

I lifted my hands. "Who knows? You heard about Liza McCarthy, right?"

Amanda nodded, a sheen of tears suddenly appearing in her eyes. "I'm just in total shock about it," Amanda said. "She was so young."

"So young," I agreed.

"What's going to happen?" Amanda asked, and I gave her the update from HQ.

"Whoa." Amanda leaned back in her chair. "That's huge."

"That's one of the reasons I came to see you. To formally introduce myself as the Delta Beta chapter advisor, pro tem."

"I'm so proud of you," Amanda sniffed. "It's so great to see your little sister succeed." Her words brought a mix of emotions, that, to be honest, made me a little uncomfortable. So I just pushed them down and ignored them, like a good Delta Beta. No need to ruin the reunion party.

My attention was grabbed by a framed photo on her desk. "I can't believe you have this picture!" I picked up the sparkly pink frame and grinned at the memories that flooded back at the sight of little nineteen-year-old Margot and twenty-year-old Amanda in the middle of the Sutton Kmart, dressed as Christmas elves. "I still can't believe you made me do that." Amanda shook her head.

"It was Christmas, we had to spread some cheer."

"You bought all those toys, and we gave them out to random kids outside the elementary school."

I couldn't help but smile.

"You always had the most fun ideas to distract me when I was feeling stressed during finals."

"It was for both of us," I said as I put the picture back.

Amanda reached out and clutched my hand. "No, you always took care of me. And now you're doing it again. Taking care of all the little Debs."

I blushed and changed the subject. Because this really wasn't about me. "I guess I need to do some paperwork with you?"

Amanda got right on the ball, as I knew she would, registering me with the college as a student advisor. We went over the Panhellenic policy, procedures, and codes of conduct, and the calendar of meetings and events of the next month. We finished with the plan for the Tri Mu Bowling Tournament the next weekend.

"Poor Liza," Amanda said. "She really hated the Tri Mus."

I nodded in sympathy. Every good Delta Beta hated the Tri Mus. "Did you know her well?" I asked. I didn't think so, but if Amanda was overcome by Liza's death, I had to be a good friend.

Amanda wobbled her head. "Yes and no. She was great with the girls, of course, a real charismatic leader. But with the college staff, she was a little more standoffish. Maybe because she hadn't gotten her doctorate yet." Amanda crinkled her nose as a sad thought occurred to her. "Maybe if I had told her I was a Deb, we could have been better friends."

"You were there for her," I assured Amanda. "She knew in her heart you were a sister."

Amanda closed her eyes and nodded, accepting my wise platitudes. "How are the girls holding up?"

I thought of the still-red eyes and hushed voices at breakfast this morning. "They're strong. They'll hold it together."

"And what about you? How do you plan to do all this? Even a temporary gig is going to be tough."

"I'm going to hold one-on-ones with the chapter officers in the next few days, get status reports from everyone. Hopefully, that will give me a good overview of the chapter. Plus, headquarters is sending me the financials to review."

Amanda nodded at the plan. "Let me know if you need help

with anything." She frowned, then said, "I should let you know, the administration is kind of freaking out about all this. I've already had about six calls this morning. You should probably expect a few yourself."

I made a note to check the voice mail at the chapter advisor's office. An image of a gold badge and a cute guy popped in my head. "Do you happen to know Lieutenant Hatfield," I asked. "At the Sutton police department?"

Amanda pursed her lips. "He comes on campus every fall to do a dating-violence-prevention thing. Are you going to ask him out?"

I rolled my eyes. So typical of Amanda to go there immediately. Let's just say that during college, she could have been kind of . . . slutty, if she hadn't been so discreet. "No way. He just seemed . . ." I searched for the words to describe Hatfield's odd behavior the night before. "A little obtuse."

"Really," Amanda said with surprise.

"Like, I don't think he understood what sorority life was all about," I explained, thinking of his complete disregard for our rituals, and his confusion that I would like to help comfort Liza McCarthy's family.

"I get that all. The. Time. Unaffiliated people just don't understand."

"Gosh darn independents," I said.

Amanda nodded in commiseration. She understood me perfectly.

Chapter Six

HOLDING A CHAPTER meeting just twenty-four hours after the last one would never be a popular thing to do. For most sorority girls, chapter meetings are like dental examinations, or going to church, or hanging out with your rich maiden aunt because she's got to leave the lake house to someone in her will. It's a required act that you don't necessarily enjoy.

I understood the sentiment. These were young college women who also had priorities like studying, exercising, and watching *Supernatural* marathons on Netflix. Chapter meetings could be grueling, with endless debates and *Robert's Rules of Order* and pin attire, requiring that sorority members get dressed up for chapter. Again, like visiting your rich aunt, you had to show some respect when you went.

So there I stood, in front of fifty slightly pissed-off, confused, grieving Debs. With a heavy heart, I informed them that I, Margot Blythe, was going to be their temporary chapter advisor.

About twenty-five hands went up. About twenty-five cell phones were whipped out. I calmly and patiently answered everyone's burning questions. Yes, the date party was still scheduled to occur. Yes, the T-shirts would still get ordered. No, I didn't know which DJ would be playing at the date party. Yes, I agreed that the Tri Mu bowling tournament was a ridiculous waste of time. Yes, we were still going to attend as a chapter and show our Panhellenic support.

The questioning got a little intense, and I blessed Liza McCarthy's memory for having the stamina and courage to face down a chapter of Debs every Monday, week after week. I thanked them for their support and friendship in the weeks to come, and invoked a quotation of Mary Gerald Callahan's that I'd always loved: "A Delta Beta sister is steadfast, in times of sorrow and despair when things look bleakest, at the end of days, when evil and corruption shall reign over the earth." That seemed to make everyone feel better.

Then I sat down in my chair off to the side of the chapter president, Aubrey St. John, who resumed conducting the meeting.

An impatient hand from a willowy, almond-skinned sister in the front row was called upon. "I'd like to know if the chapter has any contingency plans for this week."

I looked around, confused. I had just announced that I was the chapter advisor in Liza's absence. Wasn't that the contingency plan?

Another hand shot up. This one belonged to a curvy girl in a pretty emerald dress. I heard the Betas are on total lockdown."

Lockdown? I knew the death of a sorority row chapter advisor was newsworthy, but I didn't think it placed every chapter in imminent jeopardy. Just ours.

The first row girl nodded. "The Epsilon Chis have instituted the buddy system."

Another young lady in the back with a pixie cut and a deep Southern accent chimed in. "The Moos aren't even accepting mail this week."

There was a gasp throughout the chapter room. "But what about their online shopping deliveries?" someone cried.

Miss Pixie Cut looked forlorn. "They'll be delayed. Can you *imagine*?"

Chattering and murmurs spread throughout the room. I stood, addressing the chapter once again. "Ladies, I'm sure that the police will speak to each of those chapters and reassure them that whatever tragedy we endured here will not be repeated elsewhere."

Fifty sets of eyes fixed on me.

"Margot." Aubrey cleared her throat delicately. "I'm afraid that what the chapter is discussing is something altogether more . . . threatening."

I was thoroughly confused. What could be more threatening than a sudden and unexplained death?

Aubrey explained. "It's fraternity-pledge prank week."

Ah. That made a whole lot more sense.

Every year in the fall, Sutton College fraternities competed against each other to outwit, outsmart, and outprank each other. Local legend has it that long ago the pranks were committed fraternity against fraternity, mano a mano. But when the Iota Kap house burned down following an unfortunate incident involving flaming kegs, the Interfraternity Council decreed that henceforth, no pranks would be committed against fellow fraternities. But the damn IFC didn't say anything about sororities.

Since then, the fraternities still waged a war every fall, sending their pledges into skirmishes of prank-offs on the sorority houses. Apparently, as long as no house burned down, the IFC was cool with it. Most of the time, the pranks were annoying, and occasionally, they were hilarious. Like the time the doors and windows of the Tri Mu house were boarded up from the outside. (Although the fire department didn't think that was so funny.) Or the time that the Tri Mu composite was photocopied and spread across campus with GOT MILK? written over it. To this day, I know absolutely nothing about who might have possibly perpetrated that brilliant prank or who could have provided the frat with a copy of the composite accidentally misplaced from the photographer's studio when I was picking up the Delta Beta pledge portraits.

"Other sororities are instituting buddy systems?" I asked the chapter.

"And curfews," a voice from the back added.

"And *no mail*," the pixie-cut girl emphasized dramatically.

"Are the pranks that bad now?"

The chapter nodded almost uniformly in the affirmative.

"But it's not unsafe, is it?" I couldn't imagine fraternity pledges doing something that would physically harm a sorority sister.

That question was considered way more seriously than I would have liked. A sister in an unfortunate shade of yellow raised her hand. "There was that Gamma who had her eyebrows shaved off . . ."

That speculation was dismissed by the social director. "She blamed a fraternity prank, but her little sis goes to my big sister's tanning salon. She said that was totally an at-home wax job gone bad."

Fifty heads bobbed in comprehension.

"What about those Tri Mu pledges who went to the hospital?" It was the girl in the emerald dress again. Seriously, I had to ask her where she bought that. My skin would look fantastic in it.

The chapter was curiously silent on that front.

"Was it a fraternity prank or not?" I asked.

Eyes met across the room. Obviously, no one knew for sure, one way or another. I decided to let it go, but the thought that the fraternities might be out of control unsettled me for the rest of the meeting.

I asked the chapter officers to stay behind after closing rituals, which occurred faster than I'd ever seen them. The ladies—and I—flew through the chant and the *poem*, scared that someone else might drop dead. Thankfully, everyone stayed upright, which was a nice testament to Delta Beta stamina.

I rearranged some chairs for me and the five officers. As in every Deb chapter, there was a chapter president, a standards and morals director, an academic director, a social activity director, and a pledge trainer. The officers reflected the five pointed star of the Delta Beta crest, with each point standing for a character requirement of a Deb woman: leadership, ethics, scholarship, civic life, and telling other people what to do.

Some of the officers I had met the night before, and as the meeting went on, I was most impressed with their composure and maturity. The president, Aubrey St. John, was particularly impressive. A poised young lady, she spoke well, had superb posture, and seemed to immediately grasp almost all of my needs. I could tell I would rely on her greatly as the days went by.

The academic director was studious, the social activity director was bubbly, and the pledge trainer was a lesbian. Which was perfectly fine. Delta Betas loved all their sisters, even if that sister loved other sisters. I was also very impressed with the standards and morals director, or, as we Debs shorten it, S&M. I'll admit, I knew who she was before I even arrived on campus. When she'd pledged Delta Beta two years earlier, the news was trumpeted throughout the alumnae associations and in the alumnae magazine, *The Busy Bee:* She was Callahan Campbell, a direct descendant of our revered founder, Mary Gerald Callahan. The seventh generation of Callahan descendants to pledge Delta Beta, she was kind of like our sorority's royalty.

"It's an honor to work with you, Callahan," I told her, in my best non-suck-up voice.

"Call me Callie," she said with a dimpled smile. It was official. I had a girl crush.

I arranged times to meet with each of them, to understand what was going on in the chapter and address any of their substantive concerns. No one seemed to have any issues with the change of advisors, and they all stood up fairly quickly to leave, seeming to have everything under control.

Aubrey St. John stayed behind, which was both sweet and conscientious. By this point, I admit I was feeling a little out of my depth. There was a lot to do in a very short time.

"Ms. Blythe," she started to say.

I interrupted her. "Call me Margot, please," I insisted. "After all, we're sisters."

Aubrey smiled back. While she didn't have dimples, she was an adorable girl. Her hair was curled in perfect blond waves, her makeup expertly applied like a YouTube guru. She was a testament to Delta Beta womanhood. "I didn't want to ask in front of the other girls," she said, her words tentative, "but . . . what's happening with Liza?"

I reached over and patted Aubrey's hand. Concern was etched all over her face. "The police will be contacting her family soon."

"She doesn't have a family," Aubrey said. "Not really. Her parents died in a freak accident when she was in college. She told me once, over . . ." A guilty look flashed across Aubrey's face. "Drinks," she finished weakly. I patted her hand again. Aubrey didn't need to feel guilty confessing to underage drinking. Not with me. But then I remembered: I was the chapter advisor now. Maybe I should say something about it. I quickly dismissed that thought. This was a time for comfort, not chastisement. I made a mental note to chastise later.

"Does—did—she have any brothers or sisters?"

Aubrey shook her head. "That's the thing. She lost her brother in Iraq. And her only sisters were Debs."

That shot a single arrow through my heart. The Delta Beta sorority was all Liza McCarthy had in the world, and we were there for her, holding her hand at the bitter end, reciting our sacred words in unison. I could only hope for such a death.

"I'll find out," I promised Aubrey. "We'll take care of Liza."

Aubrey used the back of her hand to wipe at her cheeks. "I guess I need to show you your new office."

Chapter Seven

I WAS ORIENTING myself in the chapter advisor's office when there was a knock at the door. Without waiting for me to say anything, the door opened and in walked a cute policeman who, inconceivably, didn't seem happy to see me.

"What are you doing back here?" I asked.

"I came to see you." The flat line of his mouth showed that he wasn't that excited about it. Which hurt the ego, a little, if I'm telling the truth.

I glanced at the door in irritation. "Men aren't allowed back here."

"A man showed me back here."

I rolled my eyes. I was so right when I talked to Amanda. Hatfield didn't understand sororities at all.

"That's the house brother." Hatfield still didn't look like he understood. "He's a house brother," I repeated, a little slower this time to see if that worked.

"I know what a house brother is," he said irritably. "I just think it's a stupid name for someone you hire to wash dishes."

I so wasn't getting into this conversation. Delta Betas were expected to exhibit the highest standards of housekeeping. And who we hired to help us with the dishes was our business.

"Can I help you with something?" I asked, pointedly.

Hatfield came into the office and shut the door behind him. He leaned against a bookshelf and crossed his arms. I tried not to notice how that stretched his police-department polo shirt across a nicely built chest and his firm upper arms. He had a whole young Matthew McConaughey meets John Wayne vibe going on, all tanned, laconic, and suspicious.

"How well did you know Liza McCarthy?"

"I didn't, really," I said. "I just met her yesterday morning when I came into town."

Hatfield looked like he was trying to decide something. "They don't have anyone to release the body to," he finally said.

I nodded. "She had no family. They've all passed."

His eyes narrowed on me. "I thought you didn't know her."

"One, I learned that from a sister here. Two, I don't appreciate the implication that I am dishonest. Debs are always honest." It was in our creed.

But I couldn't waste time on being sassy with a police officer. He might throw me in the clink again. Accidentally. And I had promised Aubrey that we were going to be there for the departed chapter advisor. "So what's going to happen to Liza?"

"The coroner's holding the body for further tests. Since she doesn't have family . . ."

I cut him off right there. "She does have family. Her Delta Beta—"

Hatfield rolled his eyes. "Cut that out already."

"Excuse me?" As much as I was trying to avoid the back of a police car, I couldn't let this slide.

"Stop acting all high-and-mighty. You and I both know this sorority stuff is a crock of bull."

"I do not know that," I assured him, affecting the posture of someone most offended.

He reared his head back, studying me for a long moment. "You don't remember me, do you?"

Taken aback, I searched his face while I searched my memory. A tall drink of water with a bad attitude against sororities seems like someone I'd definitely remember. "No." I tried to be polite. "Should I?" Something occurred to me. Hatfield, Hatfield . . . "What's your first name?"

"Ty."

Ty Hatfield. I rolled the name around in my head for a moment, but nothing. There's only room for about eighty names in my memory at any given time. A hundred, max. And maybe the name Ty Hatfield rang a bell. But maybe it sounded like a thousand other names I'd learned in the last six years.

"When did we meet?" I asked, tentatively. He didn't look like we'd been close.

"Doesn't matter," he spat out. He reached for the door handle. Oh no: He didn't get to walk in here, be both suspicious and annoying, then walk out.

"Why did you come over here?" I had the distinct feeling he hadn't told me everything yet. "And what did you mean by further tests?"

Maybe I wasn't good with names. But I was pretty damn good with remembering details about my sisters.

Ty Hatfield looked at me long and hard. Under other circumstances, with those baby blues, it was something I could get used to. Right now, I felt like he was about to bring out the handcuffs. And not in the good way. "There are some inconsistencies with the preliminary report on Ms. McCarthy's death."

"Like what?"

"Like they haven't determined a cause."

I frowned. "Is that normal?"

Ty folded his arms. "You tell me."

"Oh, for heaven's sake!" I said in exasperation. "I don't know why you don't like me, but I'm not a bad person. I'm just trying to help. That's my job. Helping people."

Ty looked around the room. "This is her office?"

I had a bad feeling. "Filled with confidential sorority information," I said quickly.

He lifted an eyebrow. "Any objection to my looking around?"

"Objection," I said clearly. Big-time objection.

"I could get a warrant," he said.

"You could, if there was something illegal going on." Don't mess with the *Law & Order* mega fan. I knew all about warrants. But I gasped when a thought occurred to me. "Is there something illegal going on?"

I saw when Ty Hatfield decided to sort-of trust me. "The medical examiner doesn't think the death was natural."

My mouth formed an "O." Because if it wasn't natural, that meant it was . . . "Murder?" I whispered.

"They're doing additional tests," Ty repeated, not acknowledging the "m" word.

I sank back down in the chair. Here in Liza's office, I was surrounded by her things. It seemed unreal that someone who had sat here just hours before me was now dead and that she may have been murdered. I shivered.

"Nothing's conclusive," Hatfield said.

"It's not possible," I said, sounding pretty confident that it was true.

"Why?" Ty's eyes sharpened. For a small-town cop, he was pretty intense.

"I was there," I said quietly. "We all were. We would have seen something, heard something. Liza couldn't have been murdered. Not in front of fifty witnesses."

Ty lifted a shoulder. "One person's witnesses are another person's suspects."

I was so caught up, remembering the moment of Liza's passing that his words didn't fully impact. But then they did.

"Excuse me?" I said that a lot around Ty Hatfield, it seemed. "Are you implying . . ."

"Nothing's conclusive . . ."

I couldn't even wrap my brain around the idea, the accusation, the thought . . .

"She was our sister!" I finally said.

"The medical examiner's report shows no sign of natural death. No hemorrhage, no heart attack, no stroke."

"We have standards!"

"The people I talked to last night all said that Liza was here, in the house, all day before the meeting. According to the sociology department, she had no classes on Mondays because she saved Mondays for chapter work. The security log from her parking garage shows she left her apartment Sunday night and never returned."

"We have morals," I hissed at the policeman, coldly rattling off facts like he knew what he was talking about.

"The only people Liza McCarthy saw in her last day alive were all here, in this sorority house."

It was too much. "You obviously don't understand sororities, Officer Hatfield."

"It's Lieutenant Hatfield," he said. "And I'm pretty sure I do."

"So are you arresting someone? Are you getting a search warrant?" There was a hesitant look in his eye. He didn't have as much as he thought he did.

I took a stab in the dark. "No one believes you. Is that it?"

"The tests are inconclusive," he bit out. "And yeah, no one at the college or in town is going to call this murder until it's slapping them in their face." He took a deep breath. "That's why I need your help."

Ah. A cat-eating-the-canary grin settled across my face. Now we were getting to it. "What exactly do you need, Captain Hatfield?"

His jaw tightened before he threw an arm toward the desk. "Information. Liza's records, notes, letters, phone calls . . ."

They were things he couldn't get without a warrant. Especially if I was sitting in the chapter advisor's seat.

"Let me get this straight," I said slowly. "You've basically insinuated that Liza McCarthy was murdered by someone in this chapter, by one of her own sisters. And you want to review confidential sorority information to confirm your suspicions?"

Muscles twitched in his jaw and around his eye. "Yes." He cut me off before I could answer. "Don't you want justice for your 'sister'?"

That hit me harder than I thought it would. Of course I did. I wanted justice for all. That was in the Delta Beta creed. Or was that the pledge of allegiance? It didn't matter. They were pretty much the same thing.

I looked around the office and the piles of papers and books. It looked like Liza had used the office for her doctoral studies and not just chapter business. I recognized some of the official Delta Beta handbooks and policy manuals. But there were scribbles on notepads, sociology tests, and journals that I did not recognize. Sorting through Liza's papers was going to be necessary, no matter any impending investigation. As her sister, I had a duty to get her affairs in order, to protect the chapter, and to ensure justice was done.

Ty must have seen the look on my face. "Let me guess. You're objecting."

I held up a hand. "I'll make you a deal."

His eyebrows shot up. "A deal? You're trying to make a deal . . . with the police?"

"Sure. Why not?"

"Your arrogance is impressive."

I drew back. I was pretty sure he meant something else. Like confidence. Or competence. Or fashion sense. Whatever. I went on. "Obviously, I can't just let you go through sorority papers, willy-nilly."

"Obviously."

"I have to go through all this first." I waved my hand at the piles of paper around the room. "And I'll let you know if I find anything . . . interesting."

"What's the deal?"

I looked at him squarely in the face. "You do the same for me. I need to know the truth about Liza's death as soon as you know it."

"You're not the next of kin."

He really didn't understand. "I'm the next thing to it," I said sadly.

Chapter Eight

AFTER TY HATFIELD left, I needed something positive to focus on. So I headed back to the chapter room, where the pledges were having their weekly meeting. Despite all the drama, it hadn't escaped my notice that the Sutton Delta Beta chapter had an exceptional rush this year. Not only was the pledge class larger than usual, but they were fantastically good-looking.

I'm sure they all were made of a good moral cloth, too. But you can't judge that just by looking at someone.

The women sat in a circle on the floor of the chapter room, as only initiated members could sit in chairs. (That's not hazing, that's just Deb tradition.) Each had a notebook and pen in hand. Cheyenne, the pledge trainer, sat at the top of the circle next to an easel with posters stacked on it.

Cheyenne pointed at a poster. "Leticia Baumgardner."

A pledge busted out with the answer. "Who is the founder of Delta Beta?"

"Correct." Cheyenne smiled at the girl and pointed back at the poster. "Walnut Valley College."

"What is the college where Delta Beta was founded?"

"Correct again."

Oooh. It was Deb Jeopardy! I loved this game.

"Frisky Friedman," Cheyenne offered to the room.

A tentative hand went up. "Who is a guy we should never date?" Giggles erupted around the circle.

Cheyenne was patient with the little joke. "No. Who is the Delta Beta Olympic gold medalist," she answered.

"Bonus points," I chimed in. "Who knows Frisky's Olympic event?"

No one seemed to know.

"C'mon guys, it was heptathlon," I said.

Pens were picked up and notes were scribbled. Pledges didn't just learn this stuff for fun. They were tested on it. If they didn't get a perfect score, they weren't initiated. (It wasn't hazing. It was education.)

"What kind of a name is Frisky?" a dark-haired pledge asked.

"It was a nickname, one she picked up as a pledge. It has nothing to do with boys. Or cats," I hastily added.

The pledges looked impressed at the breadth of my knowledge of Delta Beta trivia.

Cheyenne moved on. "Dorothy."

"Oh! Oh!" A petite Asian girl on the floor said, waving her hand in the air. "The original name for Busy Bee, our mascot."

Cheyenne scrunched up her nose. "I'm sorry, your answer has to be in the form of a question."

"Fun fact!" I interrupted again. "Does anyone know why a Bee was picked to be the Deb mascot?"

Hands shot up around the circle. "Because its colors are black and gold?"

"Because they're really small and petite?"

"Because they sting like a bitch?"

"Sort of," I said. "Because bees work hard, play hard, and always listen to the queen."

Cheyenne and I exchanged a knowing smile. I could tell we both liked being the queen.

"Have you all gotten your Busy Bees yet from your big sisters?" I asked the pledges.

The pledges all smiled and nodded. Delta Beta big sisters always gave their little sisters their first plush Busy Bee. It was a cherished item that the littles kept with them for the rest of their lives. And since it wasn't a teddy bear or a bunny, there was nothing juvenile about it in the least.

Of course, I still had my Busy Bee from Amanda, back in my room at my parents' house in Florida. Because I traveled full-time for Delta Beta, it never made sense for me to get an apartment in Atlanta when I was only there six weeks of the year, so most of my personal belongings had sat in boxes for the past six years.

"Did you give a Busy Bee to your little sister?" the Asian girl on the floor asked me. She couldn't know that she had touched on a sensitive subject.

"I never had a little sister." It was the brutal truth. And six-plus years hadn't made the pain of that truth go away.

The pledges' eyes widened in shock. I bet they'd never heard something so disturbing. "It's all right," I assured them. "I'm sure it will never happen to anyone else." I was just a fluke.

"What happened?" The question came from a pale girl in the front. I had to ease their minds.

"My sophomore year, I was ready to sign up for the big-sister selection process, but my big sister got mono. As you know, the process takes a lot of time, and I couldn't help take care of my big and get her class notes and assignments and devote myself 110 percent to finding a Little, so I had to drop out." Sympathetic murmurs and sad little frowns dotted the room, and telling the story drew me back into my college years, the stress of balancing schoolwork, friends, and Delta Beta obligations.

"Junior year, I was in charge of the Delta Beta Ice-Cream-Sundae championship, benefiting our childhood-obesity philanthropy. There was a . . . conflict." I finished lamely, remembering the details like it was yesterday. I was neck deep in organizing the event and the deadline to sign up for a little sis unfortunately coincided with the day the Guinness Book of World Records investigators' visit to determine if the Debs had truly built the largest ice-cream sundae in the world. At the end of my junior year, I faced the harsh truth that I had neither a little sister nor a Guinness World Record to brag about.

"And your last year?" the Asian girl on the floor prompted me.

This one was the hardest of all to talk about because I still didn't understand *why*. "I was president of the sorority. And I didn't get matched with a Little."

Now there were gasps of horror. Even Cheyenne blinked back her visible shock. There had been all sorts of theories floated as to why I had failed to receive a little sis. Maybe people were too intimidated to request me, the president of the chapter. Maybe they didn't want a graduating senior, and I could sort of understand why a pledge would want a big who was going to be around longer than a semester. But anyone who knew me, knew that I would have been a really kick-butt long-distance big. I forced a bright smile on my face, in case these pledges got the wrong idea.

"But I want all of you to know from my example, that you can be a proud, strong Delta Beta even if your little-sister dreams don't work out like they should."

As an initiated member, Cheyenne understood better than the pledges what my admission meant. Compassion and support were in her eyes before she picked up her tablet and started again on the training process.

I pulled a chair to the back of the room and listened as facts and figures that I knew so well were repeated and memorized by a new generation. This is what it was all about: sharing history and learning traditions. This was the fabric of our lives.

The pledges finished Deb Jeopardy, and Cheyenne told everyone to pull out their Pledge Manuals and open to page fifty-five.

I knew what that was. The beginning of the standards and morals sections. Standards and morals were so vital to every sorority. Pledges were first gently corrected on bid day if they drank beer from a bottle or smoked in their letters. But it wasn't about the silly little rules. All the silly little rules contributed to something larger, something more important, reminding the pledges that their conduct reflected on the sorority as a whole, on their friends and sisters. Personally, I thought proper conduct was something that more young women needed to learn these days. And not to smoke and walk at the same time—that was just common sense.

After they had all gotten to the correct page, Cheyenne resumed her presentation. "Now, last week we discussed some of the academic rules, the required GPA, the mandatory study hours, and the expectation that all Debs will turn over their class notes at the end of a semester for other sisters to use in subsequent semesters. This week, I'd like to go over your morals. Can anyone tell me why good morals are important to Delta Beta?"

The petite Asian girl raised her hand. "Because it's in our creed?"

"Sort of, but I think it's in our creed *because* it's important to the sorority, not vice versa. Anyone else?"

"Because we're not Tri Mu?" That came from the back of the room and resulted in almost everyone snickering.

"That's sort of true, too," Cheyenne said with a wink. "But good morals define your character. Anyone can follow a rule just because it's a rule. That doesn't mean they're moral people. They just don't want to suffer the consequences when they break a rule. Morals are how you live your life when there are no rules. Morals are how you live when nobody's watching."

"I thought that was dance," a tall girl with thick auburn hair half joked.

"Yeah," another pledge nodded. "You're supposed to dance like no one is watching."

A pretty cheerleader type scoffed. "The whole point of dancing is to make sure people are watching you." Some of the other pledges nodded in agreement.

"It's the same principle with morals," I said to the room. "Yes, you can dance for performance's sake, for your dance class, or for your parents, who paid for the lessons. But if you dance while no one is watching, you're wilder, crazier. You reveal your true self then, just when it's you and the music. Morals are the things you do when no one is watching. Your sharing class notes; your forming a study group. Your showing up for work on time. These are the things that shape your character."

This is what Ty Hatfield didn't understand about the Delta Beta code. It was why I preserved the sanctity of our rituals. It was why I would always put my sisters first. It was why I knew a Deb could never murder or kill someone on purpose. It would go against everything we stood for.

Chapter Nine

WEDNESDAY MORNING, I got up with a renewed sense of purpose. After dressing and eating a quick breakfast, I headed to the chapter advisor's office and locked the door of the office behind me. It was rather futile, maybe even immature, but somehow I felt the need to lock myself in. Hatfield's visit the night before had given me a lot to think about, on top of the pile of to-do's I already had. As cute as he was, Ty did seem to be a diligent cop and rather distrustful of women. It was a shame. Women had so much to offer men.

The suggestion that Liza McCarthy had been murdered was bad enough. The suggestion that a sorority sister was the murderer was untenable. Ty Hatfield did not understand how sororities worked. Sorority women were a lot of things, but we weren't murderers.

First, I checked the office voice mail. Sure enough, as Amanda had warned me, there were about ten messages from Sutton College administrators and other Greek chapter advisors, offering both their condolences and not-so-subtle digs for information.

The last five messages were all from the same person; a Brice Concannon, the fraternity-council advisor. According to his final message, he'd been appointed by the college to be the go-between between the police, the chapter, and the administration, which I thought was ridiculous. I didn't need a man to do my talking for me. As I had nothing to share with this Brice Concannon, I focused on organizing the office.

The first round was clearing all sociology papers from the room. This was fairly easy, and in thirty minutes, I had a nice pile of books, tests, and papers that one of the chapter members could return to the sociology department. As a doctoral candidate, it looked like Liza had taught some classes, and the department would probably need these.

During the next pass, I focused on collecting the standard Delta Beta materials. The chapter bylaws and the pledge manual went on the bookshelf as I had all that committed to memory. Since I had thoroughly reviewed the monthly reports to HQ, with the GPAs and membership numbers, I shoved those up there, too.

Then I was left with the details. I set aside the order forms for the house's kitchen, intending to temporarily delegate those decisions to the house cook. There were several piles of receipts for various chapter expenses that I placed in a large brown envelope marked "receipts." I'm fairly organized that way.

Hatfield had mentioned notes and letters. Sadly, there weren't many of the latter. I found a few birthday cards that made me want to cry. Unfortunately, there were tons of notes. Half-scribbled on pieces of paper ripped from some spiral notebook, copies of Panhellenic agendas with her doodles all over them, even napkins with lists of names and numbers. I couldn't make sense of them, as haphazard as they were. I kept digging, until I found notes I did recognize, on the official forms of the Delta Beta Standards and Morals office.

Standards and morals was the worst part of the job anywhere in the Delta Beta sorority organization, but it was a duty essential to the proper development of young women. Every sorority kept its own standards for membership, some lower than others (cough, Tri Mu, cough), and when sisters failed to live up to those standards, they sat through hearings in front of the standards and morals director, the chapter president, and the chapter advisor. Consequences ranged from financial penalties, to work penalties, to the ultimate, heartbreaking discipline: yanking a sister's pin.

I recognized these forms on Liza's desk, which detailed the violations of one sister and scheduled a date for her hearing, in just three days' time. This one was being disciplined for having an inappropriate relationship with a professor. I shook my head. It was a tale as old as time. I found a folder for the S&M forms and placed them in a desk drawer. It seemed appropriate, something tawdry as that needed to be locked up.

It was when I was placing the folder in the drawer that I found the address book. A plain, black book, it had no markings to indicate whether it was official Delta Beta issue or for personal use. I suspected it was personal just because it didn't have a honeybee on it (our sorority symbol), nor a yellow rose (our sorority flower), nor a picture of a topaz (our sorority jewel).

Remembering what Aubrey and Hatfield had told me about Liza's family, I got excited when I opened the book, hoping against hope that there was a name or a number of someone who would want to get the news of Liza's passing. Maybe I would even make the call myself. I imagined the tears, the heartbreak, the jagged voice of a long-lost cousin thanking me for finding them so that they could do the right thing for Liza.

I flipped open to the "A" page. It was empty. "B" was also empty. "C" was where the entries started. They continued through "D," "E," "F," rows of incomprehensible letters, followed by ten numbers, then followed by either numbers, letters, or a mix. The first set of letters could have been names, maybe. Some of them were pronounceable and some had lots of consonants and no vowels which, unless Liza knew a whole lot of Eastern Europeans, didn't make much sense. Out of frustration, I flipped to the "M" page, in the vain hope that I'd see an entry like, "McCarthy, Long-Lost Cousin Ed." But there was just more of the same: two lines with letters, then ten numbers, then a shorter mix of letters. Clearly, this was some sort of secret journal, but it could have been for anything from her investments, to her Internet passwords, to her sociology class's grading system.

I was staring at the address book when I heard the door lock slide. The door opened and Callie Campbell walked through.

"Oh!" Callie froze when she saw me. "Sorry! I was just . . ."

"Come in," I said, getting up and shoving the pile meant for the sociology department off the chair on the other side of the desk. "Sit down," I invited her. "I'm just cleaning up in here. What can I help you with?"

Callie quickly sat down, an anxious look on her face. It was obvious she was stressed, poor girl. Who wouldn't be, under these circumstances?

When she pushed a strand of long blond hair behind her ear, I could see she was trembling. "Callie? Honey, tell me what's wrong."

"N-nothing." She took a shallow breath then followed with that brilliant smile, bracketed by those adorable dimples. "I'm S&M director, you know . . ."

"Yes," I placed my hand on the drawer pull where I had placed the forms earlier. "I've been reviewing Liza's papers."

"Oh?" Callie's hazel gaze swept the piles on the desk. "'Cause I came to see . . . if I could help, or I can just get them, keep them. You know, help you out."

What a sweetheart. Putting me first even though she was clearly overcome with the emotions of being in Liza's office. "Callie, I just don't think that's appropriate. As chapter advisor, I should really keep all the S&M forms. Especially with the subject matter."

Callie nodded and pushed her hair behind her ear again. "I see."

"Especially with the hearing in three days."

Callie's eyes widened. "Three days?"

Maybe I had it wrong. I checked my monogrammed calendar. "No. Stefanie Grossman. Saturday at two."

"Oh." Callie's shoulders relaxed. "Yeah. Stefanie."

I made a sympathetic face at the note of defeat in Callie's voice. "I know it's hard when you have to go through this with a sister." Callie still looked distressed. "When was the last time you saw Stefanie?"

Callie's brows drew together. "It's been weeks. She wasn't happy when she got written up. She just disappeared. We think she might be . . . with him." She hesitated before explaining further. "Her professor."

I nodded. Sisters rarely were happy to be brought up on standards and morals and often tried to bring other sisters down with them, or claim that favoritism was at work. It seemed that Stefanie had taken the opposite route of just walking away. It was a defense mechanism, to protect herself from being judged by her friends.

"Are you going to be able to do the hearing?" I asked. S&M hearings could be so traumatic. If Callie was this upset about it now, she'd be in for a real shock when the final judgment came.

Callie looked pained but nodded in the affirmative. I wouldn't expect anything less from Mary Gerald Callahan's great-great-great-great-granddaughter. Devotion to Delta Beta ran in the family, I was sure.

"Anything else I should know about?" I asked, hoping to distract her from the depressing topic.

"The Alpha Kappa mixer on Friday," Callie said with some force.

"What about it?"

Callie crinkled her nose. "It's traditionally . . . a busy time of year?"

"You mean . . ."

"It's crazy. A lot of girls get written up when we party with the Alpha Kapps."

I smiled reassuringly at Callie. "Don't worry, I know how to handle the Alpha Kapps," I said. After all, it wasn't that long ago that I was on that dance floor at an Alpha Kappa mixer. I knew my way around a fraternity house or two. In a totally innocent way, of course.

Chapter Ten

CALLIE HAD JUST opened the office door to leave when a brunette with corkscrew curls yelled and ran into the room. Another brunette, this one with stick-straight hair ran in on Curly's heels. They were both screaming something incomprehensible. Finally, I understood. Sort of.

"Goats?" I asked in my grown-up, completely authoritative squeal. "What do you mean, goats?"

Curly breathed hard. "Goats. In the bathroom."

"Which bathroom?" I asked both of them

"The half bath on the first floor." That was Curly. Her name might have been Stacy. Or Tracy. Lacey?

"Yes, GOATS!!!" That was the straight-haired sister. I was pretty sure her name was Emma. Or Jenna. Jemma? .

The ladies followed me down the hall to the half bath, where a small group had already gathered. Sure enough, there was a certain odor emanating from the bathroom. And a shuffling, munching sound. What the . . . I tiptoed to the door and cracked it.

"GOATS!" I yelled before I slammed the door again. A bleating came from inside. Or was it a baa?

"What do you mean?" Asha Patel was confused.

"It's an acronym," Jane told her.

"Not an acronym," I said.

"Or a disease," Jane said.

"Definitely not a disease," I disagreed. "Goats." I opened the door again. "See?"

Jane and Asha and eight other women peeked and peered into the half bath. One goat was on the floor, eating something. One goat stood on the back of the toilet tank. Another goat rested on top of the vanity, its little goat belly inside the sink. I wondered if that was a comfortable position for a goat.

"What's that one doing on the countertop?" one of the girls asked reasonably.

"It's probably pregnant," Asha said. "About to give birth in a manger like Mary."

Oh hell no. There were going to be no baby-goat deliveries on my watch, virgin or otherwise.

"Does anyone know who's in charge of removing goats from the half bath?" Jane asked the group. Again, it was a reasonable question.

Ten sets of eyes looked at me. "Me?" I asked dumbly. "But don't you need like, a goat license? Or a vet to properly dispose of a goat?"

A tall basketball player with straight blond hair burst into tears. "Don't kill them!"

So that would be wrong? "I'm not going to kill them," I said, reluctantly tossing aside my brief visions of goaticide.

"Does anyone know whose goats these are?" I yelled in my mean-chapter-advisor voice. "There are three goats in a Delta Beta bathroom. Somebody has to know where they came from."

All I got was a bunch of blank looks in response. Great. A goat mystery. That was all I needed. There was a goat sound from inside the bathroom, then two. Then the sound of splashing and a toilet flushing. "That's it," I muttered. I pulled out my phone and called 911.

"What's your emergency?" the operator asked, in a not very urgent voice.

"I have goats in my bathroom."

"Okay, is this something that you've had before or did it just start today?"

"Today," I snarled, not appreciating the implication that I always had goats in my bathroom. Who did he think I was?

"Are you having trouble breathing, pain in your chest, dizziness, or—"

I interrupted him. "Yes, no, and . . ." I grabbed at the wall with my free hand. "Maybe. I've never dealt with this before."

"Do you have someone there who can drive you to the hospital?"

"I have three goats in my bathroom! I can't go anywhere! They're going to flood the place!"

"Okay, I'm sending someone out immediately," the operator said.

I looked up at the girls around me. "Someone go out and wait for the goat exterminator." The tall blonde wailed. "I mean, the nice firemen. Asha." I got the social director's attention, her big brown eyes wide with excitement. "You know the frats pretty well, right?"

"Well . . ." She blushed and looked down, clearly misinterpreting my question. Seriously?

I waved my hand in front of her face to get her to focus on me again and not her love life. "Get on the phone and find out which stupid fraternity wants its goats back."

In unison, the remainder of the girls went "ah" and nodded in understanding. As furious as I was about three goats taking up residence in the first-floor guest bathroom, I had to give props to whichever fraternity pledges thought this up. This kind of prank took both unprecedented skill and sneakiness, two traits highly valued by the fraternity men of Sutton College.

The first responders showed up, firemen who acted like they had never removed goats from a building before, which I found a little ridiculous. These were somewhat common farm animals, if Lucy, the bubbly sister from Kentucky, was to be believed. They hemmed and hawed and got rope out and finally came up with the brilliant plan to lead the goats outside with ropes around their necks. Some heroes.

Then they left the goats out in the front yard, each tied to its own tree, and left, their fire truck clanging down sorority row as it went, causing Tri Mus and Betas and Epsilon Chis to emerge from their houses to gawk at the goats in the Deb yard. Because that was just what we needed this week. Farm animals certainly didn't help a chapter's reputation.

I called animal control about pests in the front yard. They said they didn't deal with goats.

"I didn't say they were goats," I snapped back.

"Yeah, we heard about it over the scanner. Good luck with your goats."

"Asha!" I yelled.

She appeared by my side in a jiffy. "I have it narrowed down. It definitely wasn't the Trikes."

I rolled my eyes. Trikes weren't known for animal pranks. Their pranks usually involved protractors and the scientific method. Annoying, but easy to clean up.

And so, I found myself babysitting three goats until we could catch the culprits and bring them to justice, or at least give them their goats back. And this was why I was sitting in the front yard of the Deb house, hand-feeding Honey Nut Cheerios to a potentially pregnant goat when Lieutenant Ty Hatfield strolled into the Delta Beta yard.

"Let me guess," I said. "Police scanner?"

He settled into the tree swing, his long legs stretching out. "Nah. Heard it from the meter maids downtown."

I didn't want to know how far this had gotten. I patted the nanny goat's head and pretended that I was on a farm, far, far away.

"You've got a way with farm animals," he said. I shrugged. "But you've got a way with most things."

I scratched between the goat's ears. She seemed to like it. Turned out, a goat was kind of like a larger, uglier, smellier dog.

"So what's your plan? Are you going to slap some sorority letters on these and teach them about proper etiquette and what not to wear?"

Just when he was acting nice to me, he started in on my sorority. That's how I knew that Ty Hatfield and I would never work—in a romantic sense. He didn't appreciate my sorority. And any man who couldn't do that was out the totally theoretical door.

"We're arranging for their owners to pick them back up," I informed him, like that had been my calm, well-thought-out plan all along.

"Not going to happen," Ty said. "The frat pledges don't own up to their pranks. They like to be anonymous. Like really anonymous."

I knew that. Sutton College pranks never made the most sense. Like the time the Omegas paid a marching band from a local high school to march up and down sorority row between the hours of 2 and 4 A.M. Or the time the Alpha Kapps had two hundred pineapple pizzas delivered to the Deb house. Who even eats pineapple pizza? The pranks were annoying and juvenile and probably, in the end, harmless. That's why they liked them, I guessed. They could be still be kids, do kid stuff, without any of the grown-up consequences.

"We'll find out who it was," I said calmly, stroking a goat's head.

"And then what?"

I turned my big, innocent brown eyes on him. "We'll take revenge."

Ty pretended to shudder, which really wasn't appropriate for an officer of the law. He should take a threat of revenge more seriously. But I guess I wasn't very scary, and neither was my sorority. For as long as prank week had been going on, fraternities had pranked and sororities had sat back and been pranked. It was a tradition. And there was no room in that tradition for a sorority to join in and exact vengeance. Especially a sorority as demure and polite and formerly scandal-free as Delta Beta.

Chapter Eleven

NO WOMAN WANTS to meet the man of her dreams while petting a goat. That was what raced through my head when I saw Mr. Dreamy. Slim, dark, and in a way-too-fashionable-for-North-Carolina gray suit, he flashed a devastating smile at me despite the goat/Cheerio snot I was hastily wiping on my jeans.

"Hi, can you tell me where I might find your chapter advisor?"

"My chapter advisor?" I shook my head in confusion. "I don't have a chapter advisor."

"He means you, Blythe." Ty drawled from my right.

The handsome man's smile widened. "Blythe? You're Margot Blythe? But you look too young to be an advisor! I thought you were a chapter member."

Well. He was handsome and fashion-forward and knew just the right things to say to make a girl blush. This was probably what love at first sight was like.

"I'm Margot," I assured him. "And you are . . ." My knight in shining armor?

"Brice Concannon, from the Interfraternity Council."

Somewhere, from the direction of Ty Hatfield's face, I heard a snort. Brice continued, "I left you a few messages."

"Oh yes." The goat nudged my hand forcefully because I'd run out of cereal. "How can I help you?"

"As I said on the phone, the college has asked me to be the point man for this . . ." He waved his hand vaguely toward the sorority house. "Situation."

I crinkled my nose. "Situation?"

"With a sudden death and police investigation, the college wants to ensure that the students are supported as much as possible. If there's any need for counseling, or academic assistance, or I could even help you with your interactions with the police."

Now Ty growled, something that sounded like a word Delta Betas never used in polite company.

I bit my lip as I thought about this unexpected offer. It was reassuring to know the college wanted to support my traumatized sisters, and I made sure to let Brice know that. But until we knew, one way or another, the truth about the circumstances of Liza's death—and the involvement of any other sisters—I knew it was better for me to keep my mouth shut and keep the details shared with Sutton administrators to a minimum.

"I will make sure to keep all that in mind," I promised him. "So far, the police have been pretty reasonable to work with."

Brice looked over at Ty, still lazily rocking back and forth in the swing. "So good to hear that."

Ty smirked back at Brice, the expression more challenging than anything. Police were so possessive about their investigations.

The goat nudged me again, this time burrowing under my

armpit, which was both weird and a little tickly. My inadvertent giggle didn't escape Brice's attention, unfortunately. Why could I not meet a cute guy without a goat nuzzling me?

"There is one thing you could help me with . . ."

"Name it," Brice said.

"I think one of your frats left their goats in our bathroom."

IT TURNED OUT that becoming acquainted with the Interfraternity Council advisor had its advantages. Magically, the goats were gone—collected off our front lawn by a sheepish young Agriculture major. By that time, the goats had taken up most of my afternoon, but I still had time to squeeze in one more project before the ringing of the dinner triangle, an important, long-standing Deb tradition.

Why? Because a delta is a triangle. Not all sorority traditions have to involve obscure rituals.

I booted up the chapter advisor's computer, not really knowing what I'd find. All those years as a Sisterhood Mentor, I had focused entirely on the collegiate side of sorority life and had relatively little experience with the business affairs that came along with an advisor position. When the screen lit up, I could see from the desktop and a quick look at the saved documents that Liza hadn't used the computer for any notes or correspondence. It looked like she used a Web-based e-mail system, so I couldn't even check any contacts for those long-lost relatives I had so briefly fantasized about.

I wondered how that worked when someone died. Where did your Facebook and e-mails go? Did your Facebook stay suspended in the Internet ether forever, a living testament to your last status update? What if it was something stupid, like, "Going to the gym?" I shuddered at the thought of such an inadvertent legacy. I made a mental note never to post inane status updates. And to leave my passwords with a good friend who could delete anything unfortunate in my browser history.

Poking around, I could see the last document saved was from QuickBooks. Finally, something I knew I could recognize. Rows of dollars and cents. I pulled the spreadsheet open and briefly reviewed the chapter's finances. They seemed a little spotty at first glance, to tell the truth, but if finances had been a concern, you could bet that HQ would have alerted me on that before I left for Sutton. When a chapter's not financially solvent, that's the first thing a Sisterhood Mentor has to address on her to-do list.

Something about the numbers caught my eye. I wasn't quite sure what it was, but my brain was yelling that it didn't look right. It didn't hit me right away, which is one of the main reasons why I kept turning down a headquarters job in accounting. My excuse was that my brain adds up numbers differently. (Yeah, my college algebra professor didn't buy it either.)

I was trying to focus, but then someone opened the door. Again. Maybe Liza had an open-door policy, but that wasn't going to work for me.

Headed in and caught a little off guard was the chapter president herself, Aubrey St. John. I wiped the annoyance off my face. This was the girl who'd shown me where the office was and helped me get acquainted with everything.

She, on the other hand, was clearly startled by my presence. "I didn't think you'd still be in here."

I frowned at her. "The door was unlocked."

"Right." Aubrey looked back at the door, her cell phone clutched in her hand. "I lost the key Liza gave me." She smiled charmingly. "President's privilege. Sometimes I like to come in here and study."

What a good girl she was. "You know, I bet the girls in the chapter really look up to you, with all your good habits."

Aubrey looked down at her toes in her Jack Rogers sandals, still immaculately pedicured, even in October. "I guess," she said.

"I love your skirt," I said, admiring her wool kilt.

"Thanks," she said, absently brushing the cloth. "You could borrow it if you'd like."

I surveyed Aubrey's figure. Although I was about four inches taller than her, we might be the same size around. "It would probably be too short on me," I said. "But thanks for the offer. I get so tired of my clothes sometimes, wearing the same things from my suitcase."

Aubrey's crystal blue eyes fixed on me. "Then come up and borrow something. Anytime. I'm used to sisters borrowing clothes."

My heart squeezed a little at that, it was so sweet.

"What's going on?" I asked. Something told me she hadn't come in to study. Something told me maybe she just needed to talk to someone.

"I—I just came to see if you needed anything. If you don't understand something, let me know, and I'll explain it to you. If you want." I looked at Aubrey closely. The words were right, but something was off in the delivery.

"I swear, you all are so helpful around here!"

"What do you have there?" Aubrey asked, looking at the computer.

"Chapter financials," I said, "I did have a few . . ." I was interrupted by the sound of two loud male voices coming from the hall.

Aubrey looked alarmed. Not a lot of men came into the Delta Beta house, and when men didn't enter often, their presence was mighty obvious. I was ready to storm out and set straight whatever sarcastic police officer thought he could barge in, but then I recognized the voice. It wasn't a man, it was . . .

"CASEY!" I squealed, running to the door and straight into the arms of my best friend, Casey Kenner.

I couldn't believe he was here. I turned to introduce him to Aubrey and saw that she had come around to my side of the desk and was staring at the computer screen, her face pale, her mouth open.

"Aubrey? What is it?" I ran back around to her and put an arm around her shoulder. "Are you okay?" It seemed I was asking that question every third minute lately.

She saw Casey and was even more stunned, but she still couldn't seem to close her mouth.

"Aubrey, meet Casey Kenner, from headquarters. Casey, this is Aubrey St. John, chapter president."

Casey smiled at Aubrey, with a big movie-star smile that darn near sparkled like a toothpaste commercial. Let me tell you this, Casey is gorgeous with a capital G. When I was a little girl, I used to watch classic movies with my grandma Fredrick in the summer. When I met Casey, I told him he was a dead ringer for Cary Grant and Rock Hudson's love child. And Casey is so classy, he knew exactly what I meant by that.

I know, I know. You're wondering why Casey isn't my boyfriend if he's so gorgeous and my best friend and he works for Delta Beta headquarters, right? You're saying, "Margot, that Casey sounds like the perfect man." Unfortunately, I'm not Casey's type. And if you're wondering what that means, it means Casey likes men.

You might also be wondering how Casey works for Delta Beta when he is a man. He applied for the job and simply failed to mention that fact. Since he has a gender-neutral name, he got an interview. And once he had that? Well, Casey's a lot like me. People don't turn him down very often. Casey's a Delta Beta woman in all but the extra X chromosome. He grew up surrounded by Debs—his mama, his two sisters, his mama's mama. Unfortunately, his daddy's mama was a Tri Mu. He doesn't talk about her much.

Casey was a sight for sore eyes. He was dressed impeccably, as always. Today he wore a tweed coat with suede elbow patches, a purple-striped Oxford shirt, loafers that probably cost more than a car payment, and a scarf tossed just so over his shoulder. It takes a real man to wear a scarf.

"What are you doing here?" I squealed again before hugging him. I don't really know why I was so excited to see him. Maybe I needed a break from all the grieving and dramatics at the house. I guess I was relieved to have my fun friend around to help me forget my troubles.

"I brought the files from HQ you asked for." Casey pointed at the rolling briefcase behind him.

"You're too sweet," I said for Aubrey's benefit. I'd known Casey for too long to believe that he drove across three states to bring me files he could have FedExed. Something big was going on, something he needed to be here for.

Like the sweet girl she was, Aubrey excused herself quickly, and when she did, I locked the door behind her. Casey gave the lock a pointed look. "You wouldn't believe how busy it's been in here," I said to explain the locked door before turning to him and crossing my arms. "Now. Shoot."

Chapter Twelve

CASEY'S EYES SWEPT from side to side. "Is the room secure?"

Normally, I would have laughed. But today, the joke made me nervous. Hatfield's visit and all the goats and emotions in the house had really put me on edge.

"What's in the briefcase?" I asked, toeing the thing with trepidation. With Casey, one really never knew what he packed on trips. It was one of the things I loved about him. That, and his talent at hair.

Casey waved a hand. "The reports from HQ, like I said. They sent you like, ten years' worth of documents." He rolled his eyes. Casey was a big-picture person, like me. That's why he was so good at public relations.

"And Mabel asked me to come down."

I frowned. I had just talked to Mabel Donahue that morning. Okay, really early that morning.

"Why?" I asked.

"Do you know the reason why they sent you here, to Sutton?"

I shook my head. It wasn't that big of a deal. I didn't always know the reason for a chapter visit. Sometimes a chapter had a specific problem it needed help with, like rush or a problem with the university. But sometimes it was just a well-woman checkup. I was like a gynecologist that way.

Casey's face was grim. "A month ago, they got a call from Liza McCarthy, requesting a meeting in Atlanta at headquarters."

That was interesting. "How did that go?"

Casey shook his head. "For some reason, a few days later, she called and canceled. Mabel said she was really upset and talked about quitting the chapter-advisor position. That's when Mabel decided that it was time for a Sisterhood Mentor to come and check out the chapter, generally speaking. She thought maybe it had gotten too stressful for some reason or that there was something that Liza wasn't telling her."

"Mabel didn't say anything about any of this to me this morning," I said.

Casey gave me a look that said he loved me but he thought I was ridiculous. "You called her at two in the morning."

"Why would I wait until morning to tell her someone had died?" Like that made sense.

Casey ignored my question. "She didn't really remember all this until the police officer called this morning, asking about Liza McCarthy."

I groaned at the mention of a police officer. "Hatfield."

"Who?" Casey asked.

"The police officer here who doesn't understand sororities. He's prejudiced."

Casey nodded. He understood.

I still didn't understand something. "So why did Mabel send you down here? Why didn't she just call me and tell me all this?"

Casey smiled like something was about to get good. "Because right after the po-po called, Mabel got another call from her hairdresser, who also does the hair of a Mrs. Barbra Kline."

My face was probably blank as a board. The name didn't mean anything to me. I didn't keep up with the sorority-gossip scene like Casey did. I was too busy traveling the country and saving the world.

Casey rushed on, dying to get to the good stuff. "Mrs. Barbra Kline is also known as Mabel's counterpart at a certain organization we like to call Try Moo."

Mu Mu Mu. Also known as Tri Mu. Also known as Try Moo. Or simply, the Moos. Also known as Delta Beta's sister sorority and archenemy. Yes, those two relationships coincide quite well, thank you.

Hearing the Moos' name sent a shiver all over me. "What did the hairdresser say about Mrs. Kline?"

"Mrs. Kline told the hairdresser that it was a shame about the Sutton chapter of Delta Beta, about to close so soon."

I sucked in a breath. "What? That cow!"

"I know!" Casey said, matching my indignation.

My mind reeled with the news. So far, I had seen nothing that would indicate that the Sutton chapter was having any problems serious enough to warrant suspension of chapter activities or expulsion from the campus. So basically, that meant that . . .

"Mrs. Kline is a big fat liar!"

Casey nodded like that was no big surprise. "But Mabel's nervous that Barbra Kline knows something that she doesn't. And she's nervous about Liza's death after that cop said that it wasn't natural."

I tried not to let the worry wrinkles creep onto my face. My insurance wouldn't cover the Botox. "He said pretty much the same thing to me."

"You know Mabel," Casey pointed out. "She's a little paranoid about the Tri Mus."

I worked through the implications of all this strange, yet juicy information. "She doesn't think that the Moos put a *hit* out on Liza—does she?" I asked, lowering my voice in case the room was bugged. It was almost unbelievable. But these *were* Tri Mus we were talking about.

My eyes widened as Casey nodded, slowly. I looked around the office again, wondering if it was secure. What did a bug or a mic look like, anyway? I'd have to tear the office apart again to make sure the Tri Mus didn't have some secret listening device hidden away in here. I picked up a Delta Beta stuffed honeybee off the bookshelf. I hope I didn't have to rip her apart like they did in the movies. That would be tragic.

"Is she afraid that my phone's tapped, too?" I whispered.

Casey's grim look was all the answer I needed.

BECAUSE CASEY COULDN'T stay in the sorority house (yes, I know, I said he was as good as a member, but he still had a penis, and rules are rules), I went with him to the Fountain Place Inn, an historic motel just off campus. Plus, at the Fountain Place, we could talk more openly. I didn't think the Tri Mus had the wherewithal to bug every room in Sutton.

Casey checked in, and I went up to his room with him, still feeling a little uneasy about the news from Atlanta. I remembered the inn well, from my college days. It was where my mom and dad always stayed when they visited me, in separate rooms, sometimes on separate floors. The story was that Mom snored. Or that Dad slept around with every slut on the Florida panhandle. It was one or the other.

We lay back on the bed, and Casey popped open a flask with the Deb crest on it, mixing drinks with the overpriced sodas from the motel vending machines. I told him everything that had happened in the last thirty-six hours, knowing that he would understand both my heartbreak and my concern for the chapter.

"Oh!" I sat up reaching for my phone. "We need to get together with Amanda!" It was too exciting, the thought of my two best friends finally meeting each other. We could go out and hit the Sutton bar scene, which consisted of three establishments lined up on the north side of campus. The town's forefathers had been pretty strict about that aspect of city planning. I tried calling Amanda three times, but it went to voice mail each time. On the fourth try, I received an automated message that said her voice mail was full. There must have been a Panhellenic emergency to deal with.

When it got too late to go out (we were, after all, in our late twenties now), Casey drove me back to the Deb house. I entered the secret door code—the same as the code at every Delta Beta sorority house around the country. Our tech guys at HQ said that was a security risk, but tradition was more important than potential intruders.

As chapter advisor, it was my duty to check the house and make sure all was well before going up to my room. I wandered through the first floor, picked up a few pieces of trash, and stacked a few magazines. It may surprise some to know that college women aren't always the neatest people. I opened the door to the chapter room, which was still lit softly by the small bulbs in the wooden display cases, accenting just some of the trophies and awards that the house had won in the past seventy years. There were a lot: national awards from HQ, Panhellenic awards, Sigma Chi Derby Days trophies. Looking at these physical reminders of Delta Beta's excellence only reinforced my belief that Mrs. Barbra Kline of Mu Mu Mu was full of it. Nothing was bringing this chapter down.

The last stop on my rounds was the chapter advisor's office. I flipped on a light as I went through the kitchen, turned left down the back hall, and noticed at the last minute that the office door was cracked. I was one hundred percent sure that I had locked that door when I left with Casey. Of course I had, with the tale of intersorority espionage that he was weaving. I'd never underestimate those Moos.

But the door was definitely cracked. With a pounding heart, I reached my hand out and slowly pushed the door open. Halfway through, I paused. It was absolutely idiotic to go through this door. There could be anyone in there, just waiting to murder me like they murdered Liza. I tiptoed back to the kitchen, grabbed a large stainless-steel spatula, and headed back. If someone was in there, they were going to get slapped upside the head. This spatula was industrial strength. It could do some damage.

I peeked my head into the office and gasped at what I found. Just like in the movies, the place had been torn apart. Papers and books had been knocked to the ground, the Deb Busy Bee ripped apart, the computer smashed on the floor. Next to the wreckage of the computer was the tool that had seemingly smashed the computer monitor: Liza McCarthy's Chapter Advisor of the Year Award, given by Panhellenic.

Chapter Thirteen

As late as it was, I was tempted to go upstairs to the chapter guest room, crawl under the T-shirt quilt, and sleep until the next morning brought sunshine, smiles, and a nice big nonfat, three-Equal, three-shot latte.

But no. As much as I wanted to protect my sisters, this was serious. A stuffed bee had been destroyed, for heaven's sake. I looked up the number for the police station.

Ty Hatfield drove into the parking lot without any sirens or flashing lights, which disappointed the *Law & Order* fan in me. On the other hand, the chapter advisor pro tem inside of me was grateful for the lack of attention. On sorority row, police lights could haunt us for years during rush conversations—especially two police visits in one week.

When he stepped out of the car, Hatfield didn't look as pressed and put together as he had the previous times we'd met. Instead of a police-department polo, he had on a nonregulation T-shirt with the Sutton Eagles logo on it, jeans, and boots. Seeing him in off-duty clothes sparked a memory inside me, but it quickly flitted away from all my current stress and worry. Anyway, I was pretty sure he'd been messing with me when he implied I should remember him from . . . something. Seeing him like this confirmed my first impressions. If I'd met him before, I'd definitely remember Ty Hatfield.

I sat on the front steps of the house, my knees drawn up against my chest. "You rang," he said, walking up the path. His tone was low and a little uncertain, which made sense since I hadn't told him what was going on when I called. Some things needed to be seen for themselves. And there was still the potential that secret microphones were lurking inside the house.

I led him back to the office and let him see the damage. His whole demeanor changed. His relaxed and laid-back demeanor changed in a split second, as he unconsciously adopted the same stiff-and-business posture I'd seen in all our previous visits. I'd liked the relaxed Ty Hatfield better.

"Tell me," he said.

I knew what he was asking. Like I said, I watch a lot of *Law & Order*. No matter where I traveled, there was always a station that had reruns on. It helped fill the spaces between sorority emergencies.

The details spilled from me. How I'd spent the whole day in here, getting organized and sorting through Liza's papers. And then some very rude person had trashed the place and ruined all my hard work.

He gave me a level look. Oh. "I locked up about six or so. My colleague Casey just got here from headquarters. I went with him to his hotel, and I came back about half past midnight. I was checking the house before bed when I found this."

I didn't miss the speculative glint in Ty's eyes when I mentioned going back to Casey's hotel.

But he managed to move on. "Did you see anyone else in the house?"

I shook my head. It was a Wednesday night. Most of the women had retired to bed or to the upstairs TV room. I hadn't seen anyone else downstairs.

"What about men? Anyone suspicious?"

"That's redundant."

"Not always," Ty drawled. "Anyone from campus? Colleagues?" He paused. "Brice Concannon?"

That was too specific to be the product of random brainstorming. "Brice Concannon?" I echoed. "The fraternity advisor?"

Ty's nod was dispassionate, but the set of his jaw was tense.

"Why would you think he would be here?"

"He offered to come by."

I didn't recall Brice's offer quite that the same way. "Is there something I should know about him?"

Ty looked up from his notepad and pulled his head back, observing me closely. "Just watch out for him. Sometimes he comes down on the wrong side of problems."

That was a strange warning, but given their respective positions, I could see where most everyone, and especially a fraternity representative, could come down on the wrong side of things for a man of the law such as Ty Hatfield.

"He wasn't here," I said simply.

With a businesslike "hmm," he took his phone out and made a quick call to campus police, asking them to check out Liza McCarthy's office in the sociology department.

"She has an office on campus?" I asked.

"Of course," Ty said sharply. "Why wouldn't she?"

I looked around the torn-up chapter advisor's office and the pile of sociology papers that had been previously neatly filed. "Because it looked like she did all her work here." I pointed and explained my thought process. For once, Ty didn't act like I was completely worthless.

"I'll check out her office," he said, more to himself than to me.

"Is anything missing?" he asked. I startled. I hadn't even thought about that. I was mostly pissed that someone had the gall to mess up a very organized office.

"It's hard to tell," I murmured, but I looked around anyway. After spending the whole day in the office, I had a pretty good mental list of what was in all the piles. I checked the drawers last. That's when I realized that something had been taken.

"The S&M forms," I said.

Ty's eyes nearly popped out of his head.

I sighed impatiently. Really? "Standards and Morals. They're for bad behavior."

His lips quirked distractingly. "S&M is for bad behavior?"

"I've heard it before, Hatfield!" I said, holding up a hand to cut off any other snarky comments.

His usual antisorority expression was back on the police officer's face. "Bad behavior, huh? What do you do, put them in time-out for not eating their vegetables?"

I ignored that. For a police officer, he sure didn't respect organizational rules. "They're gone," I repeated. "I put them all in a folder, right here. And someone took them."

"What kind of information was in them?"

"Confid—"

Ty held out a hand and interrupted me. "Don't say it."

"Habit," I tried to smile. But it *was* confidential information. And it was hard for me to share it. Protecting Delta Beta secrets had been an integral part of my life for nearly ten years. To talk about it with a noninitiated person was against almost everything I stood for.

But whoever had taken confidential files had violated that confidentiality first. Going to the police was ensuring that other sisters would have their disciplinary consequences kept private.

"It was paperwork for a disciplinary hearing," I said with resignation.

"For who?"

"A sister." At Ty's flat look, I continued reluctantly. "Stefanie Grossman. I've never met her. I just looked at the papers this afternoon."

"What was she being written up for?"

This was the yucky part. "Sexual misconduct."

Ty rolled his head back. "What is with you people? I thought women were over that Puritan shit."

I shifted uncomfortably. "It's a rule. It's not like the women can't . . . engage . . . in stuff."

"But they get sent to their rooms without supper if they enjoy themselves?"

"It's not like that," I insisted. "It's about . . ." I searched for the right word. "Discretion."

Ty paused. "Okay, got it."

"What?"

"They can do it, but they can't let anyone know about it?"

I scrunched up my nose. That was pretty much the rule. Yes, it was old-fashioned. Yes, it wasn't particularly enlightened. But it was tradition. It was the rule. And those of us who disagreed with the rules were going to change them the Delta Beta way: slowly, and with little to no fanfare.

Ty shook his head again. "I'll never get sororities."

Well, at least he was admitting his prejudice. Admitting you had a problem was the first step.

I gave Ty the contact information for Stefanie Grossman from the chapter roster. He walked around the office again, taking notes and gently moving items with his pen, taking care not to touch anything. "We'll get the place fingerprinted in the next few days."

"Few days?" I was aghast. On *Law & Order*, the fingerprinting team was Johnny-on-the-spot.

Ty was nonplussed. "We use a contractor. He has to come in from Greenville."

"On TV it goes much faster."

"Well, it's not like this is an emergency."

Ty was failing to see the problem.

"But what about . . . Liza?" I dropped my voice when I said her name, out of respect and solidarity. And because of Tri Mu bugs.

Ty's eyes sharpened at me. "Have some reason to believe these are connected?"

"Aren't they?" This was Liza's office, after all. "First she dies, then her office is destroyed."

Ty shrugged. "Could be. Could be some coed doesn't want her friends to know what she does to her boyfriend on the weekends."

I threw up my hands. "It's not like that." But I stopped there. Because sometimes, it could be like that. Maybe Ty was onto something about these rules.

"What about the computer?" Ty asked.

"What about it?"

"What was on it?"

I pushed back my overgrown bangs behind my ears. "Nothing much. Just chapter accounts. Financial records."

Ty toed the plastic remains. "Can I take it in?"

"Why?" I couldn't imagine.

"Tech guys on campus might be able to retrieve the files." His voice was overly calm and casual. I knew what he was waiting for. My objection. He knew he didn't have a warrant and couldn't look at the files without my permission. I could tell he was dying to see what was on the computer even if he was trying to act all cool about it.

I could object, but, really, as chapter advisor pro tem, I would probably need those files to do my job. Why not let the nice police officer try to retrieve them for me?

"Sure," I said, keeping my voice as casual as his. "See what you can get." When he looked at me in barely concealed surprise, I added, "I'll just need a copy of the files on a thumb drive, please." Our eyes met, and I could see that he saw what I was doing. And for the first time, I caught a glimmer of respect in Ty Hatfield's very blue eyes.

We scooped up the remainder of the hard drive into a Delta Beta tote bag, and, on his way out, Lieutenant Hatfield paused and inspected the doorframe. "Someone with a key got in here." I was as alarmed at him freely providing information as I was at the assertion itself. He knocked on the doorframe. "No forced entry."

A key. Something cold slithered down my back at the word, bringing it all back home again. Someone with a key meant it was someone I had sworn to protect. That sucked.

Chapter Fourteen

I SLEPT FITFULLY that night, probably not getting a full hour in at a time. As a result, not even a three-shot, nonfat, three-Equal latte had me ready for the next day. I had scheduled interviews with all the chapter officers throughout the day, between their classes, and it was imperative that I presented an alert, calm, and competent demeanor to inspire these young women. Instead, I looked less than the perfect Deb woman in my rumpled blouse and jeans, but real pants were beyond me today. Jeans were the most I could muster. At least they were designer jeans.

First up was the scholarship director, Jane Anderson, followed by the social activity director, Asha, and the pledge trainer, Cheyenne. Each report began with the assertion that things were going great overall—and then came the "but," and the omnipresent drama. Sisters complaining about too-loud music during study hours, pledges not being respectful, which fraternity the chapter would mix with next—it was almost more than I could handle. I realized that this constant flurry was the day-to-day life of a chapter advisor, and something I had never been faced with as a Sisterhood Mentor.

Aubrey St. John was scheduled next. "I know you're on a tight schedule," I said apologetically. "If you want to meet later, we can."

"No, no," Aubrey said, settling into a chair across from me. "I'm good."

"We covered most of the chapter stuff the other night after the meeting," I said. "I guess the big thing I'm trying to figure out is the chapter financial information."

I was interrupted by a shrill ring from Aubrey's phone. She shot me a nervous look. "I'm so sorry," she stammered before reaching into her purse and clicking something to either disconnect or silence her phone. "What were you saying?"

"The chapter's accounting records," I repeated. With a slight pause, I remembered the fate of the records in the crunched-up computer that Lieutenant Hatfield had toted to some nerdy IT guy on campus. Looking into Aubrey's sweet, pretty face, I felt she, of all people, deserved the truth about what was going on. As chapter president, she had almost as much, if not more, responsibility to lead these sisters than I did.

"The chapter advisor's computer was destroyed last night," I said, feeling bad that Aubrey's eyes shot open with alarm. It was a lot for a collegian to take. "Someone broke in and tore apart the office." I reached across and patted her knee. She looked really worried. "It's all right. I called the police, and they're sending someone to fingerprint the office. And Ty—I mean, Lieutenant Hatfield—took the computer to the IT department on campus to see if they could retrieve the files."

Aubrey covered her mouth with an audible "oh" sound. "But everything's going to be fine," I assured her. "They think they know who it was."

I wasn't sure why I said that. I wasn't sure that was even true.

But I wanted to reassure Aubrey, who was taking this harder than I thought she would. It always made people feel better if they thought the criminal would be caught. "Hey," I said suddenly, "why don't we just meet later about this stuff?" I wanted to let her have a moment, but then I remembered something. "Besides, headquarters sent over a bunch of paperwork for me to review. I bet everything I need is in there."

Aubrey nodded but then looked worriedly at me. "Are you sure? I really don't mind. This is my job, and I don't want to let you down." Now she looked like she was going to cry. Now I was going to cry. I hugged her then, like she was the little sister I never had. My little-sis status was a sore topic for me, but I never stopped searching for someone who would fill that spot in my heart. Right now, Aubrey St. John needed my guidance, and I'd do anything to support her, even if that meant letting her off the hook a little bit.

I felt a little emotional after Aubrey left. I remembered this particular side effect of living in the sorority house. So many post-adolescent hormones, all muddled up together. It wasn't just our cycles that got in sync; it felt like all our emotions did, too, like we were sponging off each other. Some women didn't care for that, but as an only child, I relished the feeling of being connected. It was why I first signed up for the Sisterhood Mentor program. I didn't want to let those connections go.

Today, as I started plugging back into the emotional ebbs and flows of sorority life, I wondered if, as chapter advisor, I needed more distance. Maybe that's why Liza McCarthy had lived in an apartment instead of in the chapter advisor's quarters at the house. I wondered if I should take advantage of those rooms during my stay: The tiny hard twin bed in the guest room was only going to feel smaller if this assignment lasted more than a few weeks.

If I thought I needed a break after meeting with Aubrey, it was nothing compared to meeting with Callie. It is a truth universally acknowledged that the toughest job in a sorority chapter is maintaining standards. As S&M chair, Callie not only dealt with every infraction of every rule, but she couldn't talk about it because she was sworn to secrecy. The only person she could talk to was, you guessed it, the chapter advisor, which, at the moment, was me. Awesome.

Two hours later, Callie had unburdened every little piece of dirt that she was wrestling with, ranging from academic dishonesty to just general bad behavior. Really, you'd think modern girls would know that a man who will leave you for your sister is no man at all. Throughout the conversation, I kept hearing Ty Hatfield's mocking voice from the night before, asking if I sent girls to their rooms without supper. I could see why people might laugh at sorority standards. I could see why our expectations of behavior might seem archaic. But in the world of sororities, reputation was everything. It was what sustained you; it was the very basis of recruitment. Without a good reputation, you might as well be independent.

When Callie finally took a breath, I decided it was a good time to let her know about the break-in, especially since the only thing I'd identified as stolen was under her purview. When I broke the information to Callie, she seemed stunned. "But that's confidential," she said. Her voice was flat, her eyes accusatory.

"I know," I said, feeling really bad that this breach had occurred under my watch. "But the police are having someone come in and fingerprint—"

Callie gasped, clutching her hand. "But I have a key! I go in there all the time!"

I made a face. I wasn't sure how that was going to work. "I'll ask Ty—Lieutenant Hatfield—how they know whose fingerprints are whose." I waved my hand as I thought through it. "You know? It probably won't matter. They'll probably just fingerprint the weapon that was used on the computer."

Callie still looked pale and shocked, and it was time again to give another hug to yet another traumatized college student. I hoped it didn't sound heartless of me, but I couldn't wait until we'd figured out what caused Liza McCarthy's death. Then, maybe, we could start to recover.

As I was working through yet more platitudes about time healing all wounds, I heard the blessed sound of the Delta Beta dinner triangle. "Dinner! Time for you to go!" I shot up out of the chair, put an arm around Callie, and walked her to the door. When I shut the door firmly behind her, it was the first time I'd ever been glad to be alone in a Delta Beta chapter room.

Chapter Fifteen

BANGING MY HEAD against a table felt better than most of what I'd been through today. I went ahead and banged with abandon at the table where Casey and I were having dinner at El Loco Taco, the best Mexican joint in Sutton.

"Be careful," Casey said. I felt his hand on the back of my head, stilling me for a moment. Something slid away across the table. "There. Didn't want you to get salsa in your hair."

Casey was a true friend.

"This is so not like you, Margot." Casey sipped from his margarita, one of four on the table. It was happy hour, and margaritas were two for one. Therefore, I had ordered four. "You love Delta Beta. Your blood is gold and black."

"It is," I said mournfully. "But this chapter-advisor stuff is intense. I never realized how the girls just kind of stick a knife in their heart and bleed every single emotion on top of you."

Casey quirked an eyebrow. "Sounds lovely."

"When I'm here as Sisterhood Mentor, it's different. I'm temporary. I'm fun. I'm interesting. I'm not, like, their therapist."

"I don't know," Casey mused, dipping a chip into the salsa from which my hair had been saved. "Kind of sounds juicy."

Oh it was. And how. And because I knew Casey would love it, I started spilling the tea. Starting with the S&M tea.

"God, I love girl drama." Casey sighed when our dinners were brought out.

"It's interesting, all right," I admitted. "I'm sure there will be more when we have this hearing on Saturday. Oh, and the mixer on Friday night."

Casey's eyes lit up, like only a gay sorority sister would. "Who are we mixing with?"

"Alpha Kappa," I said.

"I'm your date, of course."

I laughed. At social events, being Casey's date meant that we walked in the door together, and, three hours later, he found me and we walked out together. It was more attention than a lot of my dates gave me. I never got mad about his behavior, though. He was a bona fide social butterfly and found it impossible to stay in one place for longer than sixty seconds. Ninety seconds, tops.

A familiar dark head caught my eye. "Amanda!" I shouted at the woman walking four tables away. I'd know that superb posture anywhere. She turned, and that's when I saw that she was holding hands with the gentleman she was walking with, immediately dropped as soon as she saw me. Or maybe he dropped her hand. It was hard to tell.

She waved and smiled and came over to our table. I quickly introduced one bestie to the other, trying to ignore Amanda's smile drooping a little when she heard that Casey worked with me at

HQ. I resolved to let her know later that no one would take her place in my heart, not even my gay work husband.

"Join us," Casey urged, with such perfect manners and enthusiasm I wanted to kiss him. "I'd love to hear all about what Margot was like in college."

Amanda waggled her eyebrows implying all the stories she could tell. I wanted to remind her about that vow of silence we'd taken about all the things we did that summer. "I can't," she said sweetly. And then I looked at Mr. Hand Holder, just settling into a booth on the far side of the restaurant. She saw what I was looking at and blushed, and we shared a secret, meaningful look. *You better tell me all the details later,* I telepathically ordered her. *Promise,* she swore back.

Casey and I resumed our Mexican-food pig-out session, and, after two and a half margaritas (Casey shared his, against his will), I was almost back to feeling like the confident, always positive Delta Beta extraordinaire I was. The restaurant cleared out some, and I had a better line of sight to Amanda's table. Her date was an older man, stern and professorial-looking, which probably made sense given that Sutton was a small college town. Probably about 75.6 percent of the population worked for the college, in some respect.

I watched their body language when Casey got up to use the boy's room. They knew each other well, it was clear, but I'd have to think about some way to let Amanda know that he didn't seem as into her as she was into him. I couldn't put my finger on it, but if I had to define it, Amanda seemed a little . . . *desperate.* Which made me sad, because usually Debs are the pursued, not the pursuers.

When I got up, I was glad that Casey had driven his car to the restaurant. My body could not handle 2.5 margaritas like it used to. I had a second reason to be glad that Casey was driving when I got the call that my presence was requested at the police station. Immediately.

ON THE WAY over, I had to update Casey on my previous visit to the police station.

"Margot, no one gets accidentally arrested." He sounded like he didn't believe me. Which was strange because never in a million years would I exaggerate.

"Can you please just focus on the important things?" I was going over the progression of events that he would need to carry out in the possibly likely event that I was accidentally arrested again. "One more time."

"Yes, yes, bail money, ATM, blah blah blah."

"And what's my PIN number?"

"The year Delta Beta was founded, duh."

We pushed through the front doors of the police station. Like before, it was very quiet. I suddenly saw why I got so much attention from Captain Hatfield. He didn't have anything else to do with his free time. I wobbled a little going through the door. Luckily, Casey was there to take my arm and straighten me out.

That was when Hatfield entered the front office, holding a double cheeseburger wrapped with paper and dripping with secret sauce. He stopped dead in his tracks, glaring at me like I interrupted his evening. Then he glared at Casey, who was being a gentleman and making sure those 2.5 margaritas didn't cause another incarceration.

"What do you want?" Ty growled with his jaw locked in very John Wayne-esque impression.

"Charming as ever, Captain Hatfield," I said.

"Lieutenant Hatfield," he corrected me.

Whatever. I ignored that. "You called me."

"I didn't."

"Someone did."

"Not me."

I looked at Casey for some backup and to make sure El Loco Taco wasn't putting something hallucinatory in their margaritas these days. He nodded back, knowing what I was asking silently.

I pulled my phone out of my bag and showed him the caller ID. "Satisfied?"

Hatfield groaned. "Our assistant. I told her to call you tomorrow."

I looked around the empty station. "You have an assistant? For what?"

Casey elbowed me.

"Who are you?" Ty asked Casey, a note of challenge in his voice. Police officers were so weird when they didn't know everything.

"This is Casey. He's with me," I explained bluntly, suddenly pissed off that I was called down here for no reason.

"Should she come back tomorrow?" Casey used his debonair, impossible-to-resist voice. Maybe he wanted to smooth things over with Hatfield. Maybe he thought he had a chance. I was interested to see if he did.

"She's here now," Ty said flatly.

"What're ya eating?" I asked, my attempt to smooth things

over. In response, Ty crumpled the remainder of the burger and paper bag and threw it in the trash can. Well then.

Ty was back in his polo shirt and khakis, which I had decided wasn't my favorite look on him. Thanks to 2.5 margs, I didn't hide the fact that I was checking out his butt as he went to the desk to get something. That earned me another elbow from Casey. Whatever. I knew Casey was doing the same thing.

But then I was caught when Ty turned around, and his eyes met mine. I had a flash then, a realization that I had known him, once upon a time. The tequila just wasn't allowing me to put the pieces together. Right when I thought I had something, it slipped through my fingers.

"How do we know each other?" I asked, wobbling a little. Casey tightened his grip on my arm.

Ty shrugged, a little too studied, a little too on purpose, before he held up a pad of paper. "Fingerprint guys are coming on Saturday."

"Saturday?" I repeated the word like it was some kind of big hassle, like that was my day for biking and picnicking and listening to concerts in the park. In reality, I'd be doing what I normally did. Saving a Delta Beta chapter and watching *Law & Order*.

"Would another day work better for you?" His manners were too perfect. I knew he was putting me on.

"No," I said, matching my obsequious tone to his. "Saturday will be perfect. I'll be expecting the fingerprinters."

My tongue had trouble with that made-up word. Ty looked at me sharply again.

"Have you been drinking, Blythe?"

"Did you just call me by my last name?"

"Answer my question."

"Answer mine," I sassed back. Casey squeezed my elbow hard. I was not as padded as I looked. "Ow!" I glared at him, then transferred my glare to Officer Hatfield. I was not deterred by either man.

"I can't believe you called me all the way down here just to tell me the fingerprinters were coming."

Ty threw his hands up. "You were accidentally summoned."

Casey's eyes met mine. *See?* I said with my eyebrows.

"Since you're here, do you have anything else for me?"

He had some nerve. "No," I snapped. "You?"

"No." His answer was clipped.

Two could play that game. "Fine," I said.

"Fine," he managed between gritted teeth.

Then I turned around and left, Casey quick on my heels.

We were halfway back to the Deb house when Casey had the nerve to say, "He likes you."

I rolled my eyes. It was just my luck that the only guy who might "like" me was also someone who wanted to arrest me every chance he got.

Chapter Sixteen

I HAD TO get out of the house. I was going stir-crazy: With the chapter advisor's office still closed off, waiting for fingerprinters, I couldn't do chapter work. I called Casey and asked him if we could dig into the paperwork that HQ had sent over, with the added bonus that I could use his brawn to help me move into the chapter advisor's apartment. But he had a conference call with HQ until lunch over some hazing incident in Colorado. (Surprising. Coloradans seem too chill to haze anyone. Hazing takes a lot of effort, in my experience.)

So I broke a rule and tiptoed into the office to retrieve Liza's sociology papers. I was 85 percent sure that Hatfield would never notice they were gone. The thought of Ty Hatfield made me strangely uncomfortable. I remembered the previous night perfectly—it had only been 2.5 margaritas, after all—but enough to make me forget myself and taunt a sworn officer of the law. Something about him put me on edge, and it wasn't just his piercing blue eyes that both pissed me off and made me want to confess to something. Anything.

On campus again, I felt the romantic tug of my alma mater,

the memories of late nights and late mornings, group studies, and cute fraternity boys at the Java Jimmy food cart. The nostalgia made me stop and get a double-shot iced latte, for old times' sake, before heading into the J. Quincy Adams Building.

I figured the best place to start was the sociology-department offices, which were easy to find. I introduced myself to the receptionist, and, with the gravest voice I could muster, quietly said that I was returning some of Liza McCarthy's papers to the department. That got her all jumpy and nervous. She hustled off, saying she was going to get someone for me, which was all well and good; but the box of books was very heavy, and it was hard to hold them and drink my iced latte.

Soon enough, the receptionist called me back to an office and introduced me to Dean Xavier, sociology department chair. Interestingly, he was also Amanda's hot professor date from the night before. I dropped the box and stuck my right hand out quicker than gossip could fly through a sorority house. "I'm Margot Blythe. How very nice to meet you."

"Dean Xavier," he said as he returned the handshake.

This was interesting. He invited me to sit down, and as I did, I studied him closely. I had been right at El Loco Taco. He was older, maybe late thirties or early forties, but still in good shape, with salt-and-pepper hair and a prominent-yet-handsome nose. Thin, wire-framed glasses didn't detract from very intelligent brown eyes. Or maybe it was the glasses that made the eyes seem intelligent. Chicken, egg.

"So is your first name Dean, or is that your title?" I asked, with my sweetest smile. Okay, I was flirting. That just happened sometimes when I was around handsome older men who were also dating my best friend. It was totally innocent.

"My name. But I get that a lot around here." He smiled. Minus one for me not being creative in the slightest.

I put my grave, sad face back on as I held up the papers I had collected. "I'm not sure if you were told, but I found these in Liza McCarthy's office at the chapter house and thought they might be needed here."

Xavier leaned back in his chair, steepling his fingers. I felt like I'd been asked to stay after school. "Thank you, but I doubt there's anything in there that's necessary."

That didn't seem right. "Was all the important paperwork at her office here?"

Xavier cocked his head. "She didn't have an office on campus."

Stranger and stranger. "Where did her students go?" When I was in college, I had to go someplace to meet my instructors when I needed to explain why I'd slept in and missed the test. Again.

Xavier sniffed like it wasn't interesting at all. "To another instructor. Ms. McCarthy was no longer with the university when she passed."

"When did she get her doctorate?" I would have thought I would have heard about that, or she'd have the name "Dr. McCarthy" on all the papers sent to headquarters.

"She didn't."

"I don't understand—"

Xavier cut me off. "She was released from the program three months ago."

Oh, damn. This was kind of huge.

"Why?" It was all I could manage to say, my brain whirring at one hundred miles an hour.

To his credit, Xavier almost looked guilty about sharing the information. "Since she's passed, I guess there's no way she'll sue me. There were issues with the research for her thesis. We found that it was inappropriate and, ultimately, that it violated the Sutton College code of ethics."

This was crazy. I'd never heard of such a thing. "What was she researching? She studied sociology. There's nothing controversial about that!"

As a philosophy major, I felt I could say that about sociology. Also, I wasn't quite sure what sociology was.

Then Dean Xavier explained Liza's research, and my whole world tilted and spun out of control.

"I told all this to the police . . ." he said, in the same professorial, matter-of-fact voice that he just used to share scandalous, almost impossible-to-believe information.

A foghorn blared somewhere between my ears. I excused myself, leaving the remnants of Liza's failed degree on the floor of Xavier's office. I had a police officer to chew out.

I marched out of the building, down a curved sidewalk, and headed back to the parking lot, a thousand things running through my head. It couldn't be true. It wasn't true. I was so caught up in all the legal, moral, and ethical implications of what Xavier had said, that I wasn't watching where I was going and bumped into a pretty blond girl, whose hair was done in perfect waves and whose makeup was expertly applied. The quintessential sorority girl, Aubrey St. John.

"Aubrey!" I exclaimed, pushing my bangs off my sweaty face. "I'm so sorry, you wouldn't believe the morning I've had."

But Aubrey didn't smile back or apologize for being in my way. In fact, she looked at me blankly, like she hadn't heard anything I'd said.

That's when I saw her shirt, a pale pink tee with bright orange Greek letters plastered across her chest. Mu. Mu. Mu.

A horrified gasp came out of me. Aubrey in Tri Mu letters? Was nothing sacred in this world? I couldn't even deal with this right now. "I'll talk to *you* later, young lady," I informed her with as much menace as I could summon before I remembered where I was going. And why.

THE GLASS DOORS at the police station slammed behind me, and I stood there, arms akimbo, for someone to ask for my name and my business.

I waited for almost two minutes before I gave up. Seriously? They had no one at the reception desk? What would they do if someone came in to confess to something? Just let them hang around until they changed their mind?

"Hello!?" I called out. "Detective Hatfield!?" I decided yelling his name was the best option. If I wandered down the hall, I might be accidentally cuffed or accidentally shoved into a lineup.

Ty Hatfield came ambling down the hall, just as cool as you please a few minutes later.

"You have been holding out on me," I accused him.

There was no change on his face except for a slight squinting of his eyes, which I took as permission to continue.

"We made a deal," I continued. "We were going to share information. I even let you look through the computer."

Ty's face said he wasn't impressed. "It came back by the way." He'd just totally changed the subject.

I had to respond to that. "That was fast."

He shrugged. "Turned out, whoever destroyed the computer didn't do much to the hard drive. I have your files back in my office." He turned and started walking back down the hall. When I didn't follow, he looked back at me like, *what are you waiting for?*

I took a deep breath before taking the chance of walking down a hall at a police station when my status as a free woman might be in jeopardy if I followed him.

Hatfield's office was as boring and as plain as I'd expected, with not a cute picture frame or funny card in sight.

I accepted the thumb drive he gave me with all the icy aplomb I had in me. Then I went in for the kill.

"I just saw Dean Xavier, and he said that you knew what he told me about Liza McCarthy and her doctorate."

Ty looked inscrutably at me. I wanted to scream. I couldn't take it anymore. "How could you not tell me that Liza McCarthy was running a phone-sex hotline as a sociology experiment?"

"I thought you knew." He didn't blink, he didn't wiggle, he didn't cock his head. The man was really hard to get riled up.

"How could I have known?" My voice went up a couple of octaves, and I threw up my hands. "I don't even know . . . how to do phone sex!"

Even a cop as chill as Hatfield reacted to that one.

"This is dire," I said, ignoring the twinkle in his eyes. "One, it means that Liza was in violation of about ten Delta Beta S&M rules, including her employment contract. Two, it means . . ." *She wasn't the person we thought she was.* A chill ran down my spine.

"I thought you knew," Ty repeated, like it was all no big deal. "Thought that's why HQ sent you here. To fire her."

I sank into a chair on the visitor's side of Ty's desk. Casey had asked me that, when he arrived in Sutton. Why *had* I come? I remembered what else Casey had said, about an upset Liza calling Mabel at HQ. Had she called when she'd been fired from her doctorate program? Or was there even more going on in Liza McCarthy's secret life?

"Does this have anything to do with her death?" I was surprised at how weak my voice was. But I had never been good with people disappointing me.

Ty tilted his head, as if he was considering the possibility. "Maybe."

I knew then, without a shadow of a doubt, that Ty Hatfield was never going to be up-front about Liza's death with me. He was never going to be honest, or share information, or treat me like I had a legitimate stake in this investigation. From the beginning, he had dismissed, ignored, or mocked me. That was going to end today.

From now on, I was going to find out the truth about Liza McCarthy, her life, *and* her death. It was my responsibility to my sisters.

Ty Hatfield could bite my big fat Delta Beta butt. Well, the butt I had before Jillian Michaels took care of that particular problem area.

Chapter Seventeen

CASEY AND I set up a new office in the chapter advisor's apartment. Like the office, the apartment was tucked away in the back of the house, almost as an afterthought, when someone realized that a chapter advisor might want a little separation from the young women of the chapter. After only three days on the job, I could definitely see why some space was a good idea.

Basically a small studio, there was a bedroom that opened up into a sitting area, just big enough for a love seat, a recliner, and a desk. Casey set up his laptop and the files on the desk while I updated him on all that I'd learned about Liza McCarthy.

Casey, of course, was as horrified as I was. The thought of a Delta Beta woman phone sexing for money was scandalous. Combined with the fact that she'd been dismissed from her academic program and had lied to the chapter and headquarters for months, it was essentially unheard of. But Casey was also a man. And though he tried to hide it, I could tell he was titillated by the whole phone-sex thing.

"What are we looking for?" Casey asked, plugging in the thumb drive.

"I don't know," I admitted. "I guess we have to make sure that the chapter was still run competently, even with all the drama in Liza's life." Casey nodded in agreement. Our first priority was protecting the sorority.

With that thought in mind, it generated a second, scarier idea. If Liza had been murdered, then I needed to protect the chapter from whoever had done it. And to do that, I needed to solve the murder.

I'd never solved a murder before. But at the Miami chapter, I had disciplined a sister for chronic shoe theft, and that was pretty bad.

Casey pulled up the spreadsheets I had reviewed earlier in the week on the chapter advisor's computer. Rows and rows of numbers meant almost absolutely nothing to me, and Casey stared at them blank-faced as well. Some headings or something would have been helpful. Finally, I realized that the far-left-hand column were dates, separated by hyphens instead of slashes.

"Okay," I said, pointing at the screen. "These must be dates of when the chapter received money, right?" The second column was some sort of code. It didn't make sense to me, but the same ones were repeated, but in no particular pattern—902, 812, 421, 902, 902, 902. Probably some accounting thing from HQ. So glad I hadn't taken that job. The third column had monetary amounts. I could tell these were monetary because they each used a dollar sign and period. The final columns were a mix of codes and dollar amounts. Maybe they were account numbers? Disbursements to savings and checking accounts?

Casey thought my interpretations were reasonable, and I was

about to move on until I realized what had bothered me about the spreadsheet before.

There was no consistency. No patterns. No similarities.

Ten years in a sorority, and I was very aware of the ebb and flow of the academic calendar and the sorority calendar. No money would come into a sorority during summer breaks because women weren't in school. Same with winter breaks. On the other hand, financial records would show many, many checks received during rush, the beginning of the pledge semester, and the beginning of each month, when dues were assessed and paid. Those patterns weren't reflected on this sheet. At all.

"These aren't the chapter financials," I breathed. They were something else entirely.

A quick review of the papers Casey had brought from HQ proved that whatever we were looking at on the chapter advisor's computer wasn't the report on finances that had been submitted to headquarters. I could actually decipher those. Maybe there was hope for me in the accounting department, after all.

"So what are these?" Casey asked, looking back and forth between the laptop and the printouts.

A feeling of dread settled into my stomach. "I think Liza had another business on the side." Casey couldn't hide that he was a little excited by what the other "business" entailed: men.

"I wonder what her phone-sex name was." His voice had all the wonder and anticipation of a five-year-old boy at Christmas, waiting for Santa to bring him a special edition Versace Barbie.

I crinkled my nose. "What's a phone-sex name?"

"Well, I'm guessing she didn't tell people her name was Liza McCarthy, sorority advisor."

Oh, Lord in heaven, I hoped not. A horrible thought occurred to me. "If Dean Xavier knew about Liza's research, how many other people knew?" I gasped. "Do you think the girls knew?" I asked Casey in a voice just above a whisper.

His eyes went wide with the thought. "There's only one way to find out."

I groaned and fell into the recliner, an arm across my face. "There has to be another way."

"Well, let's think this through," he said in his best matter-of-fact way. Casey didn't get dramatic like me. That's what made him the best at public relations. "If you were running a phone-sex business, what would you need?"

"I cannot believe I'm having this conversation." It was mortifying and hilarious. I could only do this with Casey. "Okay." I tried to focus. "I'd need a phone." I thought through what I knew about phone-sex operations, which was all based on one *Law & Order, SVU* episode. "Privacy. You can't take those calls just anywhere." Casey snorted. I ignored him. "Some way to collect payment."

"And you need some way to get customers . . ."

There was a note in Casey's voice I didn't like. I really, really, *really* didn't want to pull my arm off my face.

There was a long silence from Casey, and I knew it was inevitable. I kept my eyes closed, lifted my arm, and peeked. The Web site on Casey's laptop was exactly my worst nightmare.

"Sorority Girls Gone Wild. All your wildest fantasies come true. $1.99 for the first minute; $2.99 for each additional minute."

A seriously unattractive groan came out of me. For the first time in my life, I really hated a dead sorority sister.

"How do we know it's hers?" I asked weakly. Silently, Casey pointed to the pictures on the screen. Someone had photo-shopped pale pink and bright orange Greek letters onto the silicone enhanced blessings. It was too hideous a color combination to be an accident. Whoever ran the site was someone who despised Tri Mu. And although that didn't narrow it down definitively (after all, this was Tri Mu we were talking about), it was a pretty big clue.

"Now what?" he asked.

I picked up his cell phone from the desk. "Really?" His voice was half-interested, half-horrified.

"Dial," I said, pushing his phone toward him.

"Why me? Why can't you do it?"

I gave him a "duh" face. "You're a man."

He pushed the phone back toward me. "So? I'm not any more interested in those things than you are."

"They'll be suspicious if they hear a girl's voice."

"They? They is dead."

I pushed the phone back at him. "Then you don't have to talk to anyone."

He took the phone in resignation. "Do you know how expensive this is going to be?"

"That's a corporate phone. You don't pay the bills."

Casey brightened. "Oh yeah."

I was sure the sorority wouldn't mind at all.

Casey put the phone on speaker and dialed, holding up a finger to his lips while he did. Like I was going to say anything. My mouth was sealed shut from humiliation.

A canned voice finally picked up. "Hi, Heather speaking." The "h's" were thick and breathy. "I'm so glad you called. My sisters and I are wet from our shower and are waiting for you." The "w's" were wide and deliberate. "Just one sec while we fight over who gets to make you . . ."

"Ohmigod!" I squealed, holding my hands over my ears. This was all kinds of wrong. I couldn't be a hundred percent sure, but the greeting sounded like Liza's voice. She was very breathy.

Hearing a sister talk like that was just . . . weird. Then the music came over the line, bow chicka wow wow stuff. "Really?" I asked. "How cheesy."

Casey agreed. "Do you think we're paying for this right now?"

"Ew," I said, although I had to respect the business strategy of making perverts pay through the nose for a cheap porn-reject sound track.

Finally, after three long minutes of synthesizer slow jams, we heard a click. A squeal came out of me and out of Casey, too.

"Hello, this is Hailey."

Casey's wide eyes met mine in an "oh crap" expression. I rotated my finger in a circle to get him to start talking.

"Um, hello." I had to swallow a laugh at the look on Casey's face, like a gay deer caught in heterosexual headlights.

"Hi sexy," the voice said, just as breathy and X-rated as you'd imagine.

"Hi, yourself." Sweet child of mine. This was going to take all night and be painful besides.

"Oooh, you sound hot." She sounded like she was constipated.

I bit back a giggle. Casey did not sound hot. He sounded nervous and awkward.

"What do you want to do to me today?" The voice on the other end sounded really sincere, like she really wanted to know what Casey wanted to do to her. Meanwhile, Casey was looking at me like he'd been caught in his mom's closet with her high heels on, completely clueless. Again, men. When you want them to bring their A game, they act like they'd never seen girl parts before. Which in Casey's case, could be the truth.

I grabbed a piece of paper and wrote, shoving the message at Casey's face.

"Um . . . I'd like to talk?" Casey's voice lifted on the end as he directed a silent question to me. I nodded, using my finger again in the universal "keep 'em rolling" sign.

"I love to talk dirty," she said.

"How old are you?" Casey read off my page.

The girl giggled. "Barely legal, if you know what I mean."

Oh Lord. I shoved the paper at Casey again. "Do you do this full-time?" He asked the question, then mouthed "WHAT?" to me. I know, I wasn't sure why I was asking that question either. I was under pressure.

"Oh . . . yeah, I do it all night long."

We weren't going to get anywhere with this. Casey read the next question and shook his head. I mimed ramming the pen up someplace personal, and he relented. "Do you know Liza McCarthy?"

"Um . . ." There was a long pause. When she spoke again, I could tell the slutty girl act had been compromised when she improvised, "Is that another girl you're doing? Tell me about it."

Casey had had enough. "No, I'm serious. I'm a friend of Liza's, and I want to know if you knew her."

"I—I . . ." She sounded really flustered. "I don't know what you're talking about."

I grabbed the phone from Casey. "If you know her, you can tell us, we're not going to get anyone in trouble."

The next thing we heard was a dial tone. I guessed we didn't really think through the "call-a-phone-sex-operator" plan.

After Casey recovered the color in his cheeks, I poured us both a glass of lemonade to boost our blood sugar. I looked at him, and said, "She definitely knew Liza."

Casey nodded. "Definitely."

I jammed my bangs back as I thought through the implications. "And that means Liza had employees. And the employees knew her. This could all blow up in Delta Beta's face."

We both thought about it. "I don't know how we find her employees," Casey said.

Then we both came to the same conclusion. "Liza's phone," we said in unison.

I looked around the apartment in vain because I knew it had been empty when I moved in. "She didn't live here, she lived in an off-campus apartment, for some reason," I explained to Casey.

"Because phone-sex operators need their privacy," Casey said, throwing my words back at me. I closed my eyes briefly. It was all becoming clear now.

"Right . . ." I thought aloud. "If I were a phone-sex operator, I'd want a cell, right?"

Casey nodded. "A landline ties you down too much."

I had to find Liza's phone. I thought back to the night of her death. Surely, she'd had it on her. Everyone carries their phone with them. If it had been in her pocket, it was still in her unclaimed effects at the morgue.

"How does someone get into the morgue?" I wondered aloud.

"Is that a really bad joke?" Casey had an edge to his voice.

I shot a look of apology over. I hadn't meant it like that.

But Casey had moved on. "Maybe the police? You could ask that hot police officer."

The thought of going back to Ty Hatfield for any type of assistance was untenable. I couldn't trust him to tell me the truth about any of this.

I looked at my watch. "Let's take a break," I suggested. "We can think about this over drinks with the Alpha Kapps."

The excited look in Casey's eyes showed me he thought that was a good plan, too.

Chapter Eighteen

I HAD JUST gotten out of the shower when there was a dull roar outside the apartment door, the kind only a bunch of excited women could make. Wondering what it could be this time, I pulled on a tee and running shorts, opened the apartment door, and saw nearly the whole chapter headed toward the front door. "What's going on?" I asked Ellie, a sophomore from Texas.

"The Eta Eps! They're serenading us!"

There's not much that a girl likes more than being serenaded by cute boys. That's why boy bands and *Glee* are so popular. It feeds into our feminine delight that there's a boy who's overcome his insecurities and decided the way he feels is more important than being told he's a crappy singer. Or something like that.

So, of course, when I heard that the Eta Eps were serenading our chapter, I got a little flutter in my chest even though it was probably completely inappropriate and cougar-like. But right as I joined the flood of women heading outside, something else fluttered in my head, a memory from my sophomore year.

"HOLD IT!" I yelled, stopping dead in my tracks. "NOBODY MOVE!"

But nobody listened to me. They just kept rushing toward the front door, giggling and anticipating the Tom Cruise-as-Maverick vocal stylings they'd no doubt be treated to by the Eta Eps.

I tried again, this time with feeling. "SERIOUSLY! STOP!"

All I managed to do was confuse a few of the girls in the back. The rest pushed through and lined up on the front porch. The only way I was going to get their attention was to be in front of them, preferably singing "You've Lost That Loving Feeling." I had a bad, bad, feeling about this. Eta Eps weren't known for their chivalric conduct. Just ask the Tri Mus my senior year, after they were sprayed with fire hoses during a faux fire drill.

I peeked through the front window, and, sure enough, twelve Eta Ep pledges were standing on the lawn, dressed in suits and bow ties and top hats. A little excited pitter-patter started in my cougar heart. Damn it. I looked up, trying to confirm my suspicions, but I was at a bad angle and couldn't see much besides the backsides of Debs and the goofy Eta Eps.

Think, Margot!

I had two options. I could push my way through to the front porch, cause a big commotion, and totally disappoint everyone if I was wrong about the motives of the Eta Ep pledges. Or I could slip out the chapter advisor's apartment door, nonchalantly come around the front of the house, and double-check the situation before I made a big deal over nothing.

I chose the first option. I favor efficiency over discretion.

The front door was still open, and sorority sisters packed the entry, all scrambling to see and hear the show. As predicted, the

Eta Ep pledges opened with "You never close your eyes anymore when I kiss your lips." It wasn't terribly creative, but I had to hand it to them. It was a classic for a reason. There were lots of sighs and giggles and a few catcalls, about which I'd have to speak to the ladies.

"Excuse me," I said, shoving my way through. "I need . . . to . . . get . . ." The girls were packed tight, all jostling and moving, but soon I had stepped over the threshold. Looking up, I saw what no other Delta Beta did, as entranced as they were by gangly eighteen-year-olds sacrificing all their street cred for a fraternity prank.

I couldn't see who held the cord that was connected to the net holding a hundred water balloons above the Delta Beta chapter's collective head; but if I started screaming about an ambush, someone could easily pull the cord, and all our carefully styled hair would be doomed. But if I could be sneaky, I would find the guy holding the cord, tackle him, pin him to the ground, and somehow ensure he didn't pull the cord in the fracas.

Neither option worked for me, so I decided to hold and enjoy the show until an opportunity presented itself. Maybe there would be an intermission.

But the pledges wrapped up their first song and were headed into a Billy Joel doo-wop number (adorable, if a little clichéd) when I saw movement along the right side of the house. Two Eta Eps out in the yard held up cell phones to capture the upcoming ambush. The signal must be soon. I knew I had to act fast to avert crisis.

"AMBUSH!" I screamed. "BACK IN THE HOUSE! NOW!" I waved my hands at the net of water balloons above our head, and enough people looked that it caused a chain reaction. Sisters looked and screamed, then began pushing each other and moving in all different directions.

The problem with the plan was the one I'd previously identified. By alerting the chapter to the threat, I alerted our enemy. In the next second, the cord was pulled from somewhere off stage left. The balloons fell from the front-porch ceiling and nearly fifty young women were drenched. Hair plastered, shirts transparent, just the way fraternities like. Those jerks.

They weren't going to get away with this. Eta Eps lined up in the yard, taking pictures and laughing while my girls were wet and mad and . . . sticky? Really sticky. Sticky like . . . I lifted my shirt and smelled. Grape? Lemons?

I felt coated in a gluey substance and . . . I gasped, reaching up to my hair. Other women were doing the same. I wasn't one hundred percent sure, but there was something else in those balloons besides water. Something that felt a lot like flavored gelatin. Something that was going to be a bitch to get out of fifty prideful heads of hair.

As nearly everyone tried to cram back in the front door, I moved to the porch rail instead, ignoring the crowd of Tri Mus that had innocently wandered over from their house (yeah, right).

"You!" I pointed at one of the Eta Eps in a top hat who wasn't taking pictures, the gentleman that he was. "What's your name?"

"Clark?" His voice raised as if he were uncertain about his name, but I knew that wasn't it. He just wasn't sure if I was about to kick his backside.

"Tell your brothers that this was not funny."

One of those brothers snickered at me from nearby. I focused my chapter-advisor death glare on him instead. "One day, when you least expect it, someone will get revenge. I guarantee it."

The Eta Eps listening to me were not impressed. "Yeah right," one called out.

"Girls don't prank," another one said. "They get pranked."

"That doesn't even make sense," I said, sounding entirely too much like a grown-up. "What's the point of pranking us, then?"

"Respect!" one yelled.

"Honor!" another one called out.

"Legacy!"

I rolled my eyes. Some legacy, filling water balloons full of Jell-O. Fraternity traditions were so weird.

Chapter Nineteen

THE MONEYMAKER WAS just as I remembered it from my own college days. One of the three bars allowed on the north side of campus, it sat in the middle, with Pete's Downhome Saloon on the west and Shotz, the shot/sports bar on the east. Pete's Downhome was a casual type of place that served ice-cold drafts and burgers between two and seven and peanuts in the shell all day long. Shotz changed themes and names every three years or so. When I was a freshman, it was a Daiquiri bar named the Easy Go. (Someone in town had objected to the name Easy Come.) My senior year, it changed to a martini bar, Manhattan Social; but the college kids didn't take to seven-dollar martinis. Shotz looked way more appropriate for the demographic.

But the Moneymaker was a venerable Sutton College tradition since 1973. It was the only one of the three with a dance floor big enough to host fraternity and sorority events. As such, it was home to the Greek community, and I had spent a lot of time within its hallowed halls.

It was dark, lit with neon signs and sconces that looked vaguely like fishing nets draped over bared breasts. I stood inside the door for a moment, letting my eyes sweep over the familiar wide-plank floors, the rough bar tables inscribed and carved with every symbol, number, and letter imaginable. As chapter advisor, I arrived early. The rest of the chapter wouldn't be here for another hour or so, fashionably late as ever.

Women join sororities for three major reasons, in my experience: friends, boys, and fashion. While the rank differs for each individual woman, these are the top three, for sure. And tonight, there would be all three. The ladies would party and have fun with each other, dressed to the nines, and there would be lots and lots of cute Alpha Kapps to dance with.

As chapter advisor, I couldn't be on the prowl for "boys," and I couldn't hang out with the girls as friends, but I could definitely hold my own in the sartorial department. After I had triple-washed the gelatin from my hair, Casey helped me pick out my tank dress, really the only bar-type dress I had in my suitcase—Sisterhood Mentors don't get out much. My heels added three inches to my already tall frame. Casey was a genius with hair, but even he couldn't help with my bangs. It was all Zooey Deschanel's fault.

As I expected, Casey left my side soon after we arrived and began to circulate, and as more and more Debs and Alpha Kapps entered, I got busier and busier. The underage sisters and brothers were checked and not given the stamp on the back of the hand that their elders were. Not that it mattered, but we did have the law to worry about.

When the party warmed up, I circulated to people watch in both an official and unofficial capacity. Casey was captivating a group of girls by the bar, which wasn't fair to the Alpha Kappa brothers who wished they could get some female attention. Jane and Asha hit the dance floor, jumping and singing along to songs and pulling in their sisters to form a wide circle, as girls had done since time immemorial.

I saw a blond head ducking down as I circled by a booth. "Aubrey!" I called the chapter president's name. "AUBREY!" I had to yell over the music when she pretended she didn't hear me. "I need to talk to you." I crossed my arms and tapped my foot, making it clear that she wasn't getting away from me this time.

With a quick, embarrassed glance around, she slid out of the booth more gracefully than I had ever seen anyone get out of a booth. And her dress fell perfectly, as she stood, without a wrinkle in sight. Really impressive.

Once I had her undivided attention, I started in. "Look, you need to answer for your behavior today."

She looked around again quickly. "Do we have to do this here?" Her voice was a desperate plea. I would be embarrassed, too, if I was caught in Tri Mu letters, which is exactly what I said.

I continued yelling over the music. "What in the world were you thinking?" I knew people could hear me, but after what I'd learned today, Delta Beta's reputation was at risk. "Wearing a Moo T-shirt? Do you want people to think of you like that?"

Aubrey looked stunned. "You saw me? In Try Moo letters?"

"And they were hideous," I added for good measure.

"That wasn't me, Margot, I swear." She wrung her hands roughly. "It's . . . I mean, I should have told you. Everybody knows. But I don't know how people will take . . ."

I made a motion that she should speed it up.

"You see, I have an identical twin." Aubrey bit her lip in a gesture that would have been adorable if I hadn't seen it on a Tri Mu just hours before.

I was shocked. This was so *Law & Order*. I never knew this happened in real life. "Really?" I wasn't sure I could believe this. "What's her name?"

Aubrey swallowed, hard. "Ainsley St. John," she added. "We rushed together as freshmen and because everyone had mixed us up our whole life, she decided she wanted a different sorority. You can ask anyone," she added in a rush before closing her eyes, clearly mortified. "It's hard to hide the fact that you have a twin sister at a campus this small." Her perfectly glossed mouth flattened. "Especially when she's president of another chapter."

"Your identical twin sister is president of Tri Mu?" I asked again, just to make sure.

Aubrey nodded glumly, and I took her in my arms. "You poor, poor thing," I said, stroking her hair. I couldn't imagine the trauma that Aubrey had to endure on a daily basis, especially when idiots like me mixed them up. Having a Tri Mu identical twin? Could it be worse? "I'm just so relieved. Pale pink and bright orange are not your colors."

Thankfully, Aubrey accepted my apology, and I resolved to watch what I said about Tri Mus around her in the future. I didn't want to add to her heartache and humiliation.

When I let Aubrey go back to her table, I turned and found myself face-to-face with Ty Hatfield. Before I could get a word out, he had wrapped his arm around my waist and pushed me back three steps onto the dance floor.

Out of his police polo, Ty wore a dark blue plaid button up tucked into jeans with scruffy boots. He smelled like pine trees and soap, and pressing up against him was, unfortunately, one of the better experiences of my day. I could have fought him off, but it wasn't often I got to dance, much less with a hot cop to a slow country song.

I linked my hands around his neck, his hair still slightly damp from his shower, brushing the back of my hands. Thanks to my high heels, I didn't have to look too far to watch his face in the dim light as we slowly rotated in our own little circle.

Even as I was enjoying the feeling of being in a man's arms again, I hadn't forgotten that Ty Hatfield had not been forthcoming with information to me. In fact, I had the distinct feeling he was playing some game of his own, one that I didn't understand.

"What are you doing here?" I asked, proud that I remained levelheaded and calm while pressed up against a hot John Wayne-esque rookie.

"I heard there was a party." I felt his shrug, up close and personal as his chest and shoulder muscles rubbed up against me.

I pulled back a little to get a better look at him. "You don't seem like the party type."

There was the patented Ty Hatfield squint. I was a little concerned I was getting used to his facial expressions. I could almost tell the differences between his squints. Like this one, his "slightly interested" squint.

"What type do I seem like?" he asked. I could feel the rumble of his deep voice from his chest as it pressed into mine.

I pretended I was thinking about it. But I knew my answer already. "You're the *Law & Order* type."

A rare smile was pulled out of him. "Like Elliot Stabler?"

My heart thumped extra hard at the name of my crush. "You wish," I said. Although if Stabler wasn't available, Ty Hatfield would probably do in a pinch. If he wasn't on my shit list.

"Seriously," I said, focusing back on the job at hand. "I'm chapter advisor, and it's my duty to make sure no uninvited boys are at our events."

"Boys?" Ty lifted a brow at me, and damn if my heart didn't thump extra hard again.

"Uninvited *guests*," I amended, not wanting to give him the satisfaction.

After a beat, Ty answered my question. "I'm an Alpha Kappa."

"Which chapter?" I asked, after I was momentarily distracted by his hand gently sweeping up my back.

"This one." He tilted his head toward the group of young men currently dancing to a new Miley Cyrus song. The answer stunned me. Ty had to be around my age, and if he was an Alpha Kappa who went to Sutton around my time, I would have known him. We would have been at many of the same events.

I searched his gaze, racking my memory. Ty Hatfield. Why didn't I remember him? I wondered if Ty was a nickname, short for Tyler or Tyson or Tyrion. Maybe I would have known him by a different name? Before I could coax anything from my memory, there was a tap on my shoulder. I turned to see Brice Concannon, in a crisp shirt, tie, and jacket, his dark wavy hair gelled to preppy perfection. Dang.

"Hi," I said in surprise. What a nice surprise it was. "What are you doing here?"

Ty's hand pulled me closer and I remembered what I was doing. Sort of. "Are you an Alpha Kapp, too?" I asked Brice. Maybe that's why he'd come to the mixer. "Do you know Officer Hatfield?"

"Just through official means," Brice answered.

I wondered at the tightness around Ty's mouth at that answer, but then I saw something I really had to address.

"You're an Eta Ep!" I exclaimed, pulling away from Ty and focusing on the small circle pin on Brice's lapel. I guessed fraternity council advisors didn't have to hide their Greek affiliations like Amanda had to.

"I am," Brice said proudly.

"We need to talk." I put my hands on my hips—the best pose to get someone to take you seriously. "The Eta Ep chapter perpetrated an egregious prank on my ladies today. Have you ever stuck your head in a tub of gelatin? If so, you'd know that this is serious."

But Brice was smiling, secure in his charm and Kennedy-esque good looks, which had probably gotten him through high school and college with the bare minimum of Cliff's Notes and cribbing off math-club nerds. As much as I wanted to bask in those white-teeth good looks, I wanted him to put an end to the pranks more.

"So serious, in fact," I continued, "that I might just have to press charges. Detective Hatfield? Can I do that?"

I had barely gotten the question out before he said, "Absolutely." For a man who wasn't big on immediate affirmations, the speed that he gave it made me suspicious. All of a sudden, I had a feeling Ty Hatfield wanted to impress me. Or Brice. Which one, I wasn't sure.

Brice caught on and quickly changed his tune. "Oh no, let's not. I mean, I'm not the Eta Ep chapter advisor, but I will communicate your feelings to the chapter." He hit me with another charm-blast smile. "It shouldn't happen again."

"It better not," I said, struggling to remember that I was striving for stern, not giggly and swoony. "What's with the pranks these days, anyway?" I directed the question to both gentlemen, fraternity alumni and responsible role models. "It seems like the boys have gotten more reckless and dangerous."

I thought of the fear and trepidation of the girls at the chapter meeting. "Chapters are instituting buddy systems. Women shouldn't have to live in fear on their own college campus."

Before either came up with a response, as if to prove my point, there was a commotion coming from the booth where I had left Aubrey.

I heard shouts and screams, all female, and nearly all semiprofane. I broke away from Ty and Brice and ran toward the booth, pushing and shoving my way through the crowd that had instantaneously gathered.

"Get!" I shoved at someone's back. "Out!" I pulled on a shirtsleeve. "Of my way!" A sharp elbow to a stranger's kidney. Sorry about that. Sorority casualty.

Then I saw what everyone else had gathered to see: Callie Campbell and Aubrey St. John, the chapter's president and S&M director, screaming into each other's faces and periodically grabbing a handful of nearly perfect blond hair. The scene almost broke my heart. They both had really good hair.

Chapter Twenty

I PUT CASEY in charge of the mixer, shoved Callie in my car because she was closest, and told Cheyenne to take Aubrey home.

The ride to the house was short and silent. I opened the door for Callie and followed her in, wondering what my job was here. Chapter advisor was halfway between a boss and a mom, and I had no experience with either position.

"Callie," I said sharply after we were safe in our Delta Beta haven.

"Yes?" Her voice was shaky and tentative. The entry was lit by a single lamp on a table, and I was reminded of too many nights in high school when I missed curfew and was chewed out when I got home.

I sighed. Callie was a good girl, she knew when she'd screwed up. "I'll see you at the S&M hearing in the morning. Nine o'clock sharp."

She nodded, and I couldn't tell if that was relief I saw in her trembling lips or guilt.

Upstairs, there were screams and the sound of a movie explosion. I remembered that the pledge class had their sleepover tonight. The mixers were off-limits for pledges until after initiation. Some called that hazing; I called that wise resource management. I briefly considered joining in the fun, but I remembered that I had a nine o'clock sharp meeting the next morning and my twenty-seven-year-old self needed a tad more sleep than any of the eighteen-year-olds upstairs in the TV room.

As THIS WAS a formal Standards and Morals hearing, proper pin attire was required. I dressed in a burgundy Michael Kors dress, my pearls (of course), and my sturdy Cole Haan air pumps. My Delta Beta pin was over my heart, and my monogram was on my leather attaché for note taking. Before bed the night before, I'd drafted the necessary S&M paperwork with the details I could remember, since the prefilled ones had been stolen during the break-in.

Twenty steps down the hall, and I was in the chapter room, setting up for the hearing. Three chairs on one side of the table, one chair on the other. I placed a Bible on the table. It wasn't strictly necessary, but the *Law & Order* geek in me really hoped to swear someone in one day.

Callie was the first one to arrive, dressed supercute in a J.Crew wool dress with a flared skirt and stacked wedges. I self-consciously pushed my bangs back when I looked at her perfectly arranged waves that framed her dimpled adorableness.

"Oh, Margot," she rushed out, coming to me. "I wanted to say how sorry I was for last night."

I patted her upper arm. "It's okay." I wanted to tell her that I expected better from her. Or that the descendant of Mary Gerald

Callahan—her namesake, for goodness sake—needed to be a leader. But I knew she knew those things; it was written all over her face. She felt horribly guilty, and I was satisfied that was punishment enough.

Callie settled into the left chair behind the table, and we'd been going over the forms I'd started when Aubrey walked in. Callie froze next to me, her eyes locked onto Aubrey's entrance. While Aubrey was also dressed appropriately in a twin set and trousers, there was something not quite perfect about Aubrey this morning. And that made me worried. The only time I'd ever seen Aubrey not perfect, she was actually not Aubrey at all. And even then she was almost perfect, except for her choice of clothing. Aubrey had her hair pulled back into a tight, high bun, which I'm sure was a fine fashion choice and probably necessary if she woke up late, but it only accentuated how stressed and drawn Aubrey's face was.

"Good morning, Aubrey," I said in a cheery voice, hoping to alleviate the tension that had just risen in the room. If it was this tense before Stefanie Grossman got here, imagine what it would be like when we kicked her out of the sorority.

Aubrey sat in the right chair, leaving the center one for me. I settled in and waited for Stefanie Grossman to appear.

Fifteen minutes later, the three of us were still alone in the room.

"Callie, do you have Stefanie's number?" Callie called Stefanie, and it went straight to voice mail. We gave her another fifteen. Now she was thirty minutes late. Callie called again. Still voice mail.

I peeked at my Michael Kors watch. It wasn't like I had a ton of stuff to do on a Saturday, but the girls probably had schoolwork, errands, and laundry. Still, the hearing was serious business. Our personal lives had to be set aside, and Stefanie deserved her due process. I'd even let her object.

At ten, it was clear Stefanie had skipped the meeting. "Is this like her?" I asked the ladies sitting by me. They looked up from their cell phones.

"It wasn't," Aubrey said with a sassy note in her voice, "until she got written up."

Callie crossed her arms. "Aubrey and Stefanie are BFFs," she explained to me, her voice also dripping with something unpleasant. I had to stop this before it got out of hand. Only one option was available.

"I call this hearing to order," I said in my most official-sounding voice.

"But Stefanie's not here," Aubrey protested.

Callie met my eyes and smiled. "The Delta Beta Standards and Morals manual allows for in absentia hearings, section 10.4," she recited from memory.

My heart swelled with pride. She was so good at her job!

"Okay, let's go over the paperwork," I said after I called the hearing to order.

It sucks when I am right. This was, without a doubt, the hardest experience to handle in the whole entire sorority. Reading Stefanie Grossman's name, her pledge year, and her violations out loud was heartbreaking. Aubrey kept her arms crossed the whole time, her lips pressed tightly together, and it was clear that she had some strong feelings about Stefanie's losing her pin.

Ty Hatfield's mockery of our rules notwithstanding, the Delta Beta expectations were clear. No behavior would be tolerated that would subject the sorority to ill repute and, unfortunately for her, Stefanie had been caught making out with her professor boyfriend in a bathroom during a football game. And she'd been wearing her letters. It was an open-and-shut case. I was pretty sure I heard the *Law & Order* da da DUM playing.

Then I saw something in the file that made me choke on my recitation of the S&M manual. It was only an asterisk, a footnote, as if it was a minor, unimportant detail. And maybe it wasn't pertinent to these proceedings. I knew, however, that the fact that Stefanie Grossman's boyfriend was one Professor Dean Xavier would definitely not be a minor detail to my big sister.

With a voice that was shaky for several reasons, I made the motion to terminate the membership of Stefanie Grossman for standards and morals violations. Callie seconded. We didn't need Aubrey's third. The motion passed. If Stefanie wanted to appeal, she'd have to contact headquarters.

Ironically, I was picking up the Bible when I heard a word that rhymes with "itch" come out of Aubrey.

"Excuse me?" Callie demanded.

"She didn't deserve this." Aubrey flung herself out of her chair and stuck her finger in Callie's face.

"Ladies," I said in a warning tone.

"Did you even hear what Margot read? She deserves to have her pin yanked. She's not fit to be a Delta Beta!" Callie slapped at Aubrey's finger in her face. I'm not going to lie, that finger would tick me off, too.

"Okay, that's it. It's done," I told both of them.

"Hypocrite," Aubrey snapped at Callie.

Callie's mouth dropped open. "What did you say?"

Aubrey shook her finger again. "I know, Callie. I KNOW! You know what I'm talking about."

Apparently, I was the only person that didn't know. And I wasn't sure how much I wanted to know, at this time.

"If you know so much, why don't you just say it!" Callie's voice had risen to a very high volume. "I'm so sick and tired of your trying to bring me down. Since we pledged, you've hated me. Since bid day, you've been nasty to me. And I'm done with your stupid jealousy!"

"Look!" I spread my arms out at both of them, placing myself between them. I wasn't sure I was ready to actually stop a fight, but I wanted to look like I was. "I said, that's enough! So you two hate each other. Everybody in a sorority hates each other at some point; that's what sisterhood is all about."

"I don't hate her," Callie said archly, keeping her glare on Aubrey. "She has ceased to exist for me." And with that, she turned on a heel and marched toward the door, her blond curls bouncing behind her like a shampoo commercial. Man. Even her dramatic exits were perfect.

Aubrey yelled at Callie's retreating back. "Whatever Callahan. No one buys your little miss perfect act anymore!"

Suddenly, I had a raging headache. On a Saturday. And I hadn't even had anything to drink the night before.

Aubrey collapsed into the chair and threw her head onto the table, crying. I flipped through the pages of my agenda, avoiding Aubrey's drama and wondering how it would look for a chapter advisor to quit after less than a week on the job. Would it be better or worse than a chapter advisor's running a phone-sex operation? These were difficult questions, even for a philosophy major.

Finally, I went to Aubrey and gave her an awkward pat on the shoulder. What I'd said was true. Drama was par for the course. Despising a sister who had formerly been a friend was a very common phenomenon. Too many women, too many hormones, and too many egos. They didn't have to be best friends, but they had to treat each other like ladies. It was kind of the whole goal of this organization.

"Do you want to tell me something?" I asked, the reluctance clear in my voice, praying that Aubrey did not, under any circumstances, start the story of how she and Callie started hating each other over some minor peeve on bid day two years ago. I just didn't have the energy.

Aubrey wiped her nose, took a moment to collect herself, then looked up at me, her face red and swollen. I saw the same fear and guilt that I'd seen the night before. She slowly shook her head.

Inner Margot breathed a sigh of relief. "I'll have to get to the bottom of it soon." It was a warning, between adults. Get it together before it hurts the chapter. Work it out between yourselves, so I don't have to get involved. Please.

Aubrey nodded again in understanding. "I'll end it. I promise."

I took her word for it.

Chapter Twenty-one

THERE'S A SPECIAL place in Hell for people who bang on a door early on a Sunday morning. I scrambled out of bed, made sure my girls weren't hanging out of my tank top, and mentally prepared a diatribe to be delivered to the first person I saw.

Unfortunately for me, the first person I saw was a police officer. Back in his official uniform polo, Ty Hatfield stood at the front door of the sorority house, with two other people I didn't recognize. But I did recognize their blue lab-ish coats and their tool kits. Excitement about seeing real-live fingerprinting in action warred with my high level of irritation at being wakened without a quadruple-shot, nonfat, four-Equal latte.

"What," I snarled when I opened the door.

Ty flipped open his badge, all official-like. "We're here to fingerprint the site of the break-in."

I crossed my arms. "You said you were coming Saturday." Not like I was waiting for him, or, I mean, them, or anything.

"We're here today."

Officer Hatfield, king of the obvious. Grudgingly, I had to let them in. As I walked them back to the chapter advisor's office, I caught a glimpse of myself in the hall mirror. My topknot was messy and stringy, my half-outgrown bangs bent every which way, and my tank top and boxer shorts were so not professional. I fought back the impulse to go change; I really wanted to see what fingerprinting looked like.

Fifteen minutes later, they were done, which was, like most of my experiences with male visitors on a Sunday morning, underwhelming.

And they'd left a mess behind. Fine powder coated everything. I walked the group back to the front door and Ty told the fingerprinters to go on ahead. Then he turned to me and laid those baby blues on the rat's nest on my head, my barely modest pajamas, and, finally, my black-and-gold pedicure, an homage to Delta Beta colors, of course.

"Yes?" I asked, still a little cranky from being awake.

"Do you have anything you want to tell me, Margot?"

The question caught me off guard. "Are we still doing that? The 'you-tell-me, I-tell-you' deal? Because I considered it null and void after you withheld Liza McCarthy's other job from me."

Ty shrugged his shoulders. "Wouldn't hurt to share, would it?"

Any other situation with a cute guy, I could probably do something with that statement. But not now. Not with my eyes still half-swollen from sleep. "You go first," I heard myself saying.

"The tests came back on Liza McCarthy's body." He was watching me very closely, making me wish I'd put a bra on before answering the door.

"And they're not good," I finished.

"Why do you say that?" He was suspicious.

I threw up my hands. "Because you sounded like Dr. Huang

does on *Law & Order, SVU* when he has to break bad news to someone about the cause of death, all grim and mysterious. Context clues, Hatfield." I wanted to tell him that he wasn't as good at being cagey as he thought he was, but that wasn't entirely true. He was pretty good at caginess. I was just getting better at reading him.

"So she was murdered." I was surprised at the businesslike tone of my voice. This was a murder, after all. Of a sister. But I guess my brain had gotten acclimated to the idea.

Ty nodded, once. I rolled my eyes. "Your turn," he said.

I thought about what I could share since I didn't have access to fingerprinting dust or toxicology reports. "I called the phone-sex line," I blurted out. That got a reaction out of him. Something very interesting flared to life in his blue eyes, but all he said was, "And?"

It was my turn to shrug. "Someone picked up. Someone who got real nervous when I mentioned Liza's name."

Then Lieutenant Hatfield glared at me like I was the biggest dumb-ass ever. "That could compromise our investigation!"

"Oh please," I snapped. "You don't get to have it both ways, playing games with me, pulling me into the circle of trust, then shoving me back out again."

Ty's brows furrowed together, as if I were speaking an obscure Chinese dialect. "I'm not . . ."

"Have a good day, Officer." I smiled. And then the front door to the Delta Beta house slammed in his face. Accidentally.

I HAD A few hours to kill on Sunday (is that a bad choice of words?) as Casey was busy arranging Liza McCarthy's memorial service on behalf of headquarters, which I thought was a nice gesture, especially since they weren't going to be too pleased when they found out about the phone-sex side job. Since Ty Hatfield hadn't strung yellow police tape around the door of the chapter advisor's office or told me to stay out, I decided that it was my job to clean the office. Again.

Being a chapter advisor was not as glamorous as I'd always thought.

I pulled in a big trash can from the kitchen and got ruthless about tossing items in it. The leftover parts of a smashed computer monitor, the poor, unstuffed carcass of Busy Bee, and assorted broken knickknacks all got heaped together. Then I started on reorganizing. Again. I stacked manuals, straightened books, and filed papers in folders, which went into a drawer. At the bottom of the drawer, I saw the address book again, the one with all the codes and numbers. With trembling fingers, I opened it, and this time, the codes made more sense.

The ten-digit codes had to be phone numbers.

I'd seen the numeric codes after those in Liza's spread-sheet—812, 409, etc.

The unpronounceable Eastern European names with no vowels had to be codes, as well. They made no sense to me, and I sucked at code breaking unless it was Pig Latin. And even then I got con-fused when a word started with a vowel.

I slipped the address book into my back pocket. Casey would want to see it, and maybe he'd have a brilliant flash of insight like his idea to Google "sorority phone sex number" the day before.

After straightening the office, I checked my watch. I had un-avoidable chapter-advisor duty in an hour, and I had to look as cute as I could. My hair perfect, my makeup flawless. My outfit of skinny jeans, a trendy top, and boots was as fashionable as they come. The Delta Beta chapter was headed to the Tri Mu Bowling Tournament, and we would all be on the top of our game.

It was an inviolable Panhellenic rule that sororities all supported each other. In public. We'd donate our time and money to each other's philanthropies, sit together at football games, smile and clap in unison during rush. In private, we were vicious, catty, and downright hostile. In public, we were sisters. I liked to think it taught us what real life was all about.

So that's why, on a beautiful October Sunday afternoon, the sorority women of Sutton College gathered together in a stinky, smoky, dark bowling alley to cheer each other on and support Tri Mu's national philanthropy, a good cause that we all cared deeply about: blind dogs. Or was it disabled dogs? Diabetic dogs? I could never keep them straight.

During every Delta Beta's pledge semester, she was taught the history of the sorority she had just pledged. A history that told how, in 1879, best friends Leticia Baumgardner and Mary Gerald Callahan formed a "sacred temple of sisters, sworn to love, loyalty, and secrecy" at Walnut Valley College. This was Delta Beta. Leticia and Mary Gerald selected members based on the highest standards of beauty, poise, intellect, and charity.

In 1880, women who did not qualify for Delta Beta formed their own second-rate sisterhood at Walnut Valley College and called it Mu Mu Mu. In public, the two sister sororities embraced each other, celebrating their common ancestry. Both sororities' headquarters encouraged cooperation and joint ventures. In private, Delta Beta and Mu Mu Mu were not so cooperative. Or encouraging. Or civil. But like any family, we kept our feuds private, behind closed doors and fueled with an impressive amount of alcohol.

Casey texted me that he couldn't handle being around a "herd" of Tri Mus. Not for the first time, I envied Casey's non-Panhellenic status. He got all of the good parts of being in a sorority and none of the pain-in-the-ass parts.

The Debs had picked their best bowlers to represent the chapter, and studious Jane was the captain. She was as ferocious about knocking down pins as she was about enforcing study hours. The Delta Beta sisters tried their hardest to cheer and stay excited about the tournament, but it was bowling, after all. I never could understand why Tri Mu had picked the least interesting sport as a way to raise money. But I didn't understand most everything about the Moos.

I started to drift away after the fourth time the little box came down and rearranged the pins. I was out of practice faking enthusiasm for stuff. Deciding that as chapter advisor, I should really walk around and make sure everything was in order, I started at the end of the alley where the snack bar was. If I got a giant tub of buttered popcorn, that would probably be okay, too.

I was standing in line at the snack bar when I saw two familiar heads in the shoe-changing area. It was semiblocked off by open cubbies where bowlers could exchange their shoes for strangers' old shoes. (There was nothing about that custom that I understood. One, I'd never leave my shoes where just anyone could take them. Two, strangers' shoes? Ew.)

I paid for my popcorn and extra butter and slipped in behind the cubbies on instinct, thinking that if the Panhellenic advisor was talking to my chapter president, it was probably something I needed to be informed about. I couldn't tell you why I didn't make my presence known immediately; I wasn't the type to slink behind stinky-shoe cubbies, but something about the tone of the words made me draw up short. And they were talking so softly that I had to be real still to hear.

"What do you want from me?" the blond head said.

"This is none of your business. It's been handled." That was Amanda's voice. I recognized it easily even though it had been years since we lived together in the sorority house.

"Handled? That's what you call it?" the other voice hissed.

"Do you think I need your help? Do you know who I am?" Amanda sounded like the quintessential Panhellenic queen bee.

"Do you know who *I* am? Who *I* know? One call to nationals, and this whole thing is done."

"Are you threatening me?" Amanda sounded as shocked as I was.

"It's not a threat. I already called. I'm not letting this travesty go on."

"That's not very Panhellenic of you." Amanda paused, her voice softening. "I think you need to trust the process."

"I want it done. Or I'm handling it my way." There was a rustling sound, then a perfect blond head swept out of the changing area, not looking back at me or at Amanda. I would recognize those perfect blond waves anywhere. They were Aubrey St. John's waves. In a pale pink and bright orange Tri Mu shirt.

I counted to five and circled into the changing area from the opposite way. Amanda sat on a bench, her head resting on a locker behind her, her eyes closed.

"Hey, Amanda Jennifer Cohen," I trilled, sounding as casual as possible. Amanda's eyes snapped open. "Didn't know you were going to be here!"

"Margot Melissa Blythe." She smiled, using my whole name in

response. Best friends have silly little traditions like that. "Panhellenic advisors get to go *all* the philanthropy events."

"Fun! So do chapter advisors," I said as I sat down next to her. "Somehow, it's not as much fun as it used to be."

"No," Amanda said flatly, her eyes lost in thought. "It's not."

"You look like there's something bothering you." I wanted to encourage her to confide in me without confessing that I was an eavesdropper. Not that I thought she would mind about the eavesdropping. But there could be some Panhellenic confidentiality rules that I'd violated.

She shook her head. "Sometimes, I try so hard, you know? I try to help people, but some people don't want to help themselves."

I nodded, thinking of Stefanie Grossman. If she'd just shown up to the hearing, maybe we could have worked with her, given her some other kind of disciplinary consequences to her public display of affection. But she hadn't, and we couldn't do anything other than apply the letter of the law. Then, thinking of Stefanie, I remembered the horrible information I'd learned about the man that Amanda was dating. "Sometimes we just have to do what we have to do." I sighed, thinking of the tough decisions I had to make.

"Being a grown-up sucks." I offered Amanda my popcorn, and she took a handful, still lost in thought.

Loud cheering erupted from the bowling alleys. It sounded like someone had taken the lead or struck out or something. My presence would likely be required. I gave the rest of my popcorn to Amanda, who took it with a grateful smile. "Do you want to do lunch tomorrow?" She looked so depressed, and I wanted to cheer her up. "We can do it off campus, so we're not seen together."

"I'd like that," Amanda said.

Chapter Twenty-two

AFTER RECOVERING FROM an evening spent pretending to like Tri Mu, I looked forward to meeting Amanda for lunch. She texted me the name and location of the restaurant, a little tearoom on the town square not known for attracting the collegiate crowd. It was feminine and quaint, perfect for private conversation between two sorority sisters who needed to catch up.

After we ordered our sweet iced teas and chicken salads, I decided to tackle the issue straight on, as honesty was the best Deb policy.

"I saw you talking with Ainsley St. John yesterday."

Amanda's spoon stopped stirring her tea. "Oh," was all she said.

"C'mon, Amanda. If you can't talk to me, who can you talk to? I'm your little sis. And I'm chapter advisor, now. I get the drama, believe me. With Liza's death, this week has been . . . a little much." That was an understatement, but I didn't want to burden Amanda with all the unseemly details.

"I can't even imagine," Amanda said, compassion and empathy all over her pale face. She reached out and squeezed my hand. "You're right. We should talk about our problems. We are the only ones who understand each other."

"It's so crazy. We have Liza's memorial service tomorrow . . ."

"Tomorrow?" Amanda asked.

"Well, we couldn't have it today. Chapter meeting is today." Amanda nodded in understanding.

"When's the funeral?" she asked, straightening the napkin in her lap.

"Oh, I don't know." I took a sip of iced tea. "I don't think they've released the body yet because of the investigation. And the toxicology."

Amanda's eyes got real big. "Toxicology?"

I nodded. "To determine the cause of death."

"What was it?" she asked breathlessly.

"I don't know," I said, lowering my voice while the waitress put down our plates. "Lieutenant Hatfield is being strangely tongue-tied about it."

"You two are talking about it?"

My eyes rolled around. "Sort of. He keeps saying he wants to share information, but I think he only wants me to give him information. He's not forthcoming at all, especially about—" I cut myself off. "Stuff." I finished lamely.

"Come on, Margot," Amanda's voice was chiding. "You have to tell me, especially if it's Deb related. I'm a Delta Beta, first and foremost."

That was so true. "Okay," I took a deep breath, trying to figure out how to break the scandalous news to Amanda. She wasn't going to handle it well. "Turns out, Liza McCarthy had a secret phone-sex organization on the side."

Amanda's fork clattered to her plate, but something in her eyes wasn't as alarmed as I thought she should be.

"Have you heard about this?" I asked evenly.

A guilty look crossed her face. "Rumors, only. I just thought they were vicious rumors spread by—"

"Try Moo," I finished for her. It was that obvious. Especially with the rumors that Casey had heard, originating from Tri Mu headquarters, which is what I was telling Amanda when her phone buzzed. She looked at the number. "I have to take this," she said.

"Is it Dean Xavier?" I asked carefully, my heart sinking a little at how flustered she looked at his name.

"H-how did you know?"

"When I took Liza's sociology papers back to the department, I met him then. Don't worry, I didn't say anything about you." I winked. "Much."

"Oh God," Amanda took a shaky breath, clutched her phone so tightly I thought it would break, and headed out of the restaurant.

Through the front window of the tearoom, I saw her talking on the phone, covering her mouth, and facing in toward the building.

After about ten minutes, Amanda returned to the table and pushed back her plate, which was fine because I had finished my meal while she was taking her call. "Everything okay?" I asked, trying to be discreet even though there were definite signs of trouble in paradise.

Amanda waved her hand around. "You know. Men. They're all the same. Like Officer Hatfield, they take, and they don't want to give."

I totally agreed with that statement. But if anyone could convince a man to turn his life around, it would be my big sister. She was a pretty persuasive gal.

"Look at us talking about boys just like we did in college," I mused. "Remember all those double dates with those Omega pledge brothers? What were their names?"

"John and . . ." she snapped her fingers. "Shoot. I forget. He was tall and he always smelled like—"

"McDonald's cheeseburgers!" I laughed. I hadn't thought of him in years. "Remember how you'd always get dressed in my room?"

The smile on Amanda's face faltered a bit. "Because you had the most amazing clothes, of course."

The clothes were thanks to a high-limit credit card my father had given me—to buy my silence about a certain trip he'd made to Vegas. The memory made my smile fade as well. I shook it off and adjusted the napkin on my lap. "Who would have thought that we'd both still be single all these years later?"

"Technically, I don't know if I'm single or not."

"It's complicated?"

Amanda's expression showed me just how complicated it was, and that made my decision not to bring up what I knew about Stefanie Grossman. For all I knew, Dean's fling with Stefanie had occurred while he and Amanda were on a break. Until I knew more about either situation, I needed to stay discreet, for everyone's sake.

We went on to chat about shared friends and shared interests: the new Louis Vuitton handbag she'd just bought and the latest spa treatment that reduced cellulite.

The lunch check was on Delta Beta, and Amanda had to hurry to a meeting, so I paid the tab and headed out the door, wondering if I had time to run by the Greek boutique and pick up a new Delta Beta Busy Bee for the chapter advisor's office to replace the one that someone had disposed of so violently. Then a beauty-pageant-worthy head of highlights stepped in front of me. This time, I recognized her, even without the pale pink and bright orange.

"Ainsley St. John," I said, wanting so badly to add "I presume" but feeling that would be a little over the top. "Sorry I confused you the other day for your sister."

"You're the new Debbie advisor, right?" she asked, ignoring my apology and using the nickname that Moos used for us: Debbies, short for Little Debbies, the lowbrow snack.

"I'm the pro tem Delta Beta advisor," I corrected her. "Can I help you?"

She pressed a plain white envelope into my hand. "There's a perverted Debbie phone-sex orgy going on, and it needs to stop or I'm going to bring the whole Debbie circus down."

I'm sure my face contained a whole lot of *what the hell*? "And what do you know about it?"

Her mouth twisted as she looked at the envelope currently crunched in my palm. "That's what I know. And I know the Panhellenic advisor isn't doing anything. I just saw you having lunch with her. She didn't tell you, did she?"

"She told me some jealous Tri Moo skanks were spreading rumors about my sorority." My insulting snappishness came as a reflex even though I knew the phone-sex operation wasn't just a rumor. Still, I didn't like that a Tri Mu knew about it. If Ainsley St. John knew about it, this was dangerously close to being public knowledge, and that would definitely be a lasting mark on the unsullied Deb reputation. Panic started creeping in.

Ainsley's face was bitter, and the resolve I saw there scared me big-time. This girl meant what she said. She was going to blow this whole thing up. The sad thing was she and I both wanted the same thing—to bring down the phone-sex ring. But how could I work with a Tri Mu?

I decided to give it my best shot. "Believe me, if this is true, I don't want this thing to exist."

That got Ainsley's attention. I held up my fist with the envelope. "Is this going to help or hurt people?"

Now her resolve was mixed with anger. "Both," she said with a clenched jaw.

I sighed. It wasn't the answer I wanted to hear.

CHAPTER MEETING CAME and went in a blur. I could barely pay attention to the announcements and the debates, and my usual copious and detailed notes tonight consisted of numbers and letters that I haphazardly scribbled down as my subconscious tried to work through all the details and detours I had been presented with in the past few days. Part of my difficulty was that I just didn't want to believe that any of this was true: that Liza had led a double life, that my beloved sorority was in danger of having its reputation shredded and thrown under an eighteen-wheeler. After my talk with Ainsley, I had come back to the house and looked at her envelope, immediately recognizing her evidence for what it was— proof that tied Liza to the phone-sex site. I tried to calm myself that nobody else would recognize all these phone numbers except for me, the least-likely woman to come into possession of phone-sex line records. If Ainsley had really showed this to Amanda (and I had my doubts given her obvious instability), I could see why the Panhellenic advisor dismissed it as rumors and innuendo. The numbers were gibberish unless you had the master list.

I hadn't had time to figure it all out or make peace with it, with the demands of chapter meeting, setting up the ritual items, and dealing with last-minute agenda additions. After the chapter meeting, Casey was coming to the house, and we'd go over everything, step by step. Casey would help me make sense of things.

The closing ritual was about to start, and the energy in the air shifted as the ladies reached for each other's hands. It was in this very circle, a week ago, that Liza had dropped dead. Around the room, the memory was sketched on faces, in lines that no college student should have. The thought made me angry, that someone had done this to us, that we should have such a happy moment that celebrated friendship and loyalty and sisterhood forever marred by a senseless act of violence.

The time was now, for a chapter advisor to speak up, to share inspirational words, perhaps a quotation from Leticia Baumgardner. But the words got stuck in my throat, raw and splintered. Around the room, fifty hands formed a circle with their thumbs and forefingers. Fifty mouths said words that generations had recited solemnly. Then, fifty sets of eyes gazed in horror as the door to the chapter room was wrenched open in the middle of a ritual and a man in uniform strode in.

"Lieutenant Hatfield!" I yelled, as the room dissolved into chaos. Ty barely shot me a glance as he marched to the front of the room, with his hands held high. In one hand was a piece of paper.

Chapter Twenty-three

With just a slightly raised, deep voice, Ty had the chapter's attention. He held up a folded piece of paper. "I'm Lieutenant Hatfield, from the Sutton PD. We're looking for Stefanie Grossman."

The chapter room immediately erupted into whispers and exclamations. I was at Ty's side in the next moment, yanking down on that lifted arm. "What do you want with her?" I demanded. The room went quiet at my voice. It seemed the rest of the chapter wanted to know as well.

"I have a warrant for her arrest for the murder of Liza McCarthy." I closed my eyes as the room exploded, biting back several very un-Deb-like profanities.

Ty looked at the room again. "If anyone has any information as to her whereabouts, you are legally required to inform the police." Then he met my eyes. "I'll be waiting out front if you'd like to speak with me." And then, like he hadn't just done the equivalent of unveiling a transgender stripper in the middle of the First Baptist Sunday morning service, he marched himself right out of the chapter room.

Forty minutes later, I had calmed almost everything and everyone down. There were girls crying. Some were freaking out; some were calling their mothers. Everyone wanted to know where Stefanie was and why the police wanted her. In the chaos, I saw Aubrey giving Callie the evil eye from across the room. It was clear Aubrey was still loyal to Stefanie, but she had to know that Callie's writing Stefanie up on S&M matters wasn't why the police had issued a warrant for Stefanie's arrest. At least, I hoped it wasn't.

Still, I wasn't quite clear why Stefanie was suddenly the number one suspect in Liza's murder. When I could, I made my way to the front yard to see if Ty Hatfield was still available to answer a few questions.

He was sitting in the bench swing that hung from a huge oak branch, the swing on which each pledge class affixed a small brass plaque. After all the years, the back of the bench glittered with reptilian brass scales, catching in the sunlight or the moonlight, sparkling on clear nights like tonight.

I walked slowly toward him, my arms wrapped around myself, chilled from the cool October evening. "Lieutenant," I said when I got closer.

"Ms. Blythe," he said slowly.

"Why aren't you out there, looking for Liza McCarthy's killer?" I was surprised at the bitterness in my voice.

"We can't find her. That's why I came here, to see if any of your sisters had any information." The way he said, "your sisters" made me uncomfortable. Like I was responsible for anyone who was hiding Stefanie someplace.

I hesitated for a moment. "Stefanie was supposed to come to a standards hearing on Saturday. She never showed. From what the girls told me, she stopped coming to chapter events after she was told she was being written up. She even stopped returning calls. No one's seen her."

Ty nodded, a single head bob. "I'll need you—and whomever you've been talking to—to come down to the station tomorrow to give those statements."

"Tomorrow's Liza's memorial service."

"After that. I'll give you a ride."

"You'll be there?" I was surprised. I didn't think he knew Liza.

Ty smiled, a bland expression that didn't reach his eyes. Oh, of course. The killers always came to the victim's funeral. At least, they did on TV. Maybe they did in real life, too, and Ty was hoping to catch a murderer.

We stayed silent for a long moment as Ty continued rocking on the swing, the creak of the chains hanging in the air, the moonlight turning his dark blond hair as shiny as the pledge-class plaques.

"How did you know it was her?" I couldn't contain my curiosity.

Now it was Ty's turn to hesitate. Then he seemed to decide something. "She had a personal vendetta against Liza. The only thing taken from the chapter advisor's desk was her file. Seems she wanted to keep something quiet."

I crinkled my nose. Her giving a BJ to her BF in a bathroom hadn't stayed under wraps. "But we went ahead with her standards hearing," I said. "It didn't stop us."

Ty's hand sliced through the air. "Not that. She was one of Liza's girls."

I gasped. It was my worst fear, the one that I hadn't even spoken in my head, let alone out loud. Learning everything I had about Liza, I was still praying, hope against hope, that Liza hadn't violated the sacred chapter-advisor trust and recruited her phone sexers from the chapter. It looked like my prayer hadn't been answered. I sank onto the swing next to Ty, feeling that my legs weren't all that trustworthy at the moment.

"Were there . . . others?" I asked, barely able to make the words audible.

"We had an anonymous tip," Ty responded quietly, almost gently. "We're trying to confirm that now."

"Did the tip come in a white envelope?" I couldn't look at him. When he said yes, I stood and walked back into the house without looking back, knowing he was watching me the whole time.

CASEY HELD THE white envelope in one hand and the notebook paper in his other. The piece of paper had been torn out of an ordinary college-ruled notebook, the perforations and holes all jagged on the left side.

"I don't get it," Casey said.

"These are phone numbers." I pointed at the sheet. Then I pointed at his laptop screen. "They're the same. The records on the computer were a phone log, with how many minutes were charged, the total amount and then . . ." I moved my finger across the spreadsheet to the smaller columns with the dollar signs. "The disbursements. Presumably one to Liza, one to the . . . operator."

Casey peered at the screen. "But there are three disbursement columns."

"Taxes, I don't know," I said in exasperation. I was trying to put all this together with limited information. "But this is independent verification that Liza was behind the phone-sex site."

Casey frowned at the paper and the laptop screen in succession. "How did Ainsley get the phone numbers of the johns?"

"I didn't get that part either until the police showed up in chapter meeting tonight."

I told Casey the shocking story of the police barging into chapter meeting. Casey was scandalized. "*I've* never even been in a chapter meeting!"

"Ty confirmed that they got an anonymous tip that Stefanie was the murderer. I think Ainsley must be friends with Stefanie, and that's how she found out about the phone sex and the johns. She's now threatening to expose the Delta Beta sex workers." Casey and I shivered. I wasn't sure even Casey's public-relations expertise was going to save Delta Beta now.

"You've got to give this to the police," Casey said after a long minute. "It's evidence."

"He probably already has it." I couldn't imagine that Ty wouldn't have kept a copy of the data found on the computer. He was too devious not to.

Casey didn't seem convinced. "This is serious, Margot. This isn't just Liza we're talking about anymore. If Stefanie Grossman is out there, at large, other people could be at risk."

"Are you saying—?"

"Yes." Casey looked dead serious. "If she had a bone to pick with Liza, who knows who else she's out to get? The customers? The other operators?"

An icy sliver of dread shot down my spine. "I can't let that happen."

"But we don't know who the other operators are. Unless Liza left other random spreadsheets around."

I remembered looking through the computer's drives. It hadn't held anything but these spreadsheets. But then I remembered. I jumped up and ran to the bed, where I had left the pair of jeans I had worn that day. I tore them off the bed, patting them furiously, jamming my hands in the pockets. But there were only four pockets and they weren't that deep. It didn't matter how long I held those pants, there was no address book hidden in them.

"CRAP!" I yelled. I fell to the floor, got flat on my belly and searched under the bed. No book. I tore the sheets and quilt back from the bed. No sign of anything book-related.

"Margot?" Casey joined me in the room. "What's happened?"

"There was a book!" I yelled, ramming my hands through my hair in desperation. "I found a book in Liza's desk. It looked like an address book. This big, plain black." I held out my hands to illustrate its size. "I thought it would have names of her friends, her family, but it was gibberish, just phone numbers and coded names." There weren't any other places it could have gone, and I knew I'd left it in the pocket of those jeans. "It's gone," I said, hysteria rising. "It's gone, and it's all over."

I ran to the desk where I'd put my chapter notes after the evening's commotion had died down. My scribblings during chapter meeting were all I had left of the only evidence Liza McCarthy had left behind.

In desperation, I ran to the chapter advisor's office, on the slight chance that my brain had stopped working, and the address book hadn't actually made it into my back pocket. Believe me, stranger things had happened in my brain.

When I turned left into the kitchen hall, I came face to face with Callie, her hair and makeup all smudged. I couldn't just run by her. That would've been rude.

"Callie?" She looked as surprised to see me as I was to see her. "Why aren't you with the chapter at the fro yo shop?" I had given Aubrey my Delta Beta credit card and told her to buy the chapter frozen yogurt. Fat-free frozen treats seemed the best way to get everyone in a better mood after hearing that their sorority sister was being charged with murder.

"I . . ." She faltered and looked over my shoulder at Casey, who was following me, albeit at a more measured pace. Her eyes widened, and her assumption was clear in her face.

"This is Casey. He's my friend from headquarters," I said, but I mouthed "GAY" really big at her. Hopefully, Casey would forgive me for calling him just a "friend."

"OH!" A mix of shock and wonder and a little bit of guilt from assuming the worst about me washed over her cute little dimples. "Nice to meet you," she said with perfect manners. Mary Gerald Callahan would be so proud.

"Are you feeling okay?" I asked, still noting that she looked a little rough around the edges.

She patted her hair self-consciously. "Tonight was a little . . . overwhelming." I nodded in sympathy.

"Go to bed, Callie, you'll feel better in the morning. At Liza's funeral." That hadn't come out like I wanted.

She left, and Casey and I continued to the office, unlocking the door.

"ARE YOU FREAKING KIDDING ME?" I yelled.

Everything had been knocked off the desk. And I had just cleaned this place up.

Chapter Twenty-four

THIS IS THE part where I started to cry. Huge, ugly, uncontrollable sobs. No, not because of the mess in the chapter advisor's office. That had pissed me off, and I hadn't found the address book besides.

No, the tears came at Liza McCarthy's memorial service.

I hadn't even known her. Heck, I wasn't even sure I liked her at this point.

But there's nothing like a Delta Beta funeral. Thankfully, so far, the only Deb funerals I'd gone to were of older women, former executive officers at headquarters who had devoted seventy years of their lives to the advancement of our sisterhood.

Those were emotional, of course. All funerals were sad, made you reflect on the meaning of life, blah blah blah.

Liza McCarthy's memorial service was a whole other story. Casey had arranged everything to perfection. At the Mathias Farmer Memorial Chapel on campus, masses of yellow roses plummeted around the sides of a huge portrait of Liza. He'd gotten her pledge portrait from her chapter in Cincinnati and blown it up to three by four feet. At eighteen, Liza had been radiant, her fresh face full of promise and really excellently applied eyeliner. (When the picture was this size, I couldn't help but notice.) More roses were gathered in vases around the chapel, wrapped in gold-and-black ribbon. Another arrangement featuring roses in the shape of a Delta and a Beta had been sent from headquarters. They were really going to regret that once I got back and gave them the full report on the phone sex that Liza had been involved in. Or when they read about Stefanie Grossman's trial in the news. Whichever came first.

Mabel Donahue was there, and she presented the crowd with a stirring oration, invoking the Delta Beta creed and also Liza's love of TV shows such as *Gray's Anatomy*. Several quotations from that show really made us all think.

The chapel was packed to the rafters, filled with people who had come from far and near. The whole Sutton Chapter took up the first five rows, and I was proud of their appropriate shoes and solemn facial expressions. When I first entered the chapel, I had caught a glimpse of Ty Hatfield sitting in the back row, no doubt taking notes and keeping a sharp eye out for Stefanie Grossman. If I were a murderer, I wasn't sure I'd come to my victim's memorial service filled with all my friends, but a thousand cop shows couldn't be wrong.

Amanda was there, too, as was Dean Xavier. Curiously, they didn't sit together. I guessed they didn't want to go public with their relationship yet, due to some sort of Sutton College regulations about employees dating. Hunter, the house brother, was barely recognizable in a jacket and tie, sitting just behind the chapter. I thought that was sweet, like he took his "little brother" status seriously. He also probably knew Liza pretty well since her office was right around the corner from the kitchen.

After a very long, dreary hymn about heaven or something, the chapter chaplain, a thin, redheaded girl with bright pink lipstick stood up, piously closed her eyes, clasped her hands, and lifted her face to the ceiling to lead the gathering in prayer.

"Dear Jesus Christ, our Lord and Savior, we thank you today for bright sunshine, good, good friends, and the life of Liza Jean McCarthy. She was a special flower that grew for a summer, before she was accidentally whacked by Satan, the undocumented gardener of Hell. Please let her know that we are thinking about her and hope she has lots of fun in Heaven, with you. We ask that you keep our friends close and our enemies closer. In your name we pray, AMEN."

Next came the interpretive dance, which could have been cheesy, but the hidden symbolism behind their reenactment of the chapter-meeting ritual was too evocative to ignore, especially at the end, when the dancer in black flung herself off the rear of the stage. I saw Mabel Donahue's shoulders shaking, so I assumed even she was deeply affected. It wasn't something she saw every day stuck in an office at headquarters.

When a trio of sisters slowly walked to the stage and began singing Delta Beta's "Ode to Service" in perfect, three-part harmony while Asha Patel accompanied them on the violin, that's when I lost it. And when I lost it, it was contagious. I heard sniffles spread around the chapel, then little sobs, then the bawling that echoed my own.

Any Deb would do the same. The song is really, really meaningful. They reached the final verse: "To our sisters, here and gone, our friends, true and long, we vow our oath most fervent, that you deserve our service."

It brought down the house. Hunter stood to give a standing ovation and quickly sat down when I gave him a sharp little nod. That was taking it a bit too far. This wasn't a Taylor Swift concert. This was a funeral, for Pete's sake. Have some decorum.

After the service, Casey had arranged a reception at the sorority house, so he and Mabel left together in her Cadillac, leaving me to find Ty Hatfield and see if he meant what he said about a ride to the station.

"You ready?" Ty asked me, and I tried to ignore the note of concern in his voice. I still wanted to be mad at him for withholding information.

"Is anyone ready for this?" I lifted my hands to the decorated chapel. It was a little rhetorical, but I was a philosophy major.

But it seemed he wanted to discuss something else. "I just thought you might want to change."

I looked down at my LBD. It was Calvin Klein and appropriate for both a funeral and a police station, not that I'd actually ever had the occasion to wear an outfit to those two destinations on the same day before. "No," I said shortly. "Unless you're going to throw me in a cell again."

He had the decency to look embarrassed by that. "Okay. My car's out front."

We walked out of the chapel doors, and I paused when I saw the cruiser. "I get to sit in front, right?" I asked. Calvin Klein did not belong in the back of a police car.

Chapter Twenty-five

ON *LAW & ORDER*, statements are usually given in a bleak, gray interrogation room with a two-way mirror, where officers can drink coffee and speculate on the suspects' motives outside of the perp's hearing. Not at the Sutton police station. No, we were back in Ty's office, which, while bleak, did not have a two-way mirror, as far as I could see. And there wasn't anyone playing good cop to Ty's bad cop. There was just Ty, who, if I had to be honest, had the traits of both a good cop and a bad cop. Both sides scared me a little.

He turned on a tape recorder and asked me questions about Stefanie Grossman. I felt guilty even answering since I'd never met her, but I answered honestly.

Then he turned the recorder off, and it seemed that was that. But when has that ever been that when Ty Hatfield was in the room?

"How did you know about the envelope?" he asked. I double-checked to make sure the recorder was off, and he saw me doing it.

"What envelope?" I said it to be a pain. Give him a taste of his own medicine.

Ty had the patience of a really cute saint. "How did you know we received an envelope?"

"I guessed." I met his eyes in challenge. He couldn't make me say more because it was true. I had guessed.

"You guessed."

I examined the French manicure I'd gotten before I came to Sutton. It was already ragged, the white tips chipped from recleaning and organizing Liza's office a half dozen times. "Lots of people use white envelopes. Probably a large majority of the envelope-using population, if I had to guess."

Ty leaned back in his chair and linked his hands behind his head, his elbows sticking out like pennants. "Why do you keep secrets from me, Margot Blythe?"

I couldn't help the incredulous laugh that burst out. "I could ask the same of you!"

"Where's Stefanie?" His flat question showed he really thought I knew.

"I don't know."

"Who does?" The question was a command. Would some politeness be so hard?

"I don't know," I said again. I cocked my head. "Aren't you asking other people, getting their statements? Or do you just like talking to me?"

"Yes." The single curt word caught me off guard. His eyes held me for a long moment before I recovered.

I picked up a baseball off his desk and twirled it in my fingers, then wrapped two fingers around it as if to throw. "Don't the police have ways to track people? Like GPS and credit cards and cell phones?"

Ty's jaw clamped tightly as he dropped his arms and sat up

straight again. "Her parents swear they haven't heard from her although we've got Nashville PD watching the house. There's been no activity on her cell phone or her cards. No one's seen her. She's just disappeared."

I put the baseball back on his desk. "On *Law & Order*, that usually means something really shady has gone down."

Ty looked like he shared that feeling. He reached for the baseball and tossed it into the air. Something he'd said earlier had reminded me.

"What about the phone logs?"

Ty caught the ball and stared. "What phone logs?"

"The phone-sex line. If Stefanie was one of the operators, maybe she had another phone, a disposable one, and you could trace that."

He shook his head. "We already got the records for the phone-sex number. It looks like all the operators used burners. We can't get a warrant to search all those records; there's not a close enough connection between the suspect and the warrant."

I thought the government did stuff like all the time. Apparently, Ty Hatfield was one of the good guys; or maybe this small-time PD lacked the technology.

"How many were there?"

Ty stopped tossing the ball at my question. "Margot . . ." he drew my name out.

"Just tell me," I sighed, brushing my bangs out of my eyes and behind my ear.

His eyes focused on that ear before he answered, reluctantly. "At least ten separate operators, from what we can see. Of course, it could be fewer if someone changed numbers. But we have no way of knowing."

I remembered Casey's advice to be forthcoming with the police. "There might be a way." I told him that what I'd identified as the chapter financials weren't for the chapter at all, that they didn't match up to the paperwork from headquarters—and my theory that they were phone records for Liza's phone-sex business. At some point, Ty started jotting down notes. He didn't turn on his recorder, though, and I felt grateful for that.

I paused for a moment, then decided to reveal everything. I described the address book, the numbers and letters and the codes.

"And where is this book?" Ty was still writing. When I didn't answer immediately, he looked up at me, those blue eyes seeming to know that I was leaving something out.

I closed my eyes and rushed the explanation. "It's gone."

"Gone?" The pen fell to the desk.

I lifted my hands helplessly. "It was there, in my pants when I went to chapter. When I came back, Casey was there and my pants . . ."

"Were gone?" I snapped my gaze at him. I didn't appreciate the implication that Casey had something to do with my missing pants. They weren't even his size.

"The book was gone," I said archly. "My pants were fine. Thanks for asking."

"Where did the book go?" Ty asked deliberately.

"How the heck do I know? I looked everywhere. I even went back to the office in case I'd left it there." Oh yeah. I had something else to tell him that he wouldn't like. "And the office was a mess again."

Now it was his turn to close his eyes. His mouth opened and closed like he had just lost the ability to speak.

"But it was just a mess. Not like someone ransacked it."

Ty flashed his blue eyes open. "And you can tell the difference how?"

I lifted my shoulders. For nine months of the year, I virtually lived in any number of sorority houses. I can tell the difference between types of messes.

"Was anything else missing?" Ty seemed out of sorts.

I shook my head. Just the address book. With my luck, that darned book was probably the only way any of this was going to make sense.

Ty got a call on his phone. With an irritated look at me, he picked it up. His frown only got deeper the longer he listened to whatever he heard. "Keep me updated," he said with a gruff voice, then hung up.

"You didn't say good-bye," I observed. Manners are important to me.

I became the recipient of another irritated scowl from Ty Hatfield. "What the hell is going on, Margot?"

"What?" I squealed. "What did I do?"

"That was campus police on the line. Someone broke into Professor Xavier's office."

"Dean Xavier?"

"I think he's just a professor."

I leaned back, and the realization hit me. "Someone's looking for something."

He grabbed the baseball again, his jaw tight, his grip tighter. "I swear to God, Margot, tell me what you know."

"And then there's Stefanie," I managed to say, deep in thought.

"What?" Now Ty looked furious. "What do you know?"

I shook my head as pieces clicked into place. "But no one's seen her for days. She wouldn't search Xavier's office. It doesn't make sense."

"Why not?" Ty was one step away from steam shooting out of his ears. I decided to take pity on him.

"Stefanie Grossman and Dean Xavier had a relationship. That's why she was written up for S&M violations."

"They were dating?"

"Maybe," I answered in a tone that meant maybe not.

Ty scribbled a few lines down on his ever-present pad." What is someone looking for at Xavier's office?" It wasn't so much a question as it was a demand. Again. That was fine.

"Last Friday, I paid Dean Xavier a visit. And gave him a whole stack of papers that belonged to Liza McCarthy." I paused, watching as Ty processed that. "Someone wants something that Liza had. They looked in the office, they looked in my apartment, then they looked in Xavier's office."

"Who knew you took Liza's stuff to Xavier's?"

It was a very short list.

Before I could go over that list, there was a commotion in the front of the station. A commotion that could only come from one person.

Ty muttered curses under his breath and pointed at me. "You. Stay here."

When had I ever listened to Ty Hatfield? I jumped up and followed him. I had to see the show.

At the front desk of the station, it was no longer quiet, no longer boring. My best friend Casey Kenner was yelling at the top of his lungs. "HELLO! Is anyone in this godforsaken town going to answer me?" Behind Casey Kenner was Mabel Donahue, the

Vice President of Collegiate Chapters for Delta Beta Sorority, Incorporated.

I could only see Ty from the back side, which was enjoyable in itself, but I was sure the expression on his face was priceless. His whole posture took on an "I'm the sheriff, I'm in charge" kind of vibe. Like I said, it was enjoyable from the back.

"Are you the detective in charge of the Liza McCarthy case?" Casey asked imperiously, projecting his voice like the inveterate showman he was. I wondered if I could scooch around the side to get a better look at the drama. But if I moved, I wouldn't have such a good view of Casey, and he really was the star of this show.

"Yes." Ty played the role of the taciturn, grumpy policeman well.

With a flourish worthy of a dramatic telenovella, Casey whipped out a piece of paper and presented it to Ty. "This is a subpoena duces tecum. You are hereby ordered to present property that is currently in your possession and which is the legal property of Delta Beta Sorority, Incorporated, ad nauseum."

"What property is that?" Ty asked with a dry, lazy voice. It was almost like he didn't appreciate Casey's flair.

"The aforementioned property legally consists of one cell phone belonging to Liza McCarthy. It's spelled out, habeas corpus."

In case you couldn't tell, Casey spent some time in law school.

Ty looked at Mabel. "And you are?"

"Mabel Donahue." She tilted her head like a queen. "Legal representative of Delta Beta Sorority."

"Incorporated," Casey added.

"If I say no?" Ty asked.

Casey whipped out his cell phone. "The Delta Beta attorney was hoping you'd say that. She so wants to earn that retainer."

Ty looked at Casey and Mabel for another second, then half turned to look at me. I motioned that I had no idea what was going on. This was just another of Casey's brilliant ideas. Ty made a sound of resignation, then "You're free to go, Ms. Blythe."

He was dismissing me? He cut me off before I could start arguing. "After I get your friend Mr. Kenner his item from the evidence locker." Then he stalked out of the room.

Casey and Mabel fist-bumped surreptitiously, but Mabel threw me a wink. Ty returned with the glittery phone in a depressing plastic evidence bag, and we were leaving when a totally unexpected person marched in: Amanda Jennifer Cohen, still in the same clothes she'd worn to Liza's memorial service.

I told Casey to go ahead but stayed to give Amanda a quick little hug. If Liza's service had taught me anything, it was that we should treasure the time we had with our sisters.

"What are you doing here?" I asked her. "Did Ty call you in for questioning?"

Amanda's brows shot up in alarm. "No!" She tilted her head toward the file she had under her arm. "Official college stuff. The chancellor asked me to bring this by."

"What is it?" The file looked very official, with the Sutton College seal embossed in gold on the navy binder cover.

"It's the college's Clery Act report." At my blank face, she continued. "Every year the college has to assemble their report on campus violence."

I eyed the thick binder. There were a lot of tabs in there.

"Here you go. You can look at it while I find someone to talk to." She thrust the binder into my hands, and I read the labels neatly printed out. DRUGS. ALCOHOL. WEAPONS. ASSAULT- SEXUAL. MURDER.

Was Liza McCarthy's death going to be reported in this fancy, impressive binder next year?

Amanda's heels clicked on the linoleum behind me. "Seriously? Where is everyone?"

I waved my hand at the lack of attentive personnel at the Sutton police station. "This binder's really thick, Amanda." I said, queasy at the idea of so many students being victims each year. And at the idea of so many attackers.

She shrugged. "You know college kids."

I frowned and gave the binder back to her. I did know fifty college kids fairly well by now, and I would hurt if they were hurt.

"Did I see Mabel Donahue in the front? What is she doing here?"

"They're just collecting some of Liza's effects."

"Like what? Why would Mabel want Liza's stuff?"

I decided to go with Casey's almost legal explanation. "Her phone was the property of Delta Beta."

Amanda shuffled the binder from one arm to another, nervously tapping her toes, waiting for a Sutton police officer. "God, what do the police do in this town?"

I eyed the thick collection of reports detailing a year's worth of violent incidents and substance abuse and worried for the first time that the Sutton police officers might be too busy for our own good.

Chapter Twenty-six

THE LINE BETWEEN Casey's fabulous ideas and his horrible ideas could be a really thin, invisible line.

"I don't think we should do it," I said for the forty-seventh time.

"I'm doing it," he said for the forty-eighth time.

"Casey!"

"When did you become such a wuss?"

I flashed him a final-warning look. But still, I didn't like this.

"Can we double-check, one more time?"

Casey rolled his eyes and muttered "wuss," so I punched him as I pulled up the document on his laptop again.

Once we'd gotten back to the sorority house, Mabel took one look at the phone and decided it wasn't, after all, the one that Delta Beta had issued to Liza. Funny how that works. She left for Atlanta, but not before telling Casey and me what a good job we were doing here. That meant a lot, coming from her.

After we had charged Liza's deader-than-a-doornail phone, we pulled up her call history. Sure enough, there were lots of incoming calls from the phone-sex numbers. We had learned from Casey's research that the way these things usually worked was by forwarding calls from the 1-900 line to the operators. Assuming that all the operators had disposable phones, we had no way of knowing who those numbers belonged to. Google definitely didn't help.

Liza's call history also had numbers that we had matched up to the computer spreadsheet. If we were right in our guess that the spreadsheet was a record of payments, and the ten-digit numbers were phone numbers, we now had a direct tie between Liza's phone and the phone numbers of her phone-sex employees.

Now Casey wanted to call them. From Liza's phone. I liked the detective work, but this part, I was being a baby about. For a professional sorority girl, I'm not great with confrontation.

"You need to do it." Casey shoved the phone at me.

"Why?"

"Because you're a girl. If they hear a man's voice coming from Liza's number, it will freak them out."

He had a point. It was weak, but a point.

"Margot, you know we have to do this. We have got to find out how far this goes. There isn't any other way to figure out the extent of Delta Beta's involvement in this. I can't have this coming back to bite us in the butt."

I puffed out some air, blowing my bangs out of my face. "What about the money?"

Casey's face was blank. "What about the money?"

"How were people getting paid?" I wondered why I hadn't thought of this angle before. "If we got access to Liza's checking account, we could see who she was writing checks to . . ."

"Please Margot," Casey interrupted. "It's not like that. This stuff is off the books, or in another name, or a corporation or something. It's not like Liza was writing checks from her Delta Beta checkbook."

I knew he was right. I was grasping at straws, and besides, the police had probably already pulled evidence like her bank accounts.

"Fine," I muttered. Casey dropped Liza's phone in my outstretched hand. "Let's do this."

We picked the number we'd seen most often in Liza's call record, although, interestingly, it wasn't the most frequent number in the spreadsheet. "Maybe she was high-maintenance or something. Or Liza had to train her in heavy breathing." The thought was weird and gross.

I sat in the recliner and took a deep breath before dialing. The phone rang two, three, four times and right before it should have gone to voice mail, someone picked up.

But no one said anything on the other line. "Hello?" I asked.

There was a faint click, then a rustle, then the sound of a door's being closed. I remembered what Casey had said about the operators needing privacy for verbally turning some random guy on.

"Hello?" The voice over the line was hesitant and quiet. Before I could come up with something reasonable to say (I really should have thought this through a little more and not let Casey irritate me into things), the voice said, "Who is this?"

I gasped. I knew that voice. "Aubrey?" I whispered, shocked.

"No." Although it was still a whisper, the voice was sharper, a different tone altogether. "Aubrey isn't here."

I believed the voice. It wasn't Aubrey St. John on the phone. It was her sister.

"Ainsley?"

There was another muffled sound, of a door's opening or a cabinet's closing. Then a click, and she was gone.

I pushed a palm against my forehead, sweeping my bangs away

from my face, and sought Casey's face. He was as shocked as I was.

"Well, that explains a lot," I said.

"This is the chapter president's twin sister? The Tri Mu?" Casey hadn't met Ainsley, he'd only heard me talk about her. I nodded in confirmation and he rolled his eyes. "Freaking Moos."

I got what he was saying, believe me, I did. But. "If Ainsley's been working for Liza, why is she trying to expose the ring and ruin Delta Beta's rep?"

"It's the perfect cover. She's bringing us down from the inside, the diabolical cow."

It really was the perfect cover. It was shocking, even for a Tri Mu.

"Poor Aubrey," I murmured. "To have a sister betray you like that."

"Do you think she knows? Casey asked.

I thought about it and shook my head. "No, I don't think she knows anything. You should have seen her at Stefanie Grossman's S&M hearing. She was Stefanie's biggest defender. She really thought Stefanie was innocent. She couldn't have known that Stefanie or Ainsley were phone-sex operators."

While I was still worrying about Ainsley's machinations and Aubrey's potential heartbreak, Casey had moved on. "Let's do another one," he said, running his finger over the list. "How about this 610 area code. That one comes up a lot."

Then Liza's phone rang. I don't think I've ever jumped so high. Casey let loose a swear word.

"What do I do?" I whispered, as if the caller could hear me. Casey picked up the phone, pressed a button and shoved it at me. "Answer it," he mouthed.

I took a deep, noisy breath. "Hello?"

"Hi, Heather," the man said.

My eyebrows shot up and my mouth dropped open like a fish out of water. It was a freaky pervert dude!

Casey very helpfully reached over, gently took the phone from me, put it on speaker and set it down on the recliner arm. Then he sat back to listen with an avid expression on his stupid, handsome face.

"H-h-hi," I said, irritated that my stuttering came across a lot like heavy breathing.

"I've missed talking to you," the man said.

Oh my. "I've missed talking to you, too." Casey made a keep-going motion with his finger, like I had when he made his call to the phone-sex line. Payback sucked. "So, so much." Casey threw up his hands like I was hopeless. I wasn't hopeless; I just wasn't horny. There was a difference.

"Sooooo," I drew the word out as I reached for a way to get this guy to talk. "What are you wearing?"

"My suit and tie. Remember what you like to do with silk ties?"

I closed my eyes tightly, trying not to go there. "Mm hmmm . . ." I said instead. "Lots of nasty stuff. Oh. Yeah." Casey clapped a hand over his mouth, either in shock or to keep himself from laughing, the jerk.

"What are you wearing?" The caller's voice got deep and thick. I looked down at the Delta Beta tee and jeans I'd changed into after we got home from the police station.

"Just a . . . robe," I finished lamely. "And, um, panties."

"Take the panties off," the dude ordered me.

"Okay," I said. Of course, I didn't do anything. I paused. "They're off."

"Now take the sash of your robe off, slide it out real slow."

I looked toward the ceiling and counted to ten.

"Oh yeah, like that," the guy said. I gave the phone a weird face. I hadn't made any sounds. The imagination was a powerful thing.

"You look so beautiful," he went on.

To be honest, by this point I was thinking there was something to this phone-sex business. I could sit here, in a ratty T-shirt, old blue jeans, not doing anything, get told I was beautiful, and get paid for it? I might have to rethink my moral stance.

"Tell me where you are," I said. "I want to picture you."

I heard the telltale grind of a zipper. The man laughed, low and dangerous. "I'm just outside my office. Get this, there are cops everywhere. They're next door, and they don't even have a clue what I'm about to do to you right now." That's when it started to get gross. As a general rule, the sounds of a random pervert and his overactive imagination aren't as sexy as he thinks they are.

I think I said, "oh, yes" and "oh, baby" and Casey might have moaned a few times, because he couldn't help himself, but the guy was very self-reliant. Really, he took care of most of it by himself, which, after paying 2.99 for each additional minute wasn't very economical of him.

He was on his third round of describing how big he was and how young I was when I heard the sound of a knock against wood, and a familiar voice. "Professor, we're almost finished."

"Shit," the man said, and the phone disconnected.

It was Hatfield's voice in the background—and it all fell into place.

I wondered how much money Professor Xavier had just paid to jerk off to the halfhearted sounds made by a girl in a T-shirt and her gay best friend.

Chapter Twenty-seven

WEDNESDAY MORNING, I woke up to a text from Amanda, asking me out to lunch. I felt guilty that while Casey and I had spent half the night laughing about phone-sex clients, I hadn't called her to see if she wanted to join in the fun.

Of course I wanted to see her, but there was going to be a giant elephant in the room. And I knew exactly what that giant elephant liked to do with silky ties and robe sashes.

Maybe they weren't that serious, Dean Xavier and Amanda. Maybe it was just a casual thing. But I didn't think so. I knew my big sis, and I knew she didn't waste her time on anyone that she couldn't see with the minivan and the 2.5 kids and golden retriever. She had high standards. I just wasn't sure I could tell her that her instincts might be off with this one.

We met at the tearoom again, early for lunch, at 11 A.M. I gave her a big hug.

"You look beautiful," I told her, mostly because it was true.

"You're so sweet." Amanda carefully set her clutch on a corner of the table, removing her phone and keeping it where she could see it.

I had to say something. "Amanda, is that what I think it is?"

A small, satisfied smile touched her lips. "Maybe."

"Shut up." I put a hand out. "May I?"

When she nodded permission, I picked up the fine leather accessory. Smooth, supple calfskin, exquisite handmade craftsmanship, a distinctive H on the buckle. "Hermès?" My question was whispered because this was a holy subject matter.

She tilted her head coyly. "It's secondhand. I found this great vintage shop on eBay."

"It's beautiful. And I'm mad that you're keeping all the great eBay sellers to yourself!"

She put a hand to her heart. "Margot, you don't know how much that means to me!"

I must have looked confused. She went on, "I mean, you were always the one in college who had everything. It's just flattering that maybe now you'd look up to me."

That was insane. I'd always looked up to her. She was my big sister.

"How did everything go yesterday?" When I'd left the police station, she was still waiting to see Ty Hatfield. "Did Ty sign off on your report?"

Amanda quirked her brow at me. "It's 'Ty,' is it?"

"It's a name," I said, dismissing her innuendo. "Seriously, tell me about it," I said after the waitress came and took our orders. I ordered tea and chicken salad. Amanda ordered chardonnay and chicken salad, which was surprising. It wasn't even noon yet.

Amanda pursed her lips and seemed to collect herself. "Of course, it went fine. There's always some tensions about those reports. No one likes admitting what's happened under their watch. And then he wanted to ask about that Stefanie girl that they're looking for. I didn't even know what to say, I barely knew her. All I knew was she was a Delta Beta who'd gotten herself into some trouble."

"I wonder if she had a history of violent behavior," I mused. "It seems crazy that our alumnae would recommend someone like that." Like many sororities, Delta Beta generally required a letter of recommendation from an alumna before a bid was extended during rush.

Amanda looked annoyed. "Something really needs to be done about that. Maybe I'll talk to Mabel. Is she still in town?"

"No," I said, pausing for the delivery of my tea and Amanda's chilled wine. "She left right after we left the police station."

"So she took Liza's effects with her?"

The thought of the phone made me smile, remembering the jokes that Casey and I had made last night. But then I remembered that as far as Amanda knew, the phone-sex operation was just a rumor perpetrated by the Tri Mus and I decided not to share the shenanigans that Casey had forced me to participate in. So I just shrugged, and said, "No. Turned out, the phone wasn't the sorority's," and left it at that.

Amanda reached for her glass and took a rather long sip. "Let's talk about happier things," she said brightly. "I have an announcement." She lifted her glass. "I got a promotion!"

I gasped in delight. "What! When?"

"This morning. I'm moving to administration. Vice President of Student Affairs."

My mouth dropped open. That was huge. "Congratulations, Big!" I clinked my iced-tea glass to her wineglass. "Will you be sad to leave Panhellenic?"

"No," she said definitively. "I see this move as broadening the work I can do for students. Now I can benefit the whole student body, not just the Greeks."

That was a true Deb response, right there. Always focused on the greater good.

"And," she continued, "there's a huge raise. Which is always nice in academia."

I reminded myself that Amanda had had a very difficult childhood in a West Virginia coal mine. Or close to one. Of course she deserved all the raises in the world.

Amanda ordered a second glass of wine, which she also totally deserved, and the lunch stretched into an hour—just like it used to be, me and my big, laughing and gossiping and drinking.

Her phone rang, and she checked the number. "Ugh," She said. "I'm so sorry. They're already asking me to do stuff for them."

As before, she took the call outside, which I thought was very nice manners. While I was waiting at the table, I saw a familiar blond head watching us. This time, she was dressed in all black, which looked very chic and slimming, even on a Moo.

Amanda's call took a while, so I checked my e-mail before she returned, very apologetic for taking so long. "It's fine," I said. "No one understands better than me that some jobs are twenty-four/ seven."

She nodded and drained her chardonnay. That would be her second. But I wasn't counting.

I hated to bring up a possibly uncomfortable topic, but I had to know. "So what's going on with you and Dean?"

She frowned, and settled her hands in her lap. "Dean and I are over."

"Oh," I said, with not a small amount of relief. If she and Dean were over, then maybe I was relieved of any responsibility to tell her about his preference for eighteen-year-olds named Heather and Stefanie. "That's . . . sad." It might have been sad, but I really couldn't tell from the carefully composed look she'd put on.

"Yes. Well, you know what they say. People are in your life for a reason."

The saying was, "People are in your life for a season, a reason, or a lifetime." I should know. I had had that framed and given it to Amanda for her graduation gift.

"Mr. Perfect is still out there," I said supportively.

Amanda made a dismissive sound. "Maybe. Or maybe they're all self-involved, entitled jerks." That didn't sound like Amanda; maybe Dean had hurt her more than she was letting on.

I focused back on the problem at hand. "No, you don't believe that. Remember how we made those lists in college, like Oprah told us to? The ones about defining our perfect man?" I smiled reassuringly. "Of course, my perfect man was Matt Damon and yours was Ben Affleck, so we could stay best friends and double-date all the time." I counted off on my fingers. "You wanted someone artistic and sensitive and financially independent. And someone who liked to surf." I couldn't remember why that one was on there. It had seemed important at the time. "Your artistic millionaire surfer is out there, I know it."

The expression on Amanda's face was indecipherable. Maybe she wanted to believe me, maybe she was too depressed by her breakup to believe that good things happen for people. Then she gave herself a little shake and waved at the waitress for the check. "Thanks, Margot," she said a bit condescendingly, just like a big sister. "But until Ben Affleck gets here, I'm going to have to take care of myself."

Chapter Twenty-eight

AMANDA PAID FOR the lunch, insisting that she had invited me, so it was her treat. After a friendly good-bye squeeze, she left, her Kate Spade heels snapping down the sidewalk. I counted to ten and, as I expected, I was joined by none other than Ainsley St. John, as if she'd come out of nowhere. There were so many similarities between her and Aubrey, but I was beginning to see the differences now. Aubrey's lips were poutier, her cheeks fuller. Ainsley's eyes were a tad closer together, her nose a bit sharper. They were both beautiful, as much as it annoyed me to admit that about a Tri Mu.

"We have to stop meeting like this," I drawled. Knowing that she was one of Liza's phone-sex operators made me like her a whole lot less.

"What were you two doing in there?" Ainsley demanded, pointing at the restaurant where Amanda and I had just eaten.

"None of your business," I said as politely as I could. It should have been obvious, what with the forks and the plates of food.

Ainsley's eyes narrowed on me. "I thought you would do something. That's why I gave you the numbers."

Right. The numbers. Now I concluded there might be something seriously wrong with Aubrey's twin. Or maybe she wasn't taking her meds like she should. It was just a tragedy pileup where this girl was concerned. I had taken her seriously when she'd said she wanted the phone-sex ring shut down; but that was before I knew she was an integral part of its operation.

"What do you want?" I asked, trying to sound nice. Maybe if I was nice, she'd go away. That usually worked with the overeager sales associates trying to sell me perfume at the department store.

"I want justice." The self-righteousness in her tone was shocking. Like she, of all ho-bags, had any room to demand anything.

"If people keep picking up the phone, there's nothing I can do." I looked at her accusingly. I understood that she felt victimized. My one experience the night before had definitely given me insight into the sleaziness of the business Ainsley was involved in. But she had to take responsibility and acknowledge that if she kept accepting calls from perverts, she might be helping to perpetuate the nastiness.

"Margot?" The voice came from behind me. I turned, and there was Amanda, a question huge on her face as her eyes darted between me and Ainsley. She pointed lamely at the tearoom door. "I think I left my credit card."

The three of us faced off awkwardly for a moment. I thought fast. I didn't want a mentally unstable Ainsley to attack Amanda or anything. That could cause PTSD. For Amanda and me. "She's not involved in this," I said to Ainsley. "She's not Panhellenic anymore. This is between us. Deb and Moo . . . Mu. Mu." I hoped she would ignore the slightly insulting slip of the tongue. My pledge trainer taught me better than that.

Ainsley pointed at Amanda. "She could have stopped this from the beginning." Ainsley looked back at me, ferociousness in her pretty eyes. "It was her job!"

Amanda gasped self-righteously. I put my hands out between them. "Seriously. Leave her alone." I used my sternest chapter-advisor voice, the one that really hadn't been working so well recently.

Ainsley's lip curled. "You're just as bad as the rest of them. You just won't take me seriously until I expose every last one of you slutty Delta Beta bitches." And with that dramatic statement, she whirled and stomped off down the street.

"Ainsley . . ." I called after her halfheartedly. The chapter advisor in me wanted to broker some sort of peace. The Delta Beta in me wanted her far, far, away from me. On another planet. Without hair dye or moisturizer.

Then I remembered Amanda, awkwardly standing by after being attacked for no good reason. "Are you okay?" I asked, searching her face. She nodded, and I saw that she was upset by Ainsley's uncalled-for verbal abuse of our sorority. But then, like a strong Deb woman, she pushed her shoulders back, lifted her chin, and went to get her credit card.

Chapter Twenty-nine

I WAS KNEE deep in a fascinating TLC marathon about big fat Amish gypsies when the doorbell rang. I picked up my broom, just in case I had to chase a fraternity pledge with it.

Instead, it was just Ty Hatfield.

"Again?" I asked.

"I could say the same about you," he said, pushing his way in the door. A dark-haired officer followed him: Malouf, the same one who had come the night that Liza died.

"Is Hunter Curtis around?" Ty asked.

I didn't like the sound of his voice. It was very . . . official. And not very friendly. And when a cop talks like that, it makes you stand straight and answer, pronto.

"He's probably in the dining room. We just finished dinner."

Because he was looking all official, and sounding official, and had another officer with him, my stomach felt like lead as we walked back to the dining room.

"Hunter?" I called his name, seeing the hard worker cleaning off the tables where the ladies had just eaten chicken à la king and fruit salad for dinner. "These gentlemen . . ."

But I was cut off by Ty's stepping forward. "Hunter Curtis?" There was his authoritative cop voice again.

Hunter nodded, struck mute by the same respect for law enforcement that I had.

"You're under arrest." The dark-haired officer Malouf grabbed Hunter by the shoulder and spun him around, linking both of Hunter's hands behind his lower back.

"For what?" I demanded hotly.

Ty gave me a cool look. "For burglary, destruction of property, criminal mischief."

I was shocked. Yet Hunter was not. His head hung low, and his shoulders slumped as he was led out of the house. It was to be expected that sorority sisters started gathering in the hall, their nightly activities interrupted, yet again, by police in the sorority house. If Hunter was a criminal, working for us, working among us, it was going to devastate everyone.

Ty walked slower than his partner, staying behind with me. My mind was running a mile a minute. I'd have to call HQ—again—and ask about Hunter's background employment check. They'd have to call our lawyer about liability. And Casey! I'd have to call him the second the police left to formulate a PR statement.

"His fingerprints were all over the room," Ty said under his breath.

"What?" My head spun to look at him. "What room?"

"The chapter advisor's office."

I stopped dead. "Let Hunter go, right this second."

Ty stopped and stared. "Excuse me?"

"He's the house brother," I explained calmly. "He does housework for us. His fingerprints are all over this house. That's no proof of anything."

"They were wrapped around the award used to destroy the computer." Ty's words chilled me. "They weren't accidental, housecleaning fingerprints."

I let go of the breath I was holding, slow and measured. Ty continued. "The fingerprints matched ones taken at the Beta Gamma house two years ago when their chapter room was stacked with giant blowup phalluses."

I rolled my eyes. "They called the cops about that?" I asked incredulously. Beta Gamma had no sense of humor. Ty was deadpan, and I remembered something about goats in the bathroom. I decided to focus on the bigger issue. "So Hunter broke into the office as a frat-pledge prank? He's not even a pledge!"

Ty shrugged. "Or he helped his pledges get into the house." He started walking toward the door again, paused, and looked back at me. "Have you thought about a security system yet?"

A frustrated exhale blew my bangs out of my eyes. I watched Hunter being put into the police car, then they drove off, leaving me and thirty sorority women with no one to clear our plates. This was getting ridiculous.

I hustled up some pledges to help with the kitchen cleanup, promising them a reprieve on their other pledge duties later. Until we hired a new house brother, or Hunter came back, I'd have to come up with a rotating system for the chores he normally did. I mostly focused on the inconvenience until we finished, then I remembered what else had happened the night that the chapter advisor's office had been trashed. Stefanie Grossman's file had disappeared.

Why would the frat pledges have stolen just one file from our office? It didn't make sense. But then, goats and giant phalluses and a hundred pineapple-no-cheese pizzas didn't make sense either. These were fraternities we were talking about.

Still, with the sensitive information contained in Stefanie's file, I needed to make sure that didn't get passed around fraternity row. Delta Beta's reputation would be toast.

I grabbed my purse and headed to campus.

I KNEW JUST where to find the Interfraternity Council offices. Logically, at the Commons, segregated from the sorority Panhellenic offices on the opposite side of the basement. A traditional institution founded by devout Carolina Presbyterians, Sutton College experienced the sexual-equality movement later than most, and in some ways it didn't quite catch on.

I was surprised to find Brice Concannon in his office. A man who dressed well and wore nice cologne surely had more exciting places to be than this Cold-War-era bunker.

"Margot!" He stood when I walked in, a real Southern gentleman. "May I call you Margot?"

"Of course," I said graciously.

He invited me to sit, which I did, basking in his apparent admiration and trying to resist the impulse to nervously brush my bangs off my face. The tension in that windowless office was enough to make a girl forget that she was visiting to discuss illegal activities and sexual misconduct.

When he asked me what he could do for me, I had to bring myself back to the unfortunate situation at hand. As I explained Hunter's arrest, Brice interrupted to ask, "What fraternity is he a member of?"

"Omega Omicron Rho." When Brice relaxed slightly, I understood. He was worried that Hunter was an Eta Ep, one of his brothers. I could relate.

"Do you want me to talk to their advisor?" Brice reached out for a pen to write something down, and I jerked forward to cover his hand with mine.

"It's a little more complicated than that." Following his glance at my ragged manicure, I pulled back my hand. "Pranks are one thing. We can laugh them off, we can accept them as a normal part of college life. But if Hunter's brothers put him up to this prank, it's not funny. This is criminal. Breaking and entering. Burglary."

"What did they take?"

I bit my lip. Sharing this information was dangerous if Brice Concannon wasn't a gentleman.

"I don't know if I should say. It involves a violation of our Standards and Morals code . . ."

Brice held up a hand. "Say no more. I understand."

I sighed in relief. Finally, someone who understood that I couldn't spill all the nasty beans about my sisters. Unlike Ty Hatfield, Brice Concannon understood that I needed to protect ladies' reputations.

"I'm sure the phone-sex ring has been really disruptive to the Debs."

Oh, crap.

"The what?" I tried playing innocent, which didn't wipe the amused look off Brice's face.

"There have been rumors, Margot. But if it makes you feel any better, I think they're all complimentary."

No. That did not make me feel better. Neither did what I had to say next.

"I was actually referring to another violation . . ." I swallowed and decided to come out with it. "A sister's S&M file was taken from my office. Presumably by the Omegas, Hunter's brothers."

When Brice's brows lifted at "S&M" I rolled my eyes. "It's short for Standards and Morals."

"Ah."

"This is a confidential file. If it got out on fraternity row, it could hurt reputations."

"Is the stuff in the file true?"

"Does it matter?" I snapped.

Brice shrugged. "If she did it, then she probably deserves what happens to her."

It was one thing for me to apply antiquated moral requirements to my sisters. It was another thing for a frat brother to do it.

Now I remembered Ty's warning and wondered why he'd given it. "Hunter was arrested by Officer Hatfield tonight. Do you know him?"

Brice's eyes closed briefly with a reluctant smile. "Unfortunately, yes. If he's the one that arrested Hunter, this all makes a lot more sense."

"It does?"

"Hatfield is known around town for being anti-Greek. His track record speaks for itself. Every time there's a fraternity getting in trouble, it's usually Hatfield there, writing tickets and whatnot." He waved his hand. "You know, boys will be boys. But some people have to be all uptight about it."

"Like the pranks," I offered.

"Exactly." Brice shook his head. "You and I, we understand that this is a normal part of Greek life. High jinks, crazy parties, pranks. Officer Hatfield, on the other hand, gets all bent out of shape when guys have one little party where some underaged girl brings her own Rohypnol."

Whoa.

"Well, I can sort of see his point," I ventured. "As I've tried discussing with you, I think the pranks are getting out of control. Especially if they're involving dangerous substances like gelatin or roofies."

Brice's gorgeous green eyes focused on me. "Do you want to have a drink sometime to discuss it?"

"I don't—"

"Tonight?"

"My friend Casey . . ."

"I'm cool if you want to bring her along. The more the merrier."

"Casey's a—"

Brice winked. "Yeah, I've heard the rumors about you Deb girls."

Clearly Brice was neither going to help me nor take me out. But I wanted the last word "Casey's a guy."

Brice's eyes widened. "Wow. Haven't heard those rumors. Just the ones about the phone sex."

The preppy jerk. "How ever did you hear about that?"

"One of the Eta Ep brothers is dating a president of one of the sororities. I think she's a—"

Now it was my turn to interrupt him. "Tri Mu," I muttered as I turned and left his office.

Chapter Thirty

CALLIE'S ROOM WAS on the second floor by the stairs. As S&M director, I thought she should be notified that a confidential file had probably been stolen by a fraternity. As I approached her door, I heard the familiar sound of a girl crying. Not another one.

I knocked three times. "Callie? Can I come in?"

She answered in the affirmative, and I found her curled up in her bed, a Deb T-shirt quilt wrapped around her. She was clutching her cell phone so tightly her knuckles were white.

"Callie." I went to her immediately. It broke my heart seeing her, clearly devastated by something. "What is it?"

A wet sob bubbled out of her, and I wrapped my arms around her, squeezing her. Ten years of sorority life, and I knew only one thing wrought this kind of devastation.

"Boy trouble?" I asked.

She nodded, clenching her phone into her chest. "Do you want to talk about it?"

Callie's head shook in my shoulder. "It's okay, I know," I sympathized. "Boys are so stupid."

She nodded in my shirt, and I heard the squelch of something wet from her face.

"I know, I know. Let me guess, he was supposed to call, and he didn't?"

Another shake. I was getting a little frustrated at this guessing game. "Why don't you just tell me what happened?" I said, pulling away so I could give her a chance to talk. And breathe.

"I just don't get men," she wailed. "They just don't listen, you know? They want you there when they want you, but when you want them to you know, shut up and give you a chance to talk, they're like, they're the man and they're going to do what they want to do. You know?"

"Maybe," I said. I wasn't quite sure I followed, but sometimes distraught girls just needed someone to hear them out.

"We talk every night," she sobbed. "But he said he couldn't call tonight." I hoped the phone was sturdy because she was gripping the thing very tightly.

"Why can't he call tonight?" I asked carefully. I was pretty sure she hadn't covered that part.

"BECAUSE HE'S STUPID."

Oh yeah, now that I got.

"Look," I grabbed her wrists and shook her slightly. It was hard, with her arms locked to her chest around her phone. "You are Callahan Campbell. You are a descendant of Mary Gerald Callahan, the founder of one of the greatest sororities ever created. Do you think Mary Gerald waited around and cried when a stupid boy didn't call?"

Callie sniffed. "Probably not. In 1879."

"Exactly!" I said. Point proved. "No, Mary Gerald and her best friend Leticia didn't want stupid boys running their lives. They wanted to have a place, all their own, where women could support and love each other and live together and not worry about what other people thought."

Callie cocked her head. "Family gossip has always been that they were lesbians."

I took my hands off Callie and folded them in my lap primly. "Like I said, we don't need men," I added briskly.

"I know." Callie sighed, leaning back into her pillows. "It's just hard for me. When they just won't *listen*. You know?"

I had been an advisor for a little over a week. I totally understood being ignored.

"I need to talk to you about Stefanie Grossman," I said.

"It just feels like you're not even a real person. When you're being talked at, and not to."

"It's about her file," I said. "The one that was taken from the chapter advisor's office."

"I just want someone to hear me, really hear me," she said.

"I'm concerned about the confidentiality provision being compromised," I explained.

Callie got a lost look on her face. She stared at me, then crumpled into moist sobs again. For such a cute girl, she sure was an ugly crier.

"Okay, okay. We can do it later, if you want," I said.

With a pathetic little nod, she rolled over on her side still clutching the cell phone in her hand. She was clearly too upset to handle sorority matters tonight.

"Remember Callie," I said, trying to cheer her up. "Another stupid guy will come along. Just wait. You'll see." I thought she looked a little better when I left.

FUELED BY CASEY'S magical refilling Delta Beta flask and a selection of Milano cookies, I updated Casey on my meeting with Brice Concannon and the strong possibility that whispers about Delta Beta's phone-sex participation were now running rampant around Sutton.

"At least they're complimentary rumors," Casey sighed, nibbling on a cookie.

Once again, that failed to comfort me.

When my phone rang a few minutes later, I could tell it was headquarters. (Because I had a special ringtone for Delta Beta sisters. "Independent Women" just seemed appropriate for those sassy Debs at HQ.)

Mabel Donahue was on the other end of the call. I straightened up on the couch, as if she could assess my posture over the phone. "Hello, Mabel." Casey sat up as well. "Yes, yes, he's here with me."

"Put him on speaker. You'll both need to hear this."

I did as Mabel commanded—always have, always will. "The worst has come to pass," Mabel said with a dire tone.

Casey gasped. "Lindsay Lohan pledged Delta Beta?"

"No," Mabel said. "Worse."

Casey and I exchanged a horrified glance. What could be worse?

"Fraternity mixers have been banned by Panhellenic?" I guessed.

A sigh came from Mabel's end. "Worse. The Tri Mus. They know everything."

I clutched my pearls. "Well, that's impossible," Casey said.

"I just got a call from their headquarters. They've been informed of the Sutton College chapter's involvement with a phone-sex ring. Barbra Kline was very supportive and offered their assistance."

"That bitch!" Casey said. He could use that word since he wasn't bound by Panhellenic expectations of ladylike conduct.

Mabel continued. "She offered to send one of their leadership experts to our chapter to assist us with, and I quote, our 'moral lapses.'"

I closed my eyes. The shame was too much. Thanks a lot, Tri Mu. "But wait, there's more." I broke the news to Mabel that the rumors might have already reached the fraternities.

"You two have to deal with this," Mabel said sternly. "There is too much at stake to let the Tri Mus get the upper hand."

"Their chapter president is one of the phone-sex operators," I told Mabel officially. "They have as much at stake as we do."

"How do you know this?" she asked.

Casey and I exchanged a guilty look. There was no way to explain to Mabel that we were only calling a phone-sex hotline for the most noble of purposes. And using a Delta Beta credit card, besides. "She confirmed it to me." That was pretty much true. As mentally confused as Ainsley seemed to be, she didn't deny doing what she did for money.

"All right then," Mabel sounded positive for the first time since the call began. "We have a weapon, and we're not afraid to use it. This is war. They hit us, and we hit them back. Casey, can I count on you?"

He had already grabbed his laptop to work. "Yes, ma'am. Going to the message boards now. Scandals don't exist unless they're online."

"Excellent. Margot? I assume you can control the ladies in Sutton?"

Control was a strong word, but I wasn't going to let Mabel down. "You can count on me," I promised.

Chapter Thirty-one

CASEY AND I spent the next few hours trolling greekgossip.net, shooting down Tri Mus talking trash. Word was spreading fast online; there were even memes. And if it was online, it was definitely being gossiped about via text and Instagram. It was like a never-ending virtual carnival game and, at the end of the night, more than profane. We had to face the cold, hard facts. Tri Mu had a weapon of mass destruction, and they weren't afraid to push the button. We had to come up with a plan.

I called Amanda the next morning. I thought I should give her an update on the situation, as a prominent Delta Beta in the college administration. She picked up on the third ring, sounding a little breathless. "Hey, Big, it's your little," I said.

"Oh hey, I was just about to call you." That sounded less than enthusiastic.

"Yeah?" I asked, suddenly nervous.

"I'm still officially Panhellenic advisor so I'm just going to come right out and say it."

Now I was definitely nervous. "What?"

"There's been a complaint filed against you."

I blinked hard and shook my head like there was water in my ears. "WHAT?" That was *not* what I was expecting.

"Actually two."

"Who?" The one word was all I could get out. I was dumbfounded.

"It's so ridiculous, it really is. But . . . once paperwork is filed . . ." Amanda's voice trailed off. I understood. In our world, these things were official.

"Can I come down there?" I asked. I really hated doing these things over the phone.

"Umm . . ." She paused and I imagined her looking at her trendy watch. "I'm afraid I have a meeting that's going to take most of this afternoon."

"Tomorrow?" I asked.

"You'll have to respond formally."

Damn. You'd think Amanda would cut her little sister a break. "Can you at least tell me what this is all about?"

"The first complaint is from Ainsley St. John."

I couldn't help but roll my eyes. "Amanda! Really? You and I both know that girl has let the peroxide go to her head."

"I know, I know," Amanda said in a soothing tone. "But that's why you should respond formally. Put everything in writing, saying all that. How crazy she is, all the insane things she's done."

I wasn't sure Ainsley had really committed so many wrong acts; she just seemed really intense and scary. But Amanda's advice was sound. "What about the other one? Who filed that?"

She paused, and I could hear her flipping through the papers. "The Eta Eps," she finally informed me. "They said you threatened their pledges."

I started laughing. I couldn't help it. "You can't be serious," I said. "The Eta Eps? Like anyone believes a word out of their mouths."

But Amanda wasn't laughing. "Margot, you have to take this seriously. They're one of the best fraternities on campus."

"Since when?"

"Since they pledged a bunch of nerdy guys with trust funds. Trust me. You don't want to alienate the chapter from them. They're rich and socially awkward."

"But they dumped gelatin on our chapter!" I half yelled into the phone. "Maybe they should not want to alienate us!"

Amanda's silence was chiding. Then so were her words. "This is the way things are, Margot. Successful Sutton College sororities know how to play the game. And they don't threaten fraternities."

I told Amanda I'd come by her office tomorrow, without defending myself further. All of a sudden, I was unsure of a lot of things—like whether I was really the best woman to advise this chapter.

CASEY AND I met for lunch at Cool Joe's, a burger dive on the south side of campus. Not coincidentally, it was next door to Sunset Station, the tanning salon that all the sorority girls at Sutton frequented. I complimented Casey on his new, unnatural orange glow, received at the very same tanning salon.

"It's a spray, of course. The latest in microbead delivery. I'm really impressed they have it here in Sutton since it hasn't been approved by the FDA yet."

"It looks fabulous," I said. I was always a firm believer in an almost sincere compliment.

Casey ducked his head, his eyes scanning the restaurant on alert for saboteurs and double agents. "You will not believe the things I heard," he said under his breath. It was almost certain that an Epsilon Chi worked a pole at the Silk Stocking on Wednesday nights, and that the Lambdas were still offering discounted plastic surgery to their less-cosmetically-blessed pledges. Of course, the Beta Gammas were seriously plagiarizing every single English exam, and there was proof somewhere on the fourth floor of the Samuel L. Jackson Library. (No relation to the Hollywood Samuel L. Jackson. The Sutton College forefather was dead.)

I leaned over, eagerly awaiting the coup de grace, the final nail in the coffin, the fat lady singing her precious little heart out. "And what about the Moos?"

The sparkle left Casey's beautiful blue eyes. "I got nothing."

"NOTHING?" I repeated, incredulously. How could that be? Every sorority had gossip. And no one was better at ferreting it out than a gay man in a spray-tan booth.

Casey clearly took the failure personally. "I tried, I did. I even straight up asked, 'What about those Moos?' But no one had heard anything."

We both sat and stared at our remaining lunches, too depressed to eat. Tri Mu HQ had information that would majorly damage Delta Beta's reputation, and what did we have? Big fat zero. If we couldn't fight back with some dirty gossip, what kind of sorority women were we?

Chapter Thirty-two

AFTER HOURS OF scouring the Internet to stop the spread of the true rumors about my sisterhood, I was exhausted and needed some alone time.

The closet was as dark as ever, and I tentatively shuffled until I saw the light from the window. This was my spot. This was where I could finally relax.

I pulled a cardboard box over to the window and sank down, noticing how tired my feet were, which was strange since most of the time in the hospital had been spent with my butt in a chair. The moon was clear and bright. Whether it was waxing or waning, it was nearly three-quarters full, and I watched the view that I loved. From this vantage point on the third floor of the sorority house on the bluff above Sutton, nothing had changed in the past ten years. The hallowed redbrick buildings of the college stood as they always did. The trees cast the same cool shadows. The streets wove the same basket-weave pattern.

It was Zen-like, contemplating the town like this. Not that I knew much about Zen. I was a yoga-school dropout. There was too much silence and "stay on your own mat" for my liking.

I felt my eyes grow heavy. I had already dozed twice, my head falling, my neck catching my head before my nose bounced off the windowsill, when something caught my eye as it reopened. I had to blink a few times before my zoned-out mind made sense of it.

Then I made what seemed the rational choice. I decided to go check out an optical illusion that looked like a dead body.

I let myself out the chapter-advisor door, fully intending to be back in two minutes and fall straight into bed after I'd satisfied my curiosity. What I'd seen was a play of shadows and moonlight. Or a leftover rush prop. Or, this week, a fraternity prank. If it was, heads were going to roll. Our chapter had dealt with too much drama in the past week to become the butt of some awful joke.

I followed the sidewalk to the back of the sorority house, where the yard dipped down a bit and fell into a creek. On the other side of the creek was a greenbelt with a jogging path that led to the college golf course and the dormitories. It was a convenient yet picturesque location.

She was lying in the grass, flat on her back, arms spread, still as a stone. I took a few steps back and automatically pulled my phone out of my pocket and called 911. Yes, this was an emergency. No, there were no goats. Yes, it was another dead body. The operator took my address and told me to stay where I was.

And so I did. Because the one thing I do well is rules. I follow them. I enforce them. Somewhere deep inside, I remembered that one of my rules was to help people. And even though I knew she was dead, I went back to help. I knelt beside her, put my hands on her mostly cold throat, and brushed away a piece of dark, curly hair from her face. I sat back on my heels, sticking my hands into the grass behind me, feeling the need to wipe them off on the cool, damp lawn. I felt something small and hard and closed my hand around it.

Oh, they were going to have a field day with this on greekgossip.net.

The police, the ambulance, then the coroner came. It was like a rerun of a bad sitcom, predictable and painfully unfunny.

Someone led me away from the body, put a blanket around my shoulders, asked if they could look into my eyes and shone something bright there. Someone gave me a cup of water. Someone asked me my name.

Then Ty Hatfield was sitting with me. "How did you find her?" he asked, his voice gentle.

"Dead," I said bluntly.

"I meant, how did you come to see her?"

"I looked out a window and saw a weird shadow. I had to come check it out before I went to bed."

"It's Stefanie Grossman," he said, like he wished it wasn't true.

I nodded like I wished the same.

He took my hand, and, for a millisecond, it felt nice. His skin was rough yet warm and my hand was still so cold. Then he took the glass vial out of my hand.

"I found that next to her," I said, amazed that my explanation was so calm and so simple.

Ty held it up to the light to examine it, using only the very tips of his finger and thumb. He called out to someone, who hurried over with an open plastic bag. When Ty dropped the vial into the baggie, the whoosh of adrenaline finally wore off. I was snapped out of my fugue state and back into Margot Blythe land, where things had to be done and had to be done quickly, even if I had hands that were vibrating like a Harley Davidson transmission. Even if a policeman looked like he had a million and a half questions for me.

A quick glance over my shoulder confirmed my suspicions that the entire chapter was up, watching me, the police, and the coroner loading their friend into a bag. This would not do.

I stood up, and Ty stood with me. His hand went to my forearm where it suggested that I not leave.

"The girls need me," I said to him under my breath.

The needs of the sorority never came first for him. "You need to give a statement."

"I told you everything," I insisted. My mind already had moved on, to the young women who needed explanations, too.

"Where were you tonight?"

I froze. On the TV show, even though the voice-over guy on *Law & Order says* it's the story of the victims and criminals, it's really not. It's the story of the detectives and lawyers. Those are the characters we identify with, week after week. I had always seen myself in those roles; but here I was, where I least expected it. On the flip side.

And even on the flip side of the law, I knew my rights. "Are we really doing this right now?"

"Why are you avoiding my question?"

I tossed my bangs away from my face, a defiant gesture so I could look at him straight in the eyes. "Do you think I'm going to stand here and be interrogated while my chapter—the people I'm responsible for—look on?"

Ty's expression held something I couldn't put a name to. "Do you think I'm going to let you walk away?"

"Am I a suspect?" I knew that question was asked a thousand

times on *Law & Order*. It worked just as well in real life as it did on TV.

When he didn't answer immediately, I took the opportunity to turn and walk as quickly as possible up to the house. I hustled as many people inside as I could. Those who wanted to watch the not-quite-grisly scene could stand outside and do so. I couldn't make their choices for them.

I had to answer questions, calm nerves, and assure people that we were all safe. Of course we were safe, we had nearly the whole Sutton police department on our front steps.

No murderer would dare show up. We could only hope the fraternity pledges showed as much sense.

Chapter Thirty-three

JUST AS I shut my eyes, I heard banging. Loud, fist on wood banging. I checked my watch. Somehow, I'd stepped into a time warp and it was almost eight in the morning. I hoped to God whoever it was had a venti four-shot, four-Equal coffee for me.

But no, the guy at my door didn't have coffee. He had a search warrant.

The entire Sutton police department flooded the sorority house while I got on the phone with Atlanta. While I wasn't sure of the legalities of having the girls' rooms searched, I knocked on each door and told everyone to cooperate if asked.

Turned out, they just searched my apartment. And the office. And my personal effects. The chapter room, the dining room, and the kitchen were searched, as well. Whatever judge signed that warrant must have had the same misgivings as I did about searching the personal belongings of thirty unrelated women living in a sorority house.

After making the rounds, I headed back to the advisor's apartment, just in time to see them zipping something small in an evidence bag.

"What are you taking?" I demanded.

Ty held up the bag for me and I saw a small glass vial, the sister of the one I had held in my hand the night before.

Of course, my only response was excitement. This was the clue we'd been waiting for. "Where did you find that?"

"Back of the medicine cabinet."

I was disappointed with myself. The traveler that I was, I was still living out of my hanging toiletry kit and my three-ounce shampoo bottles. I hadn't even cleaned out the bathroom cabinets. That was really sloppy of me.

In the chapter advisor's office, police officers removed a bunch of Delta Beta manuals and went through the ritual supplies in the chapter room, which resulted in another frantic call to headquarters. There was privilege to protect, and as long as I was a free woman, I was going to try my damnedest to do it.

When the search was over, Ty walked off with his colleagues, not even staying behind to chat or give me an update. I thought we'd gotten to a better place in our relationship. Apparently not.

Fifteen minutes after the police rolled out, Casey showed up at the door, grim-faced. He shoved a printed piece of paper at me. "I've been working all morning on this," he said.

I led him into the dining room because I hadn't eaten, and served up two bowls of fruity puffs with skim milk. He took one of the bowls and started eating, which was a little annoying because both bowls had been for me. After I got a second spoon, I could focus on the sheet he had given me. A reporter out of Charlotte had an "exclusive" about investigations into sex-crazed sororities.

"It's a five-part series," Casey said. "I bet I know what the investigation will reveal."

"And who gave them the exclusive," I muttered.

Casey nodded glumly and shoved a heaping pile of milk-drenched fruit puffs in his mouth. I recognized stress eating when I saw it. A similar-sized spoonful went into my mouth. "Guess who came by this morning," I said with a mouthful of cereal.

"Who?"

"The police." I paused for effect. "With a search warrant."

Casey's eyes rolled up to heaven. "Sweet Vidalia, could someone give me a break?"

He really wasn't going to like the rest of it. "Stefanie Grossman is dead."

"How?" he asked. I shook my head, thinking of the quiet, calm way she had lain in the grass. I hadn't seen any visible cause of death.

"I found her body."

"Oh, sweetheart!" Casey's hand covered mine in sympathy, but I wasn't feeling as traumatized as maybe I should have been. The night before felt like a strange, slow dream, like one of those paintings where the clocks are melting, and people have eyes in the middle of their foreheads. Plus, as harsh as it was to say, I didn't know Stefanie. She had never been in my life; therefore, her loss wasn't tangible to me.

When you find a body, you realize that it's just that. Skin, muscle, hair, a shell. A little creepy, and not something that you want to do every day, but there was something peaceful about it. It was just . . . absence. Something else I never thought I'd know.

"So aren't you going to tell me about the search warrant?"

Casey's question jerked me back to a problem that did seem real to me.

I gave him the few details that I could. "They found something in your bathroom?" Casey's eyes went wide, and I wondered if I had missed something.

"It's not mine."

"But it matches the one found at Stefanie's body."

"Oh dear," I said, rubbing my hands over my face. "That can't be good."

"I am not getting paid enough to rescue you if you get arrested, too. We'll have to just lock up the doors, and everyone will have to go home. We're done here. Delta Beta's closed."

I stilled, letting all the implications roll around my brain. Surely, no one thought that I would do something like that. Not Margot Blythe. I was the defender of the sisterhood. I wasn't the murderer of the sisterhood. Someone like me stood up for others; I didn't cut them down.

Oh wait.

"There is the one other thing I need to tell you."

CASEY CAME WITH me to Amanda's office. I wasn't sure why he wanted to accompany me, but he seemed fired up and in his PR mode. We had stopped at his hotel, where he changed into a seersucker jacket, a crisp white shirt, and a black-and-gold-striped tie, marked with a tiepin made from his mama's Delta Beta badge.

Amanda, on the other hand, was not in such snazzy attire. In a T-shirt and sweats, she looked like she'd been packing boxes since the crack of dawn. It had been a long time since I'd seen her look so rough. Even her usually sleek hair was a little frizzy. And that just wasn't Amanda.

She froze when we walked through the door, like she didn't remember who I was.

"Oh. Margot." Well that was a less-than-welcoming greeting.

"Did I catch you at a bad time?" I asked, noting the general upheaval of her office.

"What?" She looked around quickly, clearly distracted. "No . . . nooo . . ."

"I'm here about the complaints," I said, finding it odd that I had to remind her.

"She'd like to review them," Casey inserted.

Amanda looked irritated. "I already had this conversation with her."

"Okay, I'd like to review them," Casey said as smooth as you please.

Amanda cocked a finger at him. "Carey?"

"Casey."

"Right."

Clearly dismissing him, she moved behind her desk, and after flipping through a few things and shuffling an in-box, she handed me the papers. "That's Ainsley's," she said. "And the Eta Eps's is somewhere . . ."

Casey looked over my shoulder as we read Ainsley's conduct complaint against me. Neatly typed, it described how I had cornered her at the bowling alley and again inside a downtown restaurant and threatened her if she exposed information about the Delta Beta chapter.

"This isn't right," I whispered to Casey.

"What?" Amanda snapped.

"It's not right," I repeated louder for her.

"What part?" Amanda seemed exasperated. I could tell we'd caught her in the middle of packing up her office.

"Most parts," I replied a little more snappish than I'd intended. She was rubbing off on me.

Amanda frowned at the paper, then seemed to decide something. "I can't help you."

"What do you mean you can't help her?" Casey insisted hotly.

"After today, I'm no longer Panhellenic advisor. I'm moving out." She spread a hand at all the boxes, as if we couldn't tell what those strange cardboard cubes were used for.

"But you're still her friend," Casey said, with an edge to his voice.

"Of course she is," I said, putting a hand on his arm. "He's had a lot to deal with today," I explained to Amanda.

"And this should be the least of my problems." Casey glared at Amanda, but she looked at me instead.

"What's going on?" she asked.

I gave Casey a calm-down stare and focused on Amanda again. "A chapter member was found dead last night. The police woke me up this morning."

Something a lot like fear flitted across Amanda's drawn face. "That's horrible," she said, her attitude finally subsiding.

"It is, of course. Between that and the Tri Mu investigative reporter . . ."

"The what?"

Casey and I exchanged a nervous glance. I shrugged. We might as well tell her; she knew some of it anyway. "Charlotte's Channel 5 is doing an investigative piece on North Carolina sororities and the sex trade."

"You'll probably need to prepare a statement," Casey said, a little snidely, if you asked me.

Amanda's hand fluttered on her chest. "Why me?"

"Once they find out about the phone-sex deal, you don't think the reporters are going to tromp all over this campus talking to anyone who might know something?" Casey did a "please girl" look at her. "And you're the Panhellenic advisor. You know everything about everyone."

Now Amanda's hands both pressed out, fingers spread. "Not anymore! And I never did! I mean, I just heard rumors. Are you saying . . ." She looked at me, and I could see the panic rising as she processed this and the many questions and alarms that were going off in her head. We were similar in our concern for our sorority. "How did the reporter find out about the s-e-x thing?"

I shook Ainsley's complaint in my hand. "How do you think?"

Casey took that opportunity to be a little dramatic and make a point. "And that's why you should be a little more understanding when your friend needs some help. We are dealing with issues bigger than ourselves, here."

Amanda looked at him with solemn eyes. "What do you want me to do? Ignore a properly filed complaint?"

"Yes," Casey said. "That's exactly what you should do. Bury it."

"What do you think Margot? What would you do?" Amanda was asking me for advice, her voice filled with both concern and respect. I shook my head. What a difficult position for her to be in, caught between her duties to Panhellenic and her loyalty to me.

Of course, we were dedicated to our sisters, but we also had obligations to the greater good. That's what I told her. "You have to give Ainsley a fair hearing," I said, even though the thought of

Ainsley's making up lies about me pushed all my buttons. "After all, the truth is on my side," I finished confidently.

"Margot . . ." Casey's mutter was disapproving.

Silently, Amanda reached out her hand and took Ainsley's papers from me. "You are so inspirational to me," she said.

As she knew full well, that sentiment went both ways.

Chapter Thirty-four

THE SECOND HALF of *Law & Order* was always my favorite part, where the pieces started to come together, and there was some big twist that had everyone wondering if they had the right guy or not. So I wasn't too pleased when I saw the twist coming—the egotistical, cold investment banker was suddenly broke and desperate with a new motive of protecting his mother who had dementia— and there was a frantic knock at the door.

"MARGOT! DO YOU HAVE CHANGE FOR A DOLLAR?"

I sank down into the couch cushions. Maybe if I stayed very, very quiet, they wouldn't know I was in here and could find quarters elsewhere.

Bang! Bang! Bang! "MARGOT! WE NEED QUARTERS FOR THE VENDING MACHINES IN THE YARD!"

In the . . . what? I was on my feet and out the door faster than Elliot Stabler could slap cuffs on.

Sure enough, there were five vending machines in the front yard. I looked up and down sorority row. Only our house had these new additions. The Debs were slowly filtering out the house, looking at the high-fructose-corn-syrup version of Stonehenge in our yard.

I looked around again, sure that I'd see a broken-down Coke or Frito-Lay truck that had to unload its vending machines in order to fix a flat.

But I had a funny feeling.

"Quarters!" I yelled. "Who has quarters?"

One girl took a debit card out of her pocket.

I shoved my bangs away in frustration. "No. Actual coins," I bit out.

Someone else had dumped her purse to the ground, picking through the receipts and lip balms and emergency granola bars. "Here!" She yelled in triumph. "I have forty-five cents!"

A sister in running shorts ran up to me with a quarter and a dime. I eyed the machine in front of me. That would be enough. For now.

We put the coins in, hearing them slip and slither down. Then. Nothing. We all looked at each other.

"What button do we push?" The selections looked standard. Coca-Cola. Sprite. Root beer. Nothing seemed out of line. But the very fact that we had vending machines in our front yard was making me suspicious.

My fingers hovered over the buttons, like it was an action movie. If I picked the wrong one, we'd all go boom. Or we'd have a soft drink. One of those two options.

I reached for the Diet Coke button and paused. Surely, if this was a trick, someone would obviously plant a surprise under the Diet Coke button. Because this was a sorority house. Duh.

So I went to the orange drink. No one I knew drank orange soda. "Stand back everyone," I ordered. Twenty women obeyed, creating a ring of space between me and the collegians. With a steadying breath, I pushed the button for the orange soda. Nothing happened for a moment, and then the familiar sounds of metal machinery, maybe a lever, filled the air and an aluminum can rolled into the opening below.

Sighs of relief encircled me and ladies stepped forward to see what the can looked like. I, too, was momentarily relieved but when I reached for the can, I saw the Greek letters that had been glued onto it. Trikes.

My lips formed a warning, but it was too late, a cloud of orange smoke shot out ten feet, propelling a thick gas and covering anyone in its radius.

Like me.

"Someone call the police!" I yelled. "We've been hit."

THE DELTA BETA sorority learned many lessons that day. One, no good comes from vending machines. Especially ones that show up suspiciously in your front yard. Two, the police do not take vending-machine terrorism nearly as seriously as you'd think they would.

I mean, yes, they set up a perimeter around the yard, and yes, they donned hazmat suits to come over and test the orange powder that coated my skin and, to a lesser extent, five other sisters. But once they determined that it wasn't anthrax, it was like they couldn't care less. Let me tell you something. If you've never been approached by someone in a hazmat suit with a swab, it changes your life. For real.

Of course, Lieutenant Hatfield was there, taking me oh so seriously. "When are you getting that security system?" he drawled.

I spread my orange arms at the front yard. "What security system covers the outside?"

Ty considered that. "A big fence. That's what you need. With the rolled barbed wire on top."

I rolled my eyes. "And maybe some big German shepherds patrolling."

"With your luck, they'd be drugged and painted pink."

I looked at him with accusatory eyes. "That's a horrible plan. And I know what it's like to be painted." Apparently, the exploding "gas" from the can was a fine mist of paint. Like paintball, a game played by grown men pretending to be ten. "I don't know if I'll ever get this off," I said, looking at my arms. It was my bad luck that I had short sleeves on today. "I'll probably have to shower ten times in a row. I'll be all wrinkly."

Ty's eyes got a little intense and slid down my body when I said that. But it couldn't be what it looked like. I was orange, for heaven's sake. I never knew a man who liked orange paint on a lady and nothing else.

"And when are y'all going to take these away?" I demanded, trying to get his mind off my orange body in the shower.

Ty looked over the five vending machines. "Not our job."

"Whose job is it?"

He lifted a shoulder, cool as you please. "Yours."

"What are you people good for?" I demanded. "I thought you were supposed to serve and protect. Serve us! Protect us from stupid frats putting goats in our bathroom and Coke machines in our yard!"

Ty smiled a little bit at that, like my demands were amusing and not a serious plea from a concerned individual. "Margot Blythe, I believe you can serve and protect yourself." Then he took the tip of his index finger, had the nerve to pop me gently on the nose, and strolled away, like he didn't have a care in the world. Of course he didn't. He wasn't painted orange.

The police left, and we were left with five vending machines in our front yard. That's when the Debs learned another, very important lesson: Do not try to move a vending machine. I had always wondered about those stickers that showed a stick figure being crushed under a vending machine. I thought they were for people stupid enough to try to shake a machine.

I was right.

And once a machine falls over, you can't pick it back up. I left several messages around town for companies that managed these things and, lo and behold, their machines had been stolen the night before. I told them to come pick them up. For the rest of my life, I was going to be haunted by the mystery of how fraternity pledges managed to steal not one, but five heavy vending machines, stock them with paint-propellant cans, and deliver them to our yard in complete silence.

It was a mystery that ranked up there with some of the wonders of the world. Like Easter Island. Or the pyramids.

Of course the Trikes had done it. They always were the nerdy engineering fraternity.

I called over the other ladies coated in paint and told them to make a spa appointment and send the bill to me.

Then I waited until the vending-machine owners showed up and hauled the things away, making sure to tell them to dump whatever was inside. During my wait, I had a lot of thinking to do. I thought about the fraternity-prank tradition, and sorority-house security, and whether we could take care of ourselves. It really wasn't in my nature to be reactive. As a Sisterhood Mentor, when I saw problems at chapters, I moved ahead, suggested solutions, and provided leadership.

As chapter advisor here, I hadn't done that. I had been caught off guard by circumstances, by secrets revealed, and by outside forces who could mysteriously show up at night and throw our chapter into complete disarray. Forces like murderers. Or fraternities.

A sick feeling gurgled in my stomach. What if the two groups weren't mutually exclusive?

Pranks were getting more dangerous. And sorority women were feeling fundamentally unsafe. I took a deep breath and realized, Ty Hatfield was (unusually) right. I had to serve and protect myself.

Chapter Thirty-five

At the police station, I demanded to see the officer in charge of the Liza McCarthy investigation. That sounded really official.

Unfortunately, no one was there to hear my authority in person. Seriously, what was with this town?

I stumbled down the hall to Ty Hatfield's office. Was it bad that I now knew how to find it on my own? I opened the door and saw Ty behind his desk, but he wasn't alone.

Professor Dean Xavier sat across from Ty, turned, pointed at me, and said, "That's her. That's the one who blackmailed me."

I'm not ashamed to say, I shut the door pretty quickly.

Of course, I didn't go anywhere. I was still frozen in the hall, wondering what the heck the sociology professor meant by that when Ty came out in the hall. "Come with me," he said. We went two doors down to another office. It was the same as his, with a window, a bookshelf, a desk, and two chairs, except you could tell this one was currently unoccupied. "Stay right here. Do not move."

He left before I could tell him why I had come.

Five minutes later, Ty returned. "Come with me," he said again. But this time, I didn't feel like obeying his every little order.

"Look," I said, holding my cell phone up to emphasize. "I don't appreciate being ordered around. I came down here to have a civil conversation about the Liza McCarthy investigation. I don't appreciate being held in custody in an office with no Wi-Fi!"

He took a step towards me, his tall body seeming taller when he was looming so impressively. His finger went up too, presumably to emphasize. "I don't appreciate spoiled sorority girls withholding relevant information to a murder investigation. Come. With. Me. Now."

I went, although I didn't appreciate being called a girl. I was a full-grown twenty-seven-year-old woman.

We returned back to his office, and Dean Xavier was still there. He looked nervous when he saw me. Here I thought we'd left on good terms.

Ty took charge of the room. He pointed at me. "Professor Xavier, are you sure this is who you're talking about?"

Xavier licked his lips and his eyes blinked quickly. "Yes, this is who I was telling you about."

"You're making a positive identification that this woman blackmailed you."

"WHAT?" I couldn't help but exclaim. I had never officially blackmailed anyone in my whole life.

But Dean Xavier apparently disagreed. "She came to my office and said she had Liza McCarthy's records and would expose the department if I didn't do what she said."

I couldn't believe it. It was a complete falsehood wrapped up in just enough truth to make it dangerous.

"What did I want you to do?" I asked him because I was curious. I had no clue what he was talking about.

Ty looked at me like I shouldn't have said anything. But really, did he expect me to come in here and not talk? He obviously didn't know me that well.

Dean swallowed, hard. It was so obvious he was nervous. What could he possibly be scared of? *Me?* No one had ever been scared of me. Except that chapter in Miami. They were in big trouble.

"You wanted a permanent position in the sociology department," Xavier said in a shaky voice. "You said if I didn't hire you, you'd tell everyone that we knowingly approved of Liza McCarthy's unethical research."

I couldn't help but laugh in his face. "That's so stupid! One, I'm a philosophy major. Two, if I was going to blackmail you, I wouldn't publicize Liza McCarthy's research, I'd let everyone know about how you like to tie girls up and [redacted due to sorority standards]."

Dean's eyes nearly popped out of his head. Ty's eyes closed, with an "I wish I hadn't heard that" expression. Me? I wished I had thought through that statement before sending it out of my mouth.

There was an awkward silence. Ty was the first to speak. "Thank you for coming down, Professor Xavier. We'll stay in touch about the investigation." He led the still gaping professor out and when he returned to the office, I had some choice words to say.

"Him? You'll stay in touch about that investigation? But you won't keep me updated about our investigation?"

He ignored that question. "What he had to say looks very, very bad."

"Wait until you hear what I came to say."

Ty grimaced. "Now what."

"I think I know who might be behind all this."

"Who?" his voice was weary, but his eyes were, as ever, alert.

"What if this was all a stupid, misguided prank?"

"A prank?"

"The fraternities, Ty. It's prank week. We're talking about groups that are attacking women with Jell-O."

"I don't think that's the same thing—"

"And vending machines that spray orange paint."

"Really not the same thing."

I held up my hand. "I'm not saying they murdered Liza on purpose. Maybe they just were playing a joke on Liza, and it went horribly wrong."

Ty cut me off. "We know what the murder weapon was."

That was news to me. "What was it? Did it come back in the tests?"

Ty nodded slowly, watching me closely. "Botox."

I laughed at the very unfunny joke. Then I saw he wasn't joining in.

"Wait. Are you serious? You can die from that?"

"When it's injected into someone in a large enough amount."

"So someone can just walk up to me and inject me with a huge amount of Botox and I'll die?"

Ty made a face like that was no big deal.

I put my hands on my hips and stared at him.

"Well, I'd think you'd notice that," he allowed.

"Why didn't Liza notice it?"

"Maybe she did and didn't know it would hurt her." His face shuttered after that. "I'm talking way too much."

"No, you're not," I said. "You're, like, the opposite of talking too much. But this actually makes perfect sense."

"How so?"

"It's Botox, Ty. I laughed when I heard about it. Imagine what a nineteen-year-old boy would do."

"Your theory is that some fraternity members snuck into the Delta Beta house and injected Liza McCarthy with so much Botox it killed her."

I was quiet for a moment before answering. These were serious charges. I didn't want to be reckless. "Yes," I finally said. "They snuck goats into our bathroom, Ty."

"Not the same thing."

"I didn't say it was." My voice had risen a little. I was frustrated that he wasn't seeing this. "But if they can sneak goats, they can sneak a syringe."

"What about Stefanie. Why would that be a prank?

That was a good question, and I didn't have an answer to it until Brice Concannon's voice snaked through my brain. *If she did it, then she probably deserves what happens to her.* "Oh God," I gasped softly, and put a hand to my mouth.

Now Ty looked concerned. "What?"

I relayed my conversation with Brice to Ty, how I'd gone to him for help with Stefanie's file, and he'd talked about the uptight police and asked me out instead. Now I had all of Ty's attention. His eyes blazed, his jaw looked tight enough to snap. I should have just mentioned Brice to him at the beginning. Then he would have taken me seriously.

"He mentioned roofies?" Ty nearly growled.

I searched my memory. "I think he said you didn't like them."

"What I don't like is jerks like Concannon protecting fraternity members who don't think they need to abide by the law."

I was all for Greek unity. But Greeks were Americans and role models besides. We didn't put our fraternal bonds above our obligations as citizens, and if Brice was taking his brothers' side when they broke the law, I did not approve. "Will it help if I file a complaint?"

"For murder?"

"For assault," I replied. "Balloons filled with gelatin surely counts as assault and battery."

Ty considered that for a second, then shook his head. "Thank you for bringing this information to my attention."

"Are you going to investigate? Arrest someone?"

"Actually, I already have." At my blank look he continued, "Hunter Curtis."

I gasped. Another piece of evidence I hadn't even considered. "Do you think he was in on it?"

"I'll take care of it, Blythe."

My stomach dropped like it was on a roller coaster. A possible murderer might have been washing my dishes. "Hunter?"

"Do you have a response to Dean Xavier's statement?"

I saw what he was doing there. Like I wasn't going to notice a change in the topic of this conversation. But I most definitely had a response. "Bee. Ess."

"Really?"

"Really. That's my official response. You can write it down. Seriously. It's so ridiculous, I shouldn't even have to respond. Like someone like me would want a job in a sociology department." I shuddered. It wasn't an affectation. I literally shuddered at the idea of working in a sociology department.

Ty picked his words carefully, his eyes alert. "But you knew about his . . . preferences."

That was one way of putting it. I really didn't want to explain how I knew about Dean Xavier's "preferences." And not to Ty Hatfield.

My hands went back on my hips. "Look. He's not a good guy. There's no way you should take the word of a pedophile over mine."

Ty frowned. "Like, an actual pedophile?"

I rolled my eyes. "Probably not. But remember, he was dating Stefanie. She was barely of age." I paused, thinking of Xavier's strange, nearly frantic demeanor. "Speaking of which, did he even mention her?"

From the look on Ty's face, I saw the answer.

"He came in here to cook up a ridiculous story about me and didn't even ask about the murder of the student he was sleeping with." To me, that was awfully damning.

There was a long pause before Ty looked back at me, spearing me with his blue gaze. "Why would he make up a story about you, Blythe?"

Now it was my turn to frown. I couldn't think why Dean Xavier would have it out for me. "I don't know. You can ask Amanda Cohen about Xavier's character, though."

"The Panhellenic advisor?"

"And my friend. She was dating Dean Xavier, too. Although I don't think anyone's supposed to know about that."

Ty raised his eyebrows. "College policy," I said, but when I did, I realized I wasn't sure that was it. Amanda had never said why they were keeping their relationship hush-hush. "And she's a Delta Beta."

"You don't say," Ty said in a flat voice.

"I have lots of friends who aren't Debs," I said.

"Name one."

"Casey Kenner." Technically, that was true. Which was a shame because he would be such a good sister.

"Is that the guy you were with at the mixer?"

Something in his voice made me remember the dance we'd shared. There had been something there, I thought. And I felt maybe there still could be if I didn't keep finding dead bodies and being accused of blackmail.

Chapter Thirty-six

I WAS UPSTAIRS in Asha's room going over some receipts for a date party when a pledge knocked on the door shyly.

"There's someone downstairs who needs to see you."

That wasn't unusual. There was always someone who needed to see me. "It's the police," she added. That wasn't unusual either, I thought glumly.

Ty and Officer Malouf were waiting in the two-story foyer with the curving staircase. I descended the staircase as Debs ran up and down and all around. It said something about a chapter when two police officers didn't even make them blink. I was proud of their composure.

Finally, I reached them and knew something was up when Ty looked at me with a regretful resolve in his eyes. "You have the right to remain silent."

He stepped closer to me and took something shiny out of his back pocket. "Anything you say can and will be used against you."

It was unreal, like I was in my own personal episode of *Law & Order*.

"You have the right to an attorney or one will be provided to you if you cannot afford an attorney." He went a bit off script there, I thought vaguely. This wasn't real; it couldn't be real. But then the cuffs wrapped around my wrists, and I felt their cool bite.

I couldn't understand it. Delta Betas did *not* get arrested for murder. Speeding tickets, sure. Public intoxication? On rare occasions. Streaking through campus? Only once. But murder? That just didn't happen.

But this was happening. The weight of a hundred eyes was heavy on my shoulders as Ty led me to the cruiser and put me in the back—on purpose this time. I could only hold my head up and pray that someone up there gave me a Greek judge.

Ty didn't speak to me during the drive to the station, or when he walked me in the back door and put me in the holding cell. At least I wasn't alone. Hunter was in there, too.

I sat down on the opposite side of the cell from Hunter, staring down at the drain in the middle of the floor, wondering if it was used for what I feared it was used for.

"What are you in for?" Hunter said, in a tone that was maybe, kind of joking. I flashed my best prison-mama don't-mess-with-me look. He shut up after that.

Time went by very slowly on my Michael Kors watch. Finally, Ty appeared at the bars. There was a deep furrow between his eyebrows. I hadn't been fingerprinted, or arraigned, or had a mug shot taken. I wasn't sure in which order these things were supposed to go, and there was a part of me that was dying to know. But there was also a part of me that didn't want to remind him. If I could just stay here, with Hunter, in the cell, I could pretend that I was accidentally locked up again, that this was all a bad joke.

The expression on Ty's face showed it wasn't a joke. He wrapped his hands around the bars.

"How bad is it?" I asked. Might as well know.

Ty flinched. Ouch.

"You had motive. You heard about the phone-sex ring and you wanted to keep it quiet."

That was true.

"You had opportunity. You were with Liza McCarthy before and during her death."

As were fifty other sisters.

"The murder weapon was in your apartment."

The Botox vial in the medicine cabinet.

"Is that all?" I tried making a joke about it. Ty didn't laugh.

"Murder?" Hunter asked incredulously. I had forgotten he was there so I turned around and gave him a shut-the-hell-up-before-I-shiv-you-in-the-shower look.

I turned back to Ty, who continued spelling out the case against me. "Dean Xavier's statement is pretty damaging testimony."

I shook my head. It was complete horse dookie. But good luck with proving that.

"Then you found Stefanie Grossman's body, and Amanda Co-hen's statement puts the final nail in the coffin."

I froze. "Who?"

"Amanda Cohen."

"She's my big sister!"

Ty really looked regretful now. "I'm sorry, Margot."

What could Amanda have possibly said?

He answered my unspoken question. "Your altercation with Ainsley St. John."

I gaped at him. "My what? We had a discussion on a public

sidewalk, and both times Ainsley approached me, I never laid a finger on her."

Ty's gaze didn't waver.

I let it all sink in, and that's when I did a very un-Delta-Beta thing. I swore. Loudly and colorfully.

I stood up and faced Ty at the bars. He was just inches away. "I didn't do this, Ty."

He took an uneven breath. "I think I agree."

"YOU THINK?" As a suspect and an American citizen with all my unalienable rights, those words were not comforting.

He chewed on his lip, then decided to say something. "We were freshmen. It was some pledge mixer. Ice-cream social, I think. And there were some girls who were straight-up bitches."

"Why?" I asked. It would help me narrow down the pool of potential bitches.

He shrugged. "It doesn't matter anymore. The point is, you marched over and you lectured them for a good fifteen minutes on their conduct. Told them they should respect and represent their letters." His lips quirked up at the memory. "That they should be ladies."

I shook my head. It was a nice story, but I didn't see his point.

Ty frowned at the floor, his hair hanging down, partially obscuring his eyes. "Seems like someone who cares that much about proper behavior wouldn't poison a sister with a hefty dose of Botox."

For the first time, I felt a wave of hopelessness wash over me. Maybe a sister who cared about proper behavior would do exactly that. To protect the sorority she loved from a phone-sex operation that could ruin its reputation forever.

My head dropped, and my forehead rested against the bars.

They were cool and comforting for, you know, jail. I had nothing to say. No way to convince anyone that I hadn't murdered Liza. Or Stefanie. Or attacked Ainsley. Or blackmailed Dean Xavier.

And even if I did have something to say, my Miranda rights were there for a reason. Only the guilty start blabbing to the cops. I knew that much from *Law & Order*. I also knew something else.

"I want a phone call." I glanced up and saw Ty staring, just inches away from me.

Ty sighed heavily. "I don't want to have to do that."

I pushed away from the bars and put my hands on my hips. He was the one who put me behind bars; he had to deal with the consequences.

In short order, I was given access to a phone where I promptly called Casey. Mostly because his was the only phone number I knew. I always wondered about that while watching *Law & Order*. How did people know their lawyer's numbers off the tops of their heads? Or their mother's, for that matter? No one memorized phone numbers anymore in this day and age. But Casey also had two semesters of law school under his belt, and as public-relations director for Delta Beta, he knew more lawyers than Lindsay Lohan. No comment on *why* he knew so many lawyers.

While I was waiting for Casey's wheels of justice to start turn-ing, I found myself face-to-face with a real criminal: Hunter Curtis.

I tried avoiding him for a while, but that was hard in a bare room, twelve by twelve with white walls and yellowed linoleum on the floor. I could only avert my eyes toward the drain so many times before I was completely grossed out.

Finally, I couldn't avoid him anymore. "Humph." It was a pointed sound, exaggerated and obvious.

Hunter immediately looked guilty. Good. "What do you have to say for yourself?" I demanded.

He shook his head, looking stricken.

"That's it? You don't have anything to say for yourself? You betrayed us, Hunter. We trusted you. The sisters of Delta Beta trusted you. And what did you do with that trust? You trashed it just like you trashed the office."

"Miss Blythe, I'm sorry." Hunter shook his head again sorrowfully. "I can't tell you how sorry I am."

"But you did it anyway. Just because some stupid boys asked you to." I remembered my conversation with Callie the night before, about stupid boys and how we didn't need them.

"Boys?" Hunter lifted tortured eyes toward me. "What boys?"

"Okay, fine, men," I snapped, remembering that frats preferred being called men. Not like they acted like it.

That didn't change the confusion on Hunter's face. "What men?"

"Your brothers, the ones who asked you to help them with their fraternity prank."

"I didn't . . ."

"And what did you do with the file, Hunter?" I demanded, remembering the sensitive information contained in it. "Did you post it in your house? Who did you share it with?"

"God, no!" I had to say, Hunter seemed convincing in his tortured guilt. "I would never do that. I love . . ."

He broke off and swallowed hard, turning his face away from me.

"Who?" I asked, more gently this time. Then I realized. "Stefanie? You loved Stefanie?" Everything clicked into place. "You loved her and were trying to protect her?"

Hunter paused, then closed his eyes tightly and nodded. My heart melted for him. This was true love I was dealing with. Of course he was being brave and defiant. He had broken into the chapter advisor's office and stolen Stefanie's file to protect her.

Then a horrible, horrible thought occurred to me. Did he know about Stefanie's death? I moved across the cell and placed a gentle hand on his shoulder. "Hunter, did you hear about what happened, to Stefanie?"

He nodded slowly. "When Officer Hatfield said you were the one who found her."

Oh yeah. I had forgotten he was there. "Lieutenant. Lieutenant Hatfield." I corrected him. "But . . ." I searched his face. "Are you okay?" He didn't seem that broken up about his true love's dying.

Hunter lifted both shoulders in a slacker gesture. I stood, taking an angry step away from him. "REALLY?" I demanded. "Did you even love her? Now that she's gone, do you even care?" I really needed to be let out of this cell, before I really did commit murder. "Callie was right," I muttered, mostly to myself. "You're all stupid."

Hunter gasped as if *his* feelings were hurt. Whatever. I stalked to the bars and shook them, hard, which made me feel like a bad ass. "TY!" I yelled. "Get me out of here!"

Casey called a friend who called a friend, and, two hours later, I had a spitfire of an attorney drive in from Winston-Salem. Her business card read, "Bibby Hepworth, the best criminal-law attorney in North Carolina." She worked her way from county judge on down and soon, I was being released as a favor to someone's momma. Delta Beta sisterhood at its finest.

Chapter Thirty-seven

WHILE I WAS out of jail, Bibby advised that I prepare for a court hearing to be called soon. The news was not welcome. I didn't have anything left in my suitcase to wear to court. Then I remembered Aubrey's offer to lend me clothes. I'd feel a whole lot better facing some judge in an outfit that hadn't been worn three times already.

Aubrey's room was on the third floor, which was odd for the chapter president. When I lived in the house, the chapter president always lived on the second floor, just because it was livelier, closer to the action.

But maybe Aubrey liked to study in her room. Her door was decorated with a whiteboard, which was quaint in college in this day and age of texts and chats and instas; but this whiteboard was decorated with hearts and smiley faces and an inside joke or two, so I guessed some things never changed.

I knocked twice, then again. There was no answer. When I opened the door, I could quickly see that Aubrey had a single room, which, again, was probably appropriate for the president. She could have more privacy for meetings and stuff this way. A twin bed was draped with a pink-and-white-striped comforter, Lilly-Pulitzer-style sheets, and about fifteen pillows in eyelet and satin. Very girly and cute.

There were the normal sorority-house furnishings: a desk, a chair, and her own massive beanbag, which was fuzzy and black. It didn't seem to go with the eyelet and Lilly, but maybe it didn't show coffee stains.

Contrary to popular belief, sorority girls did not have massive, automated closets, with a row of designer bags showcased along the top shelves. No, in the Delta Beta house, we had tiny coffins of closets, stuffed to the brim with designer bags showcased along the top shelf.

Aubrey had pushed her house-issue dresser into the closet, which was a smart way to organize a tiny space, I had to say. I started sorting through the hanging dresses. As expected, she had lots of cute things, from J.Crew to Anthropologie to some boutique labels even I hadn't heard of. One dress was perfect, but it had spaghetti straps, which would not be appropriate for legal proceedings in October. Maybe she had a coordinating cardigan? I remember she had worn one to Stefanie's S&M hearing. I pulled open the top drawer of the dresser, intending to just do a cursory search for cardigans. The top drawer was, as I should have realized, Aubrey's womanly underthings. I was about to shut it when I saw a peek of black under the stack of Victoria's Secret Juicy boy shorts.

Tentatively, I pulled the black cover of an address book out. It looked exactly like the one I had found in Liza's drawer. The one that was missing. My fingers shook as I opened it and saw that it was, in fact, the exact one that had gone missing from my apartment bedroom.

My heart rate zoomed and, by impulse, I closed the closet door while I tried to work this out. Ainsley was the one working for Liza. And Ainsley was the one who was now acting crazy trying to get Amanda and me to "shut down" the phone-sex number. So why would Aubrey steal the book full of phone numbers? Unless Ainsley stole it and hid it here. Or maybe Aubrey stole it, to protect her sister.

I shut my eyes. Of course. Aubrey would do anything to protect her sister even if her sister was a skanky good-for-nothing Moo. It's what I would do, in her shoes, if I was cursed to have a twin sister who pledged Tri Mu.

The door to Aubrey's room opened, and I bit back a gasp and shoved the book into the back pocket of my jeans. I understood why Aubrey wanted to protect her sister, but I needed to safeguard an entire sorority's reputation. I couldn't just let this out there, not with the Tri Mus breathing down our necks.

My hand went to the doorknob and paused as I heard Aubrey answer her phone.

"Yes?" she asked.

There was a pause.

"This is she."

"No, I told you . . ." She stopped, interrupted by the someone on the other line. "No," she said again. "I won't. That was the last time, I can't do this anymore. My sister . . . she was hurt." Another pause. "I understand. But I can't help you. I quit."

The room got silent before it was filled with the sounds of Aubrey's crying softly. Well, crap. I had two options, stay in a cramped closet and pray that Aubrey suddenly didn't decide to change her clothes. Or two, come out of the closet and pretend that nothing had happened.

I flung open the closet door with a handful of dresses on hangers in front of me. "Hey Aubs! Just borrowing your dresses like you said I could! Thanks!" With a cheerful wave, I sauntered toward the door and might have gotten out safely if I hadn't heard a sniffle from the girl behind me, curled up on a massive black beanbag. My head hung low. Who was I, trying to avoid a crying girl? Crying girls were my specialty, intended or not.

I turned and faced Aubrey, looking absolutely overwhelmed. "Okay," I said, tossing the dresses on her bed. "What's up?"

She shook her head firmly, her lips pressed together, not wanting to talk. But everyone talked to me. I was the chapter advisor.

I ripped the address book out of my pant pocket. "Is it about this?"

To say Aubrey was stunned was putting it mildly. "I'm so sorry," she finally gurgled. "I know I've let everyone down."

That was it. Aubrey St. John was as much of a saint as her last name implied. "Stop, Aubrey. You're being too hard on yourself. It's your sister who needs to apologize to you."

Aubrey's red, wet face froze in confusion. "What? No. She was only trying to save me."

"I guess that's one way of looking at it. You know she went to Tri Mu HQ, right? Spilled the beans about the whole operation."

And that got Aubrey wailing again. For as much crying as I've been dealing with the past week, I really wasn't getting better at handling it. I seemed to be getting worse.

"Our sorority is ruined! Because of me!"

"Take a deep breath," I told Aubrey. "It's not you. You're not the one who was having phone sex for money. Your sister made her own choices. You tried to save her, to protect her, but ultimately it's going to be her fault." And Liza's. But it felt much better putting the blame on a Tri Mu.

Aubrey hiccuped and looked at me with wide eyes. "NO!" She shook her head and reached for my hand, nearly sending me headlong into the belly of the beanbag. "That's not it! It was me! I'm the one who had phone sex for money. Ainsley was trying to protect me!"

At that moment, I was pretty sure I was in an alternate dimension. My brain was fogged up, my ears were clogged. I couldn't have just heard what I thought I heard . . . right?

But then, everything clicked, fog and clogginess aside. Ainsley hadn't been crazy. She was the protective one, ready to do anything, say anything to get her sister out of the phone-sex ring. And when I'd called that number and heard Ainsley's voice . . .

"She picked up your phone, didn't she? That's how she found out."

Aubrey nodded glumly. "I left it in her car accidentally over summer break, right before school started. It rang and she answered and it was . . ."

"Who?" I asked breathlessly.

"Pistol Pete." Aubrey looked away. "That's what he called himself. He was a regular."

I couldn't help my lip turning up. Pistol Pete? Really? Gross.

"I tried telling her it was a guy I was dating. I thought she bought it, but then . . . my phone was missing another day and she found me at the Commons. She went nutso on me, saying she knew what I was doing, and I had to stop."

"Why didn't you?" I asked gently.

"At first, Liza just asked me to help with a sociology experiment.

She needed girls she could trust. I was honored that she'd chosen me. But then the paychecks came in and I . . ." She paused as the memory put a woeful expression on her face. "There was a pair of Jimmy Choos that matched my semiformal dress perfectly . . ."

Ah. I patted her hand. It all came back to shoes. I understood now.

"The money was nice . . . really nice. But I also felt . . . used. I saw what my sister was saying, that I needed to quit. It was just hard. And when Liza died, I thought that was it. That was my out. But . . ."

"The calls kept coming," I finished for her.

She waved her phone. That must have just been a call from a john that I heard.

"Why did you steal this?" I asked, holding up the address book.

"I had seen Liza with it a few times, she had told me that's where she kept records, for her research. I thought I could find Heather's number."

"Heather?" I remembered the call Casey had made to the hotline. The girl who had answered was Heather.

"A lot of us used fake names, but Heather was Liza's partner. I thought if I could get her direct line, I could call and ask her to take me off the list. Because I really, really do want out, Margot." Her bottom lip started trembling again. "Believe me, I do."

I did believe her. About as much as I believed anyone these days, that was.

"Do you know anything else about Heather?" I asked, wondering if maybe Heather was the key to everything.

"I just know what Liza told me a few times after she got off the phone with Heather."

"What is that?"

"That Heather is a stone-cold bitch."

A stone-cold bitch sounded like a person who would commit murder. But so did a desperate sorority-chapter president. Or a rival chapter's president. Of course, I didn't say any of this to Aubrey. On account of her being a potential murderer.

"I think Stefanie met her, though," Aubrey said carefully.

"Stefanie Grossman?" I asked, because as I recalled there were about five Stephanie-variations in the chapter.

The name made Aubrey's chin wobble, and I remembered Aubrey's antics at Stefanie's S&M hearing.

"You guys were close, weren't you?"

Aubrey used the back of her hand to dab at her mascara-rimmed eyes. "We were pledge sisters. Stefanie was like the extra triplet."

"So Ainsley knew her, too?"

"For a few years, we all lived together in the dorm. But then Ainsley got all Tri Mu on us. I ran for chapter office, and Stefanie moved in with Liza."

Whoa. The elusive Stefanie and Liza were roommates? How had I not heard this? Aubrey must have seen the shock on my face. "They kept it quiet. Liza was already skirting the rules by keeping her own apartment, and if people knew she lived with a collegiate member, they'd all think she was playing favorites."

"But she wasn't," I said slowly. "Because Liza wrote Stefanie up for her S&M violations with a professor."

Aubrey looked pained at the memory. "What happened to Liza and Stefanie's friendship, Aubrey?"

She shrugged in slow motion, as if the simple act was difficult due to the weight of the world resting on her. "Same thing as me. Liza wanted out."

The fact that Stefanie was also one of Liza's phone-sex opera-tors should have come as a bigger shock. It said a lot about what I had gone through this week that it wasn't. Still, I wanted to be clear on all this.

"So Liza wrote her up for doing Dean?" I asked.

"Liza was going legit. She told me she couldn't look herself in the mirror anymore. She had to do right by Delta Beta. And that meant starting to enforce the S&M rules. "

But this still didn't make sense. I was missing something huge, or else I was never going to narrow down exactly who killed Liza. And Stefanie. Because right now there were approximately five suspects. And one of them was me.

"I need to get into Liza and Stefanie's apartment."

Aubrey's eyes widened.

"And you're going to let me in."

IF LIZA HAD trusted Aubrey with a key to the chapter advisor's office, I was fairly sure she was close enough to Liza and Stefanie to figure out a way to break into their apartment. Turned out, we didn't need to break in. During that last chapter meeting, Liza had stored her purse in Aubrey's room. With her keys in it.

Casey was the perfect lookout, I figured. He was distractingly handsome, he could lie his pants off, and the odds of anyone in Sutton recognizing him were low. The problem was, he sucked at lookout fashion. He picked me up at the sorority house wearing tomato red chinos and a blue, red, and yellow checked shirt with a yellow paisley handkerchief neatly folded into a pocket. He looked like Chuck Bass crossed with Will.I.Am.

Liza and Stefanie's apartment was in a complex with exterior doors, and theirs was a second-floor unit overlooking a green area that smelled like dog poop. Casey stood at the bottom of the stairs to delay anyone who would come in and surprise me. I felt bad. It was really stinky down there.

I held my breath while the key slid in easily and opened the door. The apartment was in terrible shape. It was hard to tell whether it had been searched or whether the police had gone through it. The front door opened directly into the living room. There was a galley kitchen immediately behind the living room, with a small eating nook that had been turned into an office of some sort. Two doors led off the living room, one to my right and one to my left.

I perused the living room first, wondering whether I'd even recognize evidence if I saw it. After all, I hadn't recognized ten digits as phone numbers when I'd first seen those. I flipped open a few boxes of photographs under the TV stand. Some *Cosmopolitan* magazines were piled on the Ikea coffee table, which maybe came in handy for phone sex, with all those "Sixty-Seven Secrets to Please a Man" articles. In the office, there was a laptop dock but no laptop. Briefly flipping through the papers, I saw a bunch of printouts on Latin American history and a women's studies class syllabus. Those were probably Stefanie's. One thing I didn't see were any bills. Interesting. I checked under the desk and didn't see a shredder or a trash can.

In the kitchen, I flipped through the cabinets, praying that something would jump out at me. Other than a murderer, or a dead body.

With no telltale spreadsheets or bank statements with the name "Heather" on top, I chose the bedroom on the left first. From the pictures next to the unmade double bed, this had to be Stefanie's room. I teared up at the picture of a young girl with her grandma at her Bat Mitzvah. She shouldn't have ended up dead on the lawn of the Delta Beta house.

I spent too long looking at Stefanie's pictures. She had wild brown curls that she liked to toss right before a photo was taken. They always seemed to be in motion. And now they'd never move again. The thought spurred me on. It didn't matter what questionable choices Stefanie had made. She deserved justice.

I filtered through a bookcase, opening books, fanning through any pages that looked bulky. The drawers of her dresser were stuffed full of Delta Beta tees, and there was another tight squeeze on my cardiac muscles at the reminder of who this girl had been.

The apartment and the bedroom didn't seem like people had been here recently, much less been hiding out. Where had Stefanie Grossman been since the last conversation with Aubrey? Aubrey had assumed she'd been here, but I thought there'd be a lot more evidence of dirty dishes, or piled-up laundry. Not that the place was superclean, but it didn't seem like the place Stefanie had been holed up. Even the bathtub was dry. Maybe it's TMI—but if I shower every day, there's definitely residue.

Leaving Stefanie's bedroom, I crossed the living room to Liza's room, checking my watch as I did. I'd been here for fifteen minutes and hadn't heard from Casey. I hoped he was still breathing through his mouth.

I checked the same things in Liza's room, the books, the magazines, the drawers. There was nothing suspicious or noteworthy. The bathroom was similarly dry. On impulse, I picked up the Delta Beta Busy Bee on Liza's bed and gave it an absentminded squeeze, even as my eyes scanned the room for something—anything—that would help me figure all the mysteries out.

That's when my fingers felt something up the bee's butt. I

turned the stuffed animal over, revealing a seam loosely basted together. With the pull of a string, Busy Bee's butt emptied, and two zip drives fell into my hand. Jackpot. I don't know about most people, but Delta Betas don't violate stuffed animals for no good reason.

The zip drives stuffed in my pocket, I locked the front door and joined Casey at the bottom of the steps. He had his yellow paisley handkerchief tied around the bottom half of his face like a flamboyant bank robber.

"Way to be inconspicuous," I said, as we headed toward the parking lot.

"You'd think they'd get bored of crapping in one place," Casey muttered. I'm not sure Casey ever lived in an apartment complex of college students with dogs. Neither long, leisurely walks nor doggie bags were considered a requirement.

"Did you get anything?" Casey asked when we had the car doors safely closed.

"We'll see," I said.

Chapter Thirty-eight

CASEY'S HOTEL WAS closer than sorority row, so we went there to view the zip drives. He insisted on scanning them for viruses first, which I thought was mighty health-conscious of him. We couldn't know what kind of files were on them. More spreadsheets? An open letter from a serial-killer/phone-sex client admitting his guilt?

When we plugged in the first drive and double-clicked a file at random, the media player opened. And up popped a scene I was semifamiliar with: the inside of the chapter advisor's office.

"Are you kidding me?" I asked. "There really was a bug in there?"

"Holy shit," Casey said. I gave him a chastising look. There was no excuse for foul language.

There were fits and starts in the surveillance footage, either from a motion sensor or from someone's deleting scenes, or both. There was Liza, talking with Aubrey, then Callie, then the house-keeper. Then there was Callie, opening the door when the office was empty. Then the door opened again. Hunter.

Then they were kissing.

And undressing.

And . . . "OH MY GOD!" I cried out, covering my eyes.

"Holy SHIT!" Casey yelled. This time I didn't correct him. There was a time and a place for everything.

There was no audio, thank goodness, and Casey let me know when it was safe to look again. A minute later, Callie and Hunter were back at it again, this time against the bookshelf. Then on the desk. Then the chair.

I closed my eyes and told Casey to review the rest. Nothing else was on the zip drive but pictures of Callie and Hunter doing it like bunnies in the chapter advisor's office.

I was really scared of the second thumb drive. Even Casey gave it a speculative thought. The fact that he even paused was something.

He waited until I was ready to plug it in.

I took a deep breath. "Do it."

I expected the media player to pop up with a video, but instead, it was a sound recording. With lots of heavy breathing, lots of talk about being tied up, and lots of Dean Xavier. I wasn't sure if I could prove it was him until the phone-sex operator very clearly said, "Yes, DEAN, DO ME DEAN." And then he said, "Don't call me Dean." Which probably wouldn't prove his identity since you can't prove a positive with a negative (or something like that). But he did finish with, "Call me Professor Xavier," which helped me out a lot.

After about ten minutes' worth of freaky-deaking, I motioned to Casey, who fast-forwarded to see if we had anything else good on there. Like a woman's voice identifying herself as Heather, confessing that she was going to kill Liza McCarthy on a Monday night, but our luck had run out.

"So Liza had these in the butt of a Busy Bee? Why would Liza put them there?"

I had been thinking about it. "One, she wanted to keep them safe. But you know what? I think someone knew about these."

"Why?"

"The Busy Bee in the chapter advisor's office was torn open when Hunter trashed the place. I don't think that was a coincidence. Maybe Hunter knew the recordings were in there, and he wanted them?"

"But how would he know he was being recorded? Or where they were?"

"And what did he do when he didn't find them?" I asked rhetorically low. "And this was all after Liza was killed. So either she told Hunter before she died . . ."

"Or someone told him after."

No doubt there were huge pieces of the puzzle that I was missing. But I knew how to knock out a bunch of the corner pieces.

"Are you thinking what I'm thinking?" I asked Casey.

"We need to go find that camera."

"Yeah. That, too."

I HAD TO fill out some chapter-advisor paperwork first. Yes, I know that sounds boring, but it was really vital. Then Casey and I headed to the police station.

For once, there was someone at the front desk. Will wonders never cease? His name tag identified him as Deputy Winchester.

Casey argued some legal mumbo jumbo about a prisoner's rights under the Geneva Convention which, I had to say, impressed the heck out of me. The most international law I knew about was diplomatic immunity, and that was only because so many scumbag diplomats were also creepy pedophiles on *Law & Order.*

Deputy Winchester rolled his eyes and said we'd come during visitor hours anyway, which seemed like a good cover story for him.

Hunter was still sitting in the cell, now dressed in a county-issued scrub set. "Why haven't you paid bail yet?" I asked. Surely a Sutton College fraternity brother could spare some cash to help a friend out.

"Mom and Dad are on a cruise down the Rhine. They're trying to teach me a lesson."

I almost felt sorry for him.

Casey pulled up two chairs to the bars. I set the laptop on one of them. The second chair was for Hunter's next visitor. Just a few minutes later, Callie Campbell walked slowly down the hall, her blue eyes big and scared. "What's going on Margot? Why did you say there was urgent chapter business here?" Her gaze sought out Hunter's, and the pain in them was obvious to even Shakespeare, dead in his grave, all the way back in England, who was impressed by how Romeo and Juliet these two were.

"Sit down, Callie."

She responded immediately to the inherent authority in my voice and sat in a chair with a view of the laptop screen.

I began with an official statement. "In compliance with rule 10.9, subsection C (1) of the Delta Beta sorority Standards and Morals manual, I am hereby inciting an emergency standards and morals hearing, under my authority as a properly instituted chapter advisor."

There was no evidence of Callie's adorable dimples as her face went ashen.

I handed her the S&M paperwork I had filled out and, as she started to review it, Casey pressed play on the laptop. As we'd seen earlier, there was nothing very notable about the first minute or so of the video, and Callie ignored it, as her horror grew while reviewing the pages I'd written up. But Hunter saw the screen immediately and knew what it meant. "Where did you get that?" he whispered urgently.

"Where do you think we got it?" I asked him.

He shook his head, mute as he and Callie burst onto the screen. His strangled sound made Callie look up, startled. And then she saw what was on the laptop.

"What?" she squealed. "What is that?" Panicked, she looked up at Hunter, who was now at the bars, gripping tightly. "You taped us? You pervert! Asshole!"

"I didn't. I swear, baby, I did it for you."

Casey and I exchanged a look. Now that was a line.

Callie buried her face in her hands. "Turn it off! Turn it off!"

"Callie, baby, I swear, listen to me, I never would have done it, but she said she was going to take your pin. And I knew that would destroy you."

I held up a hand. "Who told you she would take Callie's pin?"

Hunter brushed both hands in his thick hair, looking like a very sad Romeo. "I don't know. She never gave me a name. She blackmailed me into breaking into the office, and she said she needed the evidence in there. In the stuffed bee."

"What about the computer?" I asked.

"She told me to get rid of it."

"And the file?"

Hunter stilled, his stricken eyes focused on Callie. "She wanted that, too."

"You stole Stefanie's file?" Callie's voice was strangled. "You are a bigger idiot than I thought! I could get in trouble for that. I'm in charge of that file!" She stood and screamed the last bit. The dramatic flair surprised me.

"But if it's gone, how do they even know about it?"

"You are so dumb!" Callie exploded. "You think if you steal the file it just goes away? Delta Beta is way more organized than that!"

"Thank you," I said. Hunter looked devastated.

"Hunter, back to the point, please." I snapped my fingers.

"What's the point?" He groaned dramatically, sitting on the bench, his head in his hands.

"If you don't tell me the truth, I will pursue this S&M hearing against Callie. Her pin will be taken because of her involvement with a house brother, in direct violation of S&M manual section 24 B."

Callie's response was a soft cry. I would have felt bad for her, but she was leverage and had clearly broken a major S&M rule.

I pressed my advantage and focused on Hunter again. "So someone called you out of the blue and blackmailed you into breaking into the office to steal Stefanie's file and getting the evidence out of the stuffed bee. What did you do when you didn't find it?"

Hunter slowly raised his head and looked at me, a question clear on his face. "But I did find it."

Casey held up his hand in a "stop" gesture. "What did you find?"

Hunter tilted his head towards the laptop. "A thumb drive."

Casey and I exchanged a long glance. "Hunter . . ." I drew his name out slowly as my brain worked through that information. "When did you get the call blackmailing you?"

"The night after Liza died."

"Did you recognize the voice?" That question came from behind us, from a voice I recognized as belonging to one Ty Hatfield.

Hunter looked surprised at that question, like he'd never even considered it. "No. I got texts from an unknown number."

"Did you know what you were supposed to get out of the Busy Bee?" I asked.

"They just said it was a thumb drive, and if I didn't get it, they were going to tell the Delta Betas about me and Callie."

"And did you actually look at it?"

Hunter's lip curled at me. "I know she doesn't believe it," he said, nodding at Callie. "But I'm not an idiot. I listened, and it was just some pervert talking dirty. It had nothing to do with me and Callie."

"What I want to know is who did you give the drive to?" Ty asked, ignoring Hunter's question.

"I was told to drop it off in a trash can at the Commons," Hunter said. "Right next to the fraternity advisor's office."

Chapter Thirty-nine

Ty brought me and Casey back to his office. At my unspoken suggestion, Casey shut the laptop. We left Callie to fume at Hunter. Or kiss him, whichever she chose.

Ty shut the door behind us and spread an arm inviting us to sit down. I chose to stand, and Casey stood with me like the best friend he was. Since we didn't sit, Ty didn't either. It was like a shoe department face-off at the Nordstrom semiannual sale.

"I interviewed Hunter, and he didn't tell me any of that," Ty ground out.

I could tell that the good lieutenant was a little frustrated, but I wasn't sure how he spoke at all when his jaw was flexed that tight.

"He's a romantic guy. He was trying to protect his girlfriend," I said, surprised I was making excuses for Hunter now.

"He thought his parents were bailing him out."

"That too," I said, "or his fraternity advisor."

Ty's blue eyes locked onto mine, and we communicated telepathically for a moment, long enough for Casey to notice. "What? What are you two up to?"

"The question is, what are the frats up to?" I asked. "Have you talked to Brice Concannon yet?"

Casey perked up. "Oh, the cutie patootie?"

"The cutie roofie patootie." I reminded him.

He frowned. "Phooey."

"Well?" I demanded of Ty. "Or do I need to take care of this myself?"

"We should totally do it," Casey affirmed.

"No!" Ty half shouted. "I'm still in charge here. You do not approach Brice Concannon without my approval!"

"Someone's a little territorial," Casey said under his breath.

Ty's jaw clenched again. That wasn't a good sign. "And where did you get the surveillance footage?" He was shifting gears, and I decided to go along with it, for the moment.

"So that's a complicated question," I started to say, thinking quickly. "Because it seems like, according to Hunter, there were multiple copies, anyway."

Now Ty's eyes narrowed. Very scary. "Really, who could say where one gets anything," I hedged. Ty reached for the baseball on his desk and squeezed hard. I spoke quickly. "But I'll give you permission to find the hidden camera that you didn't find during your search warrant."

From the way his jaw was working, maybe I shouldn't have added that part. "And you might be interested in this," I took out the second thumb drive, the one with Dean Xavier's heavy-breathing serenade.

"I'm sure this is admissible in court?" Ty asked with a sigh as he plugged it into his computer.

I made a little "maybe" noise. Who knew? Casey, with his year's worth of law school, also shrugged. Even the experts weren't sure about "admissibility."

The recording didn't get any more enjoyable the second time around, and Ty shut it off right after the "call me professor" part. He unplugged the drive and held it up. "It would help if I knew where this came from."

I went for it. What was he going to do? Arrest me? "Liza McCarthy's apartment."

The lieutenant's blue eyes sharpened with attention. "When?"

"Today."

"You do understand that you're a suspect in her murder."

"You were serious about that?" I asked.

Casey snickered. Ty, not so much.

I sobered up. "Yes, I know there's a lot that looks bad for me. But I've just given you two other suspects and a whole lot more leads you wouldn't have without me."

"Or you've just drummed up evidence to falsely accuse someone else. That's what their attorneys are going to say!"

Oh. I hadn't thought of it quite like that.

"Look," Casey interrupted. "We can go round and round about whether Margot killed Liza."

That did not sound like a good idea. My eyes bugged at my supposed best friend.

"Or," Casey continued, "we can solve this once and for all."

"How?" Ty looked like he was steeling himself for something preposterous like a good old-fashioned murder suspect walk-off.

"A sting."

A heavy silence filled the spaces in the room as we all ruminated on that one. Have I said how much I loved Casey's ideas? I've always wanted to be in on a sting.

It was clear the wheels in Ty's head were turning. And so were mine. I could see it now. Me, in an all-black bodysuit, with lace-up boots and some kind of high-tech microphone/earpiece combo wrapped around my long dark braid, Lara Croft style.

"You've got to narrow down the suspects," Casey said, reasonably.

"Except for me, I'm already out," I added. Ty gave me a look that said he wasn't completely sold on my innocence yet. "We've got a whole bunch of people who want to keep their involvement with Liza McCarthy secret, bad enough to kill. But we don't even know who all of them are."

"So we need to round them up and winnow them out," Casey added. We were so in tune with one another.

"Before I agree to anything, you have to tell me everything." Ty's brows rose. "EVERYTHING. No holding back because of some B.S. sorority-secrecy rules."

Casey and I exchanged a glance and agreed silently that this was our best plan of action.

"First of all, I'd like to go on record and say that I'm pretty sure the Tri Mu sorority started all of this," I started off. Ty smiled like I was being a smart-ass, but I was being about 85 percent sincere.

I sat in the chair in front of Ty's desk, and Casey followed my lead. I outlined what I knew about the phone-sex ring and how Liza's proposed sociology experiment had either turned into something darker or the research was just her cover all along. We knew that at least two members of the Deb chapter had been employed by Liza. One of them, Stefanie Grossman, was now deceased. The other, Aubrey St. John, had a twin sister who was demanding that the phone-sex ring be taken down and had gone to our rival sorority headquarters with the information.

"See what I mean about Tri Mu?" I muttered before continuing.

We knew that Liza had been fired from the sociology department and had called Deb HQ upset about something a few months prior.

From Aubrey's account, Liza had wanted to disband the phone-sex ring. Hunter had been blackmailed by an unknown person into getting the evidence of Dean Xavier's participation and Stefanie Grossman's S&M file.

The thumb drives had presumably been found in two locations: the chapter advisor's office and her apartment. And there was a hidden camera, put in the office by another unknown person. Finally, I had to point out that the fraternity pranks were seriously out of control.

"Violating stuffed animals, secret sex tapes, and hefty doses of Botox are right up the fraternity-prank alley," I said.

"Sounds like a party," Casey murmured.

"You left out something," Ty said when I was done. My mouth was dry, my cheek muscles were sore from talking so much. What could I have left out?

"That black address book," he said. "The one that went missing from your apartment."

I brightened. "Oh. I found that."

Instead of being happy about that, Ty looked pissed. "Where?"

I crinkled my nose. "Aubrey's closet?" I said it that way because I knew that I'd get the whole Ty Hatfield, heavy sighing-eye rolling-head naggy thing for conducting "illegal searches" or something. "I was borrowing clothes, and I just happened to see it in her bureau," I said defensively.

Ty leaned back in his chair, his arms bent out at the sides of his head. I had seen him do that motion before, when I was in police custody. Call me crazy, but I had a feeling those experiences behind bars were going to forever affect my relationship with this man.

"What do you have in mind?" he finally said.

I smiled. "First, I need a black bodysuit."

IN THE END, I didn't get to wear a black bodysuit with high-tech gadgets on my belt and badass lace-up boots. But that didn't mean I couldn't find some on my favorite shopping sites as soon as I got rid of the whole murder rap.

No, we had argued and cajoled and negotiated and come up with the stupidest scheme. I want to go on the record officially and announce that this stupid scheme was the idea of one Officer Ty Hatfield.

But just the first part was Ty's idea. The second part was all mine. You'll see which is which.

Mandatory invitations went out to all of Panhellenic, under the auspices of the Panhellenic advisor. Once Ty called Amanda, she was only too happy to help out. After all, as she kept reminding us, she wasn't going to be the Panhellenic advisor anymore. All five sororities were required to be in the G. G. Hankler Auditorium on campus to hear a presentation on the evils of Botox. And even though I was nervous about it, I made sure that all Delta Betas would be there. No Sutton sorority member was getting special treatment; except for Ainsley St. John, who, her sister told me, had a meeting at the Panhellenic offices.

Even stupider, Casey was selected to give the presentation, he of the unlined brow and unnatural orange color. But he was the one with public-relations experience, and he could whip up a convincing fifteen-minute slideshow with very scary images yanked from the Internet.

We all knew that this plan might not work, but it was our first step to identifying who, if any, were the other unknown sex operators in Liza's ring. I'd gone on record suggesting that if it proved unsuccessful, we were pulling a sting on the fraternities next; in my opinion, there was still something fishy about these pranks on innocent women, and it looked like Ty agreed with me. Or at least, he nodded vigorously when I brought up the black bodysuit again.

Ty sat in the front row of the auditorium, and I sat off to the side, on the stage, so I could have a good view of the seats and the women occupying them.

When all the sororities filed in, Casey went to the mic and introduced himself as Dr. Casey Kenny, Plastic Surgeon to the Stars. An alias and a glamorous fake job? Casey had all the fun.

Right away, the first slide was shocking. Apparently, Botox was some kind of paralyzing agent. Which was really scary, especially with what had happened to Liza and Stefanie.

Then Casey used some facts and figures, blah blah blah. Then he got into the good stuff. He flipped a slide, and it showed a world-renowned actress in a recent action-adventure movie. The picture was from a scene where she was screaming that her lover was shot. Her face was contorted in every painful way except for her forehead.

Then he showed a young starlet, barely twenty-two, shiny and plastic-y. "Your age," Casey pointed out with a delightfully dire tone in his voice. "And that's with photoshop."

Something about seeing the unnatural face on a huge projection screen really made you think. Personally, I wondered how she got her pores so small.

After another slide or two that caused some of the sorority women to gasp and cringe, I nodded to Ty. There really wasn't a reason to let this go on so long except that Ty felt strongly that Botox was dangerous, given the murders and everything.

In the front row, he acknowledged my signal, and surreptitiously pressed a button on his cell phone. We weren't sure how long this part was going to take, so we waited, as Casey pointed out another Botox horror story that made a few Betas in the back cry.

Then it started happening. When Ty had pressed the button, it had started a redial of the phone-sex hotline. He had programmed it to redial every thirty seconds, knowing that when the hotline picked up, it would forward the call to another and another available operator. Sooner or later, if there were phone-sex operators in our auditorium, we would know. No college woman could ignore her phone for that long.

A phone rang in the Beta section, hastily answered. Another Beta had her phone on vibrate, but she checked her screen. Two Epsilon Chis got theirs out. A Tri Mu grabbed her phone and acted like she was leaving to take the call. And yes, I saw two Delta Betas receive calls.

Some of them could be coincidences. But not all of them. My heart sank, knowing that we had just added more sisters and friends to the ever-growing suspect list.

Then the unthinkable happened. Another phone rang, loudly. I recognized the ring tone. Beyoncé was singing in my purse.

I jerked the phone out and saw an unknown caller ID. My head jerked up to see Ty's inscrutable gaze. This was not happening.

As we had decided, Casey informed the audience that there had been a threat and that they'd need to exit in a single-file line out the back. What he didn't tell them was that police officers would ask those who had been seen with their phones to step to the side.

I had to do the same. I had a sick feeling in my stomach. Everything clicked into place. Accidents took on a whole other meaning. Little things that I had ignored were really big, important things.

I didn't have to walk to Ty. He was next to me in a moment. For some reason, I handed him my cell phone. "You have to go to the Panhellenic offices," I managed to say through my rising nausea.

"Why?"

"Because Ainsley St. John is about to be murdered."

Ty grabbed a radio from his belt and called a code in. "I need someone at Sutton Student Center, Panhellenic offices looking for Ainsley St. John."

He gave me a hard look, and I held up a hand to stop him from saying whatever he was about to say.

"I promise I'll tell you everything. But you have to make sure that Ainsley St. John stays alive."

Casey stepped up. "I'll make sure Margot doesn't leave the country."

That didn't have the effect on Ty that Casey intended. He paused, gave us a very intimidating look, turned, and jogged off the stage. I hoped he could stop an attempted murder. For Ainsley's sake, and for mine.

Chapter Forty

CASEY AND I stood alone on the stage of the auditorium together, silent for several minutes. Which had to be a new record for us.

"Margot," he finally said slowly. "Were you . . ."

"NO!"

"But your—"

"NO."

Another long pause. "Good. Because you really suck at phone sex."

I shot him my you-better-not-be-taking-the-last-brownie look.

"I heard you, remember? When we accidentally called that professor?"

Yeah, I remembered. And he was right, I would be just horrible at phone sex. But I didn't want that to be my argument in front of a jury.

Everything looked bad for me, right now. Every. Single. Thing. I could only pray that Sutton's finest got to the Panhellenic office in time.

"Do you want to talk?" Casey asked. I loved that about him.

I shook my head.

"What do you want to do? Besides head for the Canadian border?"

I thought for a moment before I had the perfect plan.

After returning to the chapter advisors apartment, I leaned my head on Casey's shoulder on the little love seat in the chapter advisor's apartment. We had Milano cookies, beverages topped off with Casey's magically refilling flask, and an episode of *Project Runway*. Nothing was more reassuring than Tim Gunn. Even when a garment was a disaster waiting to happen, Tim Gunn could see a way out of it. It was a much better message for me now than my other favorite show. On *Law & Order*, someone was either dead or locked up at the end of each episode. Not what I wanted to think about.

When my phone rang, I nearly jumped out of my cozy honey-bee slippers. I listened to the short message, hung up, and looked at Casey, who was waiting with inquisitive eyebrows.

"I've been summoned," I said. "And I've already worn all my innocent clothes to the police station."

Casey took the challenge seriously. When I walked through the doors of the Sutton police station, I was styled by Casey Kenner. My trusty black skinny jeans were an obvious choice. The high-heeled boots were mine. The black-leather blazer he borrowed from Kelli on the second floor. The gold Delta Beta T-shirt with the black Greek letters topped off the ensemble. Make it work, Delta Beta style.

Ty Hatfield met me at the front door, his blue eyes sweeping over me with some kind of amusement.

"How's Ainsley," I asked first. I really did care about that, first and foremost.

"Alive and well, thanks to you."

I let out some air I'd been holding since I first put the pieces together there on the stage.

"Campus security found her cornered in the Panhellenic offices, a syringe full of Botox pointed at her neck."

"Oh God," I breathed, my hand reaching out to steady myself. I couldn't help but think of how, a few minutes later, Aubrey would have lost her only sister.

"And?" Ty knew what I was asking. He nodded his head for me to follow him, and I did, down the same hall that led to his office, but we passed it, going farther, then right down another hall. That's when I saw it. The two-way mirror. The cops drinking coffee and watching the scene unfold inside the interrogation room. I actually felt my heart go pitter-patter. It was exactly like I had imagined it would be.

And then I saw inside the interrogation room and my same pitter-pattering heart stopped and sank like a stone.

"You knew it was her, didn't you?" Ty's voice was low and kind in my ear. Neither his voice nor the fact that he was right made this any better.

I nodded. I had known. It hadn't meant that I hadn't prayed that I was wrong.

Sitting in the interrogation room, her hands twisting in front of her, was Amanda Jennifer Cohen, my big sister.

Chapter Forty-one

Ty took my elbow and led me into a nearby office. The lights flipped on when we walked in. "It all made sense when my phone rang," I told him. "Until then, I thought I was just having bad luck. That all these things were just accidentally pointing to me, setting me up. But when the phone rang, I knew someone had deliberately been setting me up to make it look like I was the killer."

I smiled at Ty sadly. "And Amanda was the only one who knew why we were calling all the sororities together. I need to go talk to her. Will you let me?"

Ty wasn't sure. "If I let you go in and talk to her, there's no privilege or confidentiality. Everything in that room can be used in a court of law." I wondered if he was worried about Amanda's confessing something, or if he thought that I would.

"It's okay," I assured him. "I won't confess to anything you don't already know about."

When I walked into the interrogation room, Amanda smiled at me. It was a habit, I realized. Something she did, not something she felt.

"Why did you do it?" I asked, when I settled into the metal chair across from her.

Her fingers stopped squeezing each other for just a moment. "Remember when I was a senior and the chapter's representative for the Miss Greek pageant?" I nodded. She continued, "And the Beta Gams and Moos joined forces and bought that ad in the *Sutton Eagle* implying that the Debs used drugs to stay skinny? You and I marched down to the newspaper offices and bribed the editor with a cute wrapped gift basket full of alcohol to get him to collect all the editions off campus so the Delta Beta name would be protected."

I remembered.

"It was like that," she said. "Liza was going to tell everyone about the phone-sex line. She had called Mabel Donahue. She threatened to go to the Sutton chancellor's office. And then Liza said she was going to tell the Delta Beta Sisterhood Mentor when she arrived. I had to protect Delta Beta."

The queasiness came back in my stomach. "That's not like what we did in college, Amanda. People were hurt. People died."

She did a little eye roll.

"What happened, Amanda?" So much was wrapped up in that question for me.

"I heard a Beta Gam gossiping about a really great way to make some cash. I followed the trail and found out it was Liza," she said, like we were gossiping about old friends from college. "I came out to her then. As a Delta Beta sister, I couldn't approve what was going on." Amanda flinched at the memory. "Then she cut me in."

I put a hand to my mouth. "A bribe?"

Amanda's expression pleaded for understanding. "Do you know what that was like for me? Finally becoming successful? The purses, the shoes? Not having to worry about money? Margot, sometimes the line brought in $3k a night."

Even knowing the lengths she had gone to, my heart ached for the girl she once was. The girl from West Virginia desperate to fit in at the preppy college.

"It was easy, too easy. I thought I could handle the rumor mill. Liza would keep the cash flowing. The business grew in leaps and bounds until a man screwed it all up."

"Dean Xavier."

Amanda nodded. "We'd been seeing each other on and off for the past year. I wasn't into his teenager thing, so I suggested he call this phone-sex line. Might as well make some money off your boyfriend's kink, right? That's when it all started to go wrong."

"He put the pieces together."

"Liza was embarrassed and started getting all judgmental about it. She said she didn't feel comfortable using college girls anymore once a professor knew about it, so she quit and said she was going to come out with the truth."

"But Dean specifically said that Liza was cut from the program?"

"He said that because her death gave him the perfect opportunity to rewrite history. Liza's being cut from the doctoral program because she was a bad-girl phone-sex worker sounds much better than the truth: He was obsessed with calling teenagers and telling them to tie themselves up."

"And you blackmailed him to get a promotion out of the Panhellenic office." I filled in the blanks again.

Amanda looked unrepentant. "Do you know how many crying girls I deal with on a weekly basis?"

I could guess.

But I wanted to stay focused, not least because there were about five police officers outside the room who were hanging on my every word.

"You blackmailed Hunter to break into the office."

She shrugged. "I needed the dirt on Dean. Stefanie's file was proof of his inappropriate relationship with a student, and I knew we had a recording of one of his calls somewhere. Getting Hunter to do it was easier than sneaking in and out of the house again. Especially with you there. When Liza was alive, I'd come in the chapter advisor's apartment door and wait there to talk."

I knew exactly how Amanda had come in and out of the house so easily. Because the house had had the same security code for the past thirty years.

Talking about Amanda going in and out of the chapter advisor's apartment and seeing Liza brought to mind pictures of a Botox vial in a medicine cabinet. And the memory of a woman collapsing in front of a chapter of sorority sisters.

"Why did you have to do it in front of the chapter, Amanda?" The plea in my words was sincere. It wasn't just the murder that was evil. It was the inexcusable timing. No young person needs to see that.

As different as this Amanda was now, I saw that my question touched a part of her that I knew and recognized. A little wrinkle appeared between her brows (which would have been a big wrinkle if she hadn't been injected with a killer virus). "I misjudged the dose," she finally said. "I never thought she'd walk out of the apartment and into that meeting." Neither of us said anything for a moment. Then Amanda said, "I did better the second time."

Stefanie. The thought made my heart ache.

"At least I made sure you found her," Amanda said softly. "I knew you wouldn't want her to stay out there for long."

Tears sprang to my eyes. So that was Amanda's version of sisterhood. Following the proper etiquette for leaving a body behind. Killing a sister to protect the sisterhood.

"Why Stefanie?" I asked, surprised by the strength of my emotion. "Why did you have to kill her?" I asked.

Amanda turned her head slowly. "I didn't plan it. She and Dean had grown close over the phone. Then they were sleeping together. When I found her at his place, she accused me of doing something to Liza, and I just snapped."

There was a shimmer in Amanda's eyes. "I never meant for it all to happen like this, Margot. I just wanted to protect the things I loved. Like Delta Beta. "

"And your $3k a night." I said quietly. Painfully, I acknowledged Amanda's innate selfishness, which I'd never wanted to see.

"You would do the same," Amanda insisted. "I know you would. You always put Delta Beta first. And that's why I had to stop Liza from telling you about the business. Once you knew, you'd never look up to me again."

On that, she was right. I couldn't look at her anymore. I couldn't talk to the woman who had, after all, not only committed two murders and attempted a third, but had tried to set me up. Me. Her little sis.

I found I had to ask the big question—why had she set me up? Because I'm that kind of girl, who pushes, even when it's smarter to stop.

Amanda did look sad and regretful. "You're my little sis. And you're such a good Delta Beta. I thought you might take another one for the team."

And then I got up and left.

Chapter Forty-two

I PUNCHED THE code on the keypad at the front door of the sorority house. It was the date our sorority was founded. December 16, 1879—12-18-79. For ten years, every time I had entered that number, it was a reminder of the history of the best, most inspirational, strongest sorority ever established. It was a reminder of the 150 years that sisters had stuck together, united in love and loyalty and friendship.

Until now. Now it was a reminder that one of our own had tried to corrupt us from the inside. Phone sex. Blackmail. Murder.

I didn't let Amanda see what she had done to me. Even someone with a big open heart can close it off when pride demands it. But now the full, earthshaking reality of what had happened was sinking in.

I went to the chapter advisor's apartment and left the badass black-leather jacket on the floor. I kicked off the boots and ripped off my Delta Beta tee. I dug a plain gray tank top and a black Juicy hoodie out of my suitcase and put those on instead. Anything with Greek letters was a painful reminder. Even my Busy Bee slippers hurt my heart. I put fuzzy socks on instead, wrapped my arms around a pillow, and let the tears come.

It would probably sound idiotic to most people that my heart was broken by Amanda's betrayal. She wasn't a relative; we shared no genes or family. But in my heart, she was still my sister. I talked to her like a sister and held her in my heart as close as any sibling.

She obviously hadn't felt the same, and I was devastated. My loss was real, acute, and would stay with me for the rest of my days.

Minutes or hours later (I wasn't sure how much time had passed, at that point), there was a soft knock at my door. I ignored it, knowing I was in no shape to advise or console or admonish anyone. I was no chapter advisor today.

The door opened anyway, and in walked Casey, then Aubrey, then Callie, Asha, Cheyenne, Jane, and more faces that I had to come to know and love over the past ten days.

Aubrey sat on my bedside, her beautiful face creased with concern. "Casey came back and told us what happened. What can we do for you?"

My face crumpled again. I had let them all down. I was supposed to be helping *them*. I couldn't be the one who needed help. I was the worst chapter advisor ever. "I'm sorry," I sobbed to the women who were in my charge. "I should have known what she was doing."

"Even the police didn't know," Casey said as he crawled onto the bed next to me. "Why should you have known?"

Because I was the one in charge. "Because she was my big sis," I said.

"So?" Aubrey and Casey said in unison.

"I feel like . . ."

"She dumped you," Casey suggested.

"She cheated on you," Aubrey said.

That wasn't it. "I feel like it didn't matter as much to her as it did to me."

Casey and the rest of the girls nodded. They knew what *it* was. Friendship, loyalty, sisterhood, the whole ball of wax. The things that were important to me turned out to be of little value to Amanda after all.

"She's the loser, then," Callie said.

"Yeah, she's missing out."

"She doesn't know what's important in life."

The young ladies around me all indicated their agreement. I knew they were right. My heart might be broken, but, in the end, at least my heart was in the right place. Here in Delta Beta, with friends. Amanda would never have that—especially in prison.

"Thank you." I smiled shakily.

Asha pushed a stuffed Busy Bee into my arms. "Here. It always makes me feel better when I hug one of these." I took it gratefully and held it tight.

"Speaking of which . . ." Cheyenne looked meaningfully at her sisters gathered around, in the small bedroom. "We wanted to ask you something."

I steeled myself. I didn't know if I could answer any more difficult questions about murderous sorority bitches.

"You told the pledges that you never had a little sis," Cheyenne continued.

"I just never got matched up," I said sadly. "It was probably for the best." Considering what happened when I had a big sis.

Jane cleared her throat. "We wanted to know if you would be our honorary big sister."

I looked up, expecting to see that this was some kind of consolation gesture. But the faces around me were sincere, warm, and open. "Really?" I asked, my heart opening up at the thought.

Asha nodded at the Busy Bee. "You've been the best big sister to all of us even though we know it hasn't been the best of times for the chapter."

Aubrey chimed in. "You've looked after us."

"And helped us through tough times," Cheyenne said.

"And listened," Callie added. "Most of the time."

"That sounds like an awesome big sister, to me," Casey said, reaching out and putting his arms around the nearest Debs.

I squeezed the Busy Bee to my chest, feeling the Delta Beta love warming me completely. "Thank you. I accept."

EARLY THE NEXT day, I called Aubrey and Callie into the chapter advisor's apartment.

"Ladies," I began. "A lot of information has come out about your behavior in the past week and a half. And I think you both knew what the other was up to." Aubrey and Callie exchanged cautious looks underneath their lashes.

I held up two pieces of paper. "These are your S&M reports."

Both of the girls' perfectly shaped eyebrows shot straight up. "Delta Beta procedures mandate that I write you both up for your violations. Of which there have been many, some of which were recorded on film." I let that sink in, then dropped the papers.

"But I'm willing to bend the rules this time." They relaxed until I said, "On one condition."

"What?" Callie said quickly.

"Anything," Aubrey said soon after.

"You mend your fences. Forgive each other. Start fresh. I know you've probably never been close. But bid day was long ago, and you two are both leaders in this chapter. You have both learned so much, and I just think you shouldn't waste the opportunity to have a true friend."

They both looked tentatively at me and each other.

"So you'll ignore everything if we just agree to be friends?" Aubrey asked.

"And you agree to never ever have phone sex for money again," I said pointedly. Then I gave Callie the same glare. "And you agree to never ever molest another house brother on my desk."

Aubrey gasped, then tried to cover it up with a cough.

"What if he quits the house-brother position?" Callie asked.

"No, not on my desk!" Honestly. Did I really have to say that twice?

Aubrey bit back a giggle, and Callie had to smile, too.

"Thank you," Callie said softly.

Aubrey nodded in agreement. I could only smile back at both of them. My heart was too far up my throat to say anything.

Casey dropped in at the house not long after that. He had checked out of the hotel and was headed back to Atlanta.

"So, what's the status of the Charlotte reporter?"

Casey rolled his eyes. "Journalists are such a pain the rear." They're all 'the public has a right to know.'" He made little quote marks with his fingers and sighed. "But it's actually worked out that Amanda was the Panhellenic advisor."

"Really?" I couldn't imagine how Amanda helped anyone with anything.

"She wasn't allowed to tell people her sorority. No one knew what she was." Casey smiled. "And I'm not telling. The reporter agreed with me that the Botox murder was a much better angle than the phone sex, so we'll see." He shrugged. "The good news is, I heard you'll be here as chapter advisor."

I avoided his eyes. I had indeed called Mabel after leaving Amanda at the police station, giving her a very detached and calm statement about the events of the day. And she, after calling Amanda a few choice names that were not Mary Gerald- and Leticia-approved, bluntly assessed the situation as being totally [redacted to protect the dignity of a Delta Beta national officer] up. "We need you there, Margot, more than ever. Please consider staying on as chapter advisor," she said.

I had just heard my big sister confess to murder after trying to frame me for it. I wasn't in the best mind-set to consider any permanent job offer, much less one at the Sutton chapter. There were too many memories. Too many ghosts.

"I told Mabel I'd think about it," I said.

"Someone has to bring this place together again."

I hated the feeling that swept over me when he said that. "Or maybe I'm the one that tore it apart."

Casey grabbed my hand and yanked it. "Don't ever say that, Margot. You were the one who put these women first, every single time. No one else had their best interests at heart. Not Liza, not Amanda, not the police. You. And they know that. And maybe you just stay for a month or so. Just knowing you're here is going to be the best thing in the world for these Debs. They'll see a real woman in charge. A woman who's strong enough to put others first."

Then he hugged me, smelling deliciously expensive, like the way anything Gucci should smell.

"I'll miss you," I said into his sweater vest. Casey was one of the few men on planet earth who could pull a sweater vest off.

"I'll miss you, too." Casey smoothed my hair. "Now wash your face. You don't want these women to have a role model who looks like she can't properly apply eyeliner."

I used the back of my pinky to wipe under my eyes. Casey was right. Leticia and Mary Gerald would not approve.

Chapter Forty-three

IT WAS NEARLY midnight, and gray wisps of clouds covered the moon and cast shadows over the trees surrounding the sorority house. I opened the front door very slowly, slipping out into the night in a black L.L. Bean fleece and dark-rinse skinny jeans. I looked around. No one was around, and sorority row was deserted.

Silently, I crossed the grass and sat in the old swing hanging from the oak, the one with the brass plaques and all of the memories attached.

I waited, watching the play of moonlight and wind dance with the shadows on the still-green grass. It was October, and there would be a frost soon, even in North Carolina, and that grass would fade to brown. After four years at Sutton College, I remembered the change of seasons well. They had been a revelation for a Florida girl like me.

With the sounds of the wind in the leaves above me, I didn't hear his approach until it was too late. When he sat down on the swing next to me, it sank on his end with his weight. There in the moonlight, Ty Hatfield was a calming, strong presence, as steadying as the tree that we hung from. He smelled like laundry detergent and something sweet, like he'd just stopped by a fall carnival and indulged in a caramel apple.

"Did I call 911 and not remember?" I finally asked, deciding to lead off with a joke.

"Nope." He pushed off the ground with his feet, pushing us against the wind.

"So what's new?" The question was casual, like I hadn't been a murder suspect in the past forty-eight hours.

"Just thought I'd come by, make sure everything was okay here."

"Well, that's ridiculous," I snorted.

"Yeah, well, I'm a worrywart."

"If everything wasn't okay, I'm sure I could handle it by myself."

"I'm sure you could."

We rocked back and forth, thanks to Ty's boots levering toes to heels as he pushed us along. A gust of cool air blew through my hair, and I took a deep breath, savoring the scent of fall in the wind.

"Fatfield," I said, my voice barely rising above a whisper.

Ty paused, turning his head to look at me.

"I remember you." It all came back to me. "I didn't recognize you because you look so different now."

Ty sniffed. "Amazing what losing fifty pounds can do."

I shook my head. "It's not just that. You're older, more mature, more . . ." *Manly, hot, experienced.* Pick one. But I didn't say that aloud. "The girls were calling you Fatfield." I remembered them. Lilah DuBrow, Jenna Gallo, Alicia Allen. Bitches, yes. And sisters, unfortunately. "I just did what any Delta Beta would do."

There was a slight pause before Ty swung his arm across the back of the swing and stared at me, intense and serious. "No, Margot. Not every Delta Beta would stand up for a fat pledge whose own brothers wouldn't defend him."

My heart softened at those words. Because of Amanda, I now could truly empathize how that freshman felt when his sworn friends abandoned him. I understood where his cynicism came from, but I wasn't ready to be as black-and-white about fraternal organizations as he was. "Maybe there are a few bad apples, but the principles are still worthy. The Delta Beta founders set standards that—"

Ty's dry laugh interrupted me. "You're going to still do that, now? After all this?"

"Do what?" I asked, confused.

"Act like there's something magical about your sorority that makes the world perfect? All your little perfect princesses, spreading peace, love, and rainbows."

Yes, he was mocking Delta Beta, but I could see his point. The fact that I saw where he was coming from disturbed me. A lot. But getting arrested and blamed for murders and assaults you didn't commit changed the way you saw the world, I guessed.

"I don't see anything wrong with seeing the good in people," I said softly.

"Even with everything that's gone down?" Ty shook his head in disbelief.

I nodded. "Even with everything that's gone down." My echo of his words was quiet and a little more affirmative.

"Do you want to talk about it?" It was one of my favorite phrases. Only the best people used it.

I pushed back the tears that had been threatening since I had left Amanda in the police station. "I'll be okay," I said. I had gotten pretty tough. Jail could do that to a person.

We sat on the swing, our feet pushing back and forth in unison, the only sound the creak of the chains tied to the big oak's branch.

"So, what's next for Margot Blythe?" His questions were often statements, but I heard the inquiry in those words, just the same.

It was a good question.

I needed to call Mabel to tell her I'd stay in Sutton until a new, reliable, moral, nonadvantage-taking chapter advisor was hired. "I'll probably stay here, for the time being."

Stay. Here. Time. Those were words I hadn't really used since . . . well, since ever. Even as an adolescent, I felt restless, ready to go, explore, adventure. Being a Sisterhood Mentor allowed me to keep moving, keep traveling. But if the last ten days had proved anything, they had proved that adventure could come even when you stayed in one place.

That was kind of deep. Even for a philosophy major.

"Oh," was all Ty Hatfield said.

I had to comment. "That's it? No snarky retort? No snide implications about hoping your overtime gets paid or setting up extra staff to deal with sorority girls?"

Ty's head bobbed. "Nope. Think you got it."

Oh, him. I elbowed his flannel-covered side, and wondered if he was always that warm and cozy or if it was just tonight.

"I think you'll be good for this place," Ty said after ten swings back and forth had passed.

"What? Delta Beta?"

Ty's shoulder rubbed against mine when he shrugged. "Here. Sutton. The college."

That was nicer than I expected, but I didn't understand the comment. "Why would I be good for the college?"

Ty spent longer than I would like thinking about his answer. "Goats. You're pretty good with goats."

I smiled as if he'd given me a huge compliment. It probably was. Not many women could say they were good with goats. It seemed like something that would define a woman's character.

We sat and swung, and five minutes later, a group of Debs walked down the front steps, dressed all in black. They sat down on the steps and talked quietly among themselves. Another group noiselessly walked down the street and convened on the sidewalk. They, too, were in dark clothes and sneakers, their hair pulled back into ponytails and tucked under hats and headbands.

At nearly half past midnight, I estimated there were almost fifty young women loitering in the front yard of the Delta Beta house, all of whom were in black or gray clothing. I reached into the pocket of my fleece and pulled on a black ski mask.

I heard Ty's tortured sigh next to me. "Blythe . . ." he groaned under his breath. I had to turn my head all the way to see him because the ski mask severely limited my peripheral vision. In one moment, his face was shadowed by tree branches, and in the next, the clouds parted, and he was illuminated. Those normally guarded blue eyes were full of suspicion and . . . could it be? Humor?

"There's no law against wearing a ski mask, Lieutenant Hatfield." I picked up the Super Soaker that had been resting next to me on the swing. Now Ty groaned louder.

"Do I want to know?" he asked with resignation.

"Nope," I said, mimicking his single-word intonation. "I plead the Fifth."

"The Fifth?"

"The Fifth Amendment. I don't want to incriminate myself." I stood, and the swing sank lower on his end.

Turning back to the house, I saw fifty women pick up assorted shapes and sizes of water guns, settling hats and masks and bandannas around their faces. Nothing to see here, Officer, all completely innocent. There isn't anything illegal about a bunch of sorority sisters playing with water guns, dressed in all black in the dead of an October night. Move along.

With a signal, we started jogging down sorority row, cutting through the Epsilon Chi yard and following an alley toward fraternity row. As we dipped out of sight, I was pretty sure the law was still watching me.

Jane had looked up the average date of first frost in Sutton and compared it to the Farmer's Almanac predictions for the year. In about two weeks, Mother Nature would do her thing, and leaves that were now green would turn yellow and brown. After a full winter, spring would hit Sutton in March, but even then, it would take another six weeks or so for the grass to grow back completely. By then, it would be nearly the end of the school year, with graduation looming. All of fraternity and sorority row would be initiating another batch of fresh pledges, eager to be taught the lessons of their new secret societies.

By then, they would know.

But tonight, no one would have proof of any wrongdoing, any mischief, any ill intent.

Yes, fifty sorority women in all-black gear spraying water guns at the lawns of fraternity houses might look a little funny. But as I told the girls, there was nothing illegal about any of it. And I should know. I was practically the expert on the North Carolina criminal code by this point.

Five fraternity houses were lined up in a row, so we split up into five squads of ten. Each squad moved efficiently and quickly, wasting no time. At each house, a Delta Beta sorority sister whipped out a can of whipped cream and sprayed in huge letters a single word, spread from border to border. In the morning, the whipped cream would be dissolved. The remaining women sprayed the contents of their water guns along the lines of the whipped cream. The liquid was clear and lightweight, but it wasn't pure water. It was water with a whole lot of salt in it. Jane called it a "solution," and I agreed that it was solving a problem. By the time the salt water had faded the grass, the first frost would make the results faint, if not invisible. As the winter progressed, the salt water would kill the grass, and when spring returned, the message carved out in the salted grass would be clear to even the most drunk fraternity brother.

DON'T.

MESS.

WITH.

DELTA.

BETA.

If anyone called the police about that next April, well, I'd deal with Lieutenant Hatfield myself.

THE LADIES OF Delta Beta relaxed over mugs of hot chocolate, laughing and giggling and reliving the Dirty Dozen techniques that had been employed by almost everyone. Becca had thought for sure she'd seen someone looking out the window at the Alpha Kappa house and had dived behind a bush. Christina had accidentally shot Asha in the bottom with a load of salt water and Asha had retaliated with a spray of whipped cream. As for me, I had left my Super Soaker jammed under the hood of a shiny silver BMW that looked just like Brice Concannon's, parked in front of an apartment building between here and fraternity row. I liked imagining the look on his face and the paranoid thoughts that might run through his mind the next morning. Maybe he'd think twice about participating in sketchy parties from now on. The left-over cans of whipped cream were held high, there was a cheer, and more whipped cream was sprayed into steamy, fragrant mugs.

Maybe the fraternities would prank us even harder next year. Maybe teaching the chapter to fight back wasn't the best example I could have given them. Maybe we should have found a more ladylike way to make our point, as Leticia Baumgardner and Mary Gerald Callahan would have liked.

But as I sat there and looked over the chapter, I noticed how, in one evening, their bond had strengthened, ties been formed, and memories had been made, even after we had been continually tested and knocked down. Maybe our sisterhood would survive just fine, after all.

Acknowledgments

ONCE AGAIN, THIS book could not have been published without the help of many women who supported me, urged me to take action, and didn't let me take no for an answer. Thanks to Jill, who empowered me to get this book out there. A million thanks to my agent, Cassie Hanjian, who would be one of Margot Blythe's role models, because she is determined, passionate, and has really good hair. Thanks to Trish Daly, who believed in me, and Margot, who makes the editing process as easy and fun as a sorority mixer.

To my lunching writer sisters, Ophelia and Alexandra, who always tell me exactly what I need to hear.

And finally, my sorority sisters. This book is 100% fiction, but it started with a spark from you. Thanks for sharing your light.

Look for Lindsay Emory's
next Sorority Sisters Mystery,

RUSHING TO DIE

Available November 2015 from Witness Impulse

About the Author

LINDSAY EMORY is a native Texan and recovering sorority girl. She is also the author of the contemporary romance *Know When to Hold Him.*

@Lindsay_Emory
www.lindsayemory.com
www.witnessimpulse.com

Discover great authors, exclusive offers, and more at hc.com.